A Scream in the Silence

Stockbridge felt hollow in his gut as he walked, heard the adornment clattering in his deep pocket. A trapper would have had the time and the reason to make such a thing. And not necessarily for himself, but for a son he loved and missed. Stockbridge had, with a lead ball he had removed from a famed Colorado lawman. His son had been wearing it on his belt buckle the day he died.

Nearing the horse, Stockbridge took care to look for signs of anyone approaching. He did not see dust kicked up anywhere against the clear sky to the east and west of the looming peak. He did not hear anyone calling, or hooves pounding. He moved cautiously, his shotgun loaded and ready. He saw the tracks the horse had made coming to this spot—from the west, higher up on the Peak Road.

This man did live here, then.

Finally reaching the horse, he heard nothing but wildlife and wind—

Until he heard Mrs. Keeler scream his name.

RALPH COMPTON

○

BLOOD OF THE HUNTERS

A Ralph Compton Western by

JEFF ROVIN

BERKLEY
New York

BERKLEY
An imprint of Penguin Random House LLC
penguinrandomhouse.com

ISBN: 9780593100738

First Edition: May 2020

Printed in the United States of America
1 3 5 7 9 10 8 6 4 2

Cover art by Dennis Lyall
Cover design by Steve Meditz
Book design by George Towne

THE IMMORTAL COWBOY

This is respectfully dedicated to the "American Cowboy." His was the saga sparked by the turmoil that followed the Civil War, and the passing of more than a century has by no means diminished the flame.

———◆———

True, the old days and the old ways are but treasured memories, and the old trails have grown dim with the ravages of time, but the spirit of the cowboy lives on.

———◆———

In my travels—to Texas, Oklahoma, Kansas, Nebraska, Colorado, Wyoming, New Mexico, and Arizona—I always find something that reminds me of the Old West. While I am walking these plains and mountains for the first time, there is this feeling that a part of me is eternal, that I have known these old trails before. I believe it is the undying spirit of the frontier calling me, through the mind's eye, to step back into time. What is the appeal of the Old West of the American frontier?

———◆———

It has been epitomized by some as the dark and bloody period in American history. Its heroes—Crockett, Bowie, Hickok, Earp—have been reviled and criticized. Yet the Old West lives on, larger than life.

———◆———

It has become a symbol of freedom, when there was always another mountain to climb and another river to cross; when a dispute between two men was settled not with expensive lawyers, but with fists, knives, or guns. Barbaric? Maybe. But some things never change. When the cowboy rode into the pages of American history, he left behind a legacy that lives within the hearts of us all.

—Ralph Compton

PROLOGUE

The Colorado Line & Telegram
October 17, 1883

FROM GUNNISON TO HELL
by Otis A. Burroughs

Until a year ago, it was said that if you were looking for restored health, then you needed to look no further than one John Daniel Stockbridge, M.D. The folks in this bustling city of twenty-five thousand good and honest Christian souls have nothing but fourteen years of happy memories of lives saved, babies born, and grave news delivered with care and heartfelt compassion.

Since a year ago, it was whispered that if you were a black mask looking for sudden death, then you also needed look no further than John Daniel Stockbridge, M.D. These whispers became shouts two mornings past, in a vacant lot south of the Kansas

River, just west of the railroad bridge. That was when and where this man is said to have killed an unbeloved cuss by the name of Asa Preston.

Nobody knows much about the deceased, other than that in the three weeks he had been in Gunnison he gambled, had a felonious temper, and was behind in his hotel bill. From his possessions, examined after his demise, he appeared to travel under a variety of names. What has been assembled by your obedient servant through these documents and telegrams ranging from Topeka through Lincoln and back to Gunnison is that at one point, the unmourned soul called Asa Preston was formerly one Adam Piedmont, a practitioner of land-grab schemes. From the only known description, the corpse appears to have been the same man who took the lives of Dr. Stockbridge's beloved wife, Sarah Jane; his fifteen-year-old daughter, Polly; and his ten-year-old son, Rance.

That description comes from the doctor's brother, the honorable Jed Stockbridge, now commissioner of the General Land Office in Wichita. Mr. Stockbridge, Esquire, told this reporter, "As I said seven years ago, I believe this is the same man who tried to usurp a claim at my assaying office. My brother would not confirm this to me. He said that he had to clean his own soul of this. Apart from that remark, written to me in a state of deepest misery, I have not had a communication from John."

The identity of the killer was never legally adjudicated because Dr. Stockbridge refused to testify and there was only hearsay that they had a grudge against the family.

What is interesting about Dr. Stockbridge, and only adds to the unsavory mystery, is that he closed his practice and appeared to vanish. Prior to this week, he was not known to have set a bone or sewn a wound. Nor was the killer in possession of a medical kit, a horse, or even a grip—only the double-barreled, highly polished waterfowling shotgun he used to dispatch Adam Piedmont most emphatically, and only after he had been shot upon.

It is for this reason that we bequeath to him the sobriquet Dr. Vengeance. As the gentleman is still somewhere among us, I will endeavor to find him and pry from his unsympathetic mouth the full and no doubt captivating story of . . .

Dr. Vengeance!

CHAPTER ONE

THE BLACK BEAR bore the scars of a life lived in the mountains.

The animal lumbered on all fours under a fading sun, his leather-bottomed paws and long blue-gray claws sure on the granite-and-gneiss surface.

He was not yet ready to winter. There was a presence—mostly scents but also sounds and movement—that was unaware that this was his territory. It was unafraid. That meant danger to the bear, his mate, and their cubs.

The threat had to be chased away or destroyed.

The foothills sloped north from the Oónâhe'e River, where the bear made its home. The terrain was treed and still free of the snows that had fallen in the higher elevations. The soil, already frozen, bore no tracks, but that did not matter. The bear's sense of smell was greater than that of its prey, greater than even that of the gray wolves that stalked him in packs.

None challenged him in what the Cheyenne had named *Náhkòheósévóse*—the Bear Paw Mountains.

Yet in his sixteen winters, the bear had learned that no animal, not even one that weighed four hundred pounds and could rear to a height of six feet or greater, could afford to be careless. His fur was marked by conflicts with other bears, with mountain cats, with wolves. If not the wolves, then a dislodged rock or storm-weakened tree or landslide could deliver instant death. The bear's head bore the scar of a tumble on slick rocks by the river near his den.

But this was not a wolf the black bear sought. It was a different scent, a different enemy, one who walked upright and could kill from a distance, from behind a boulder or atop a tree. A foe who dressed in the skins of his kind but was otherwise frail and easily broken.

The last of the full moon threw a pale ivory cast over the pines and oaks that stood above and below him on the gentle incline. An occasional cloud briefly blanketed the entire landscape in darkness, and the crunch of fallen leaves now and then dulled his hearing. That did not stop the large nose from dipping, rising, seeking the scent he had picked up by the cave, the smell of the upright killer, the stench of dead hides upon its weak shoulders—

The double-spring steel trap clanged shut an instant before the bear howled. He fell, writhing, swatting at the sharpened metal teeth that chewed through fur and flesh, digging into bone. The creature roared as it twisted on its back, each move causing the teeth to bite deeper, wider. The more the bear struggled, the more its wound opened and the more blood spilled onto the crushed leaves. It coated the animal's lower leg and poured onto the exposed rock, making it slippery for the men who emerged from hiding. They appeared suddenly, as if the trees had suddenly birthed them, and slowly converged on the fallen beast. Even though the bear was held fast in a trap that was securely chained to a tree trunk, they were not incautious.

They would not have survived the Civil War and eighteen years in the wilderness had it been otherwise.

There were six of them, all in furs and most with caps—fur or Confederate 1st Virginia Infantry. With a seventh, the cook, back at their mountain compound, they called themselves the Red Hunters—just that.

The one man who was bareheaded came forward with a drawn Bowie knife, its blade a spectral white in the light of the moon. He was Captain Promise Cuthbert, and he was here to kill. Like climbing, logging, lovemaking, it was a skill that waned the less it was practiced.

There was a lean six feet of Promise Cuthbert, with black hair that covered the back of his neck and tumbled over two eyes of different colors, one blue, the other hazel. His mouth was a slash cut into a face that had the cheekbones and complexion of a skull.

How often, in the wild, beyond pickets, had he drawn this blade and seen it shine. It almost had moods to him—calm and cold under the moon, fierce and bloodthirsty when used by the fire of a campfire, a flash of lightning when called upon in daylight. The shine attracted the bear's attention and, with effort that caused the chain to rattle, he stood awkwardly on his three good legs to face what looked like a big white fang. But the movement caused the trap to tug, and the three limbs locked in an unsteady stance—

"Stay down," the approaching man said, his voice deep and raw.

"Papa needs new shoes," said another.

The bear showed its own teeth in a mouth wide
and foul from a recent kill, though it appeared to be
more grimace than threat. Cuthbert showed his own
wide smile back.

"You're gonna die," he said. "It's gonna happen."

As the man neared, the others closed in behind him.
Four of those other men held Springfield short rifles in
their cold, bare hands. One held a knife—not a Bowie
like the captain's but a custom weapon that was 9¾
inches overall with a 5⅛-inch drop-point blade and a
bone ivory handle. There was no cross guard, just a
three-brass-rivet attachment, so the cutting edge
could be thrust in as far as the holder felt like pushing. The Springfields were new. They had replaced
the old Sharps rifles the men had carried for more
than a decade.

The guns had been the contribution of Woodrow
Pound, the freed slave who had hooked up with Cuthbert and the others when, migrating west, they found
him half dead by the Kansas River in Topeka. The
slave had escaped before the War and kept moving
west, aimless and alone. A six-foot-seven mass of
man, with a long face and a big knob of a chin, Pound
was a master with anything sharp or pointed, and he
was too rich a find for even former Confederates to
leave behind. They'd had plans and the ailing man
had needed help. In the almost twenty years since
then, the former log splitter had become invaluable
to the team. Pound's initiation had proved that. His
job had been to slip into the camp of a U.S. Army
patrol one night, cut loose the horses, and make off
with the new Springfield rifles while the men, half
awake, chased their mounts.

Pound secured ten guns and stuffed a dozen boxes
of ammunition into his canvas bag.

The men were happy to be rid of the worn-out

Sharps. Anywhere else in the world—on a farm, on the sea, in the desert—a man was as strong as his sinew allowed. But here in the Rockies, in God's unfinished wilderness, he needed more.

His eyes narrow in his sun-blasted face, the fifty-year-old Cuthbert stopped just out of range of the bear. Holding the knife waist-high, he glared at the animal, his smile flinching wider with each weakening bellow from the big mouth, with each futile tug of the chain.

"You are not the master here," Cuthbert snarled. Without turning from the beast, he said to the men behind him, "Take it."

The four Springfields erupted as one and the top of the head of the big beast was lost in waves of red. Animal brain and bone were blown across the oak behind it. But only across the top of the head. The pelt would go to shoes and at least two coats, while the snout and the teeth had commercial value. Though the men lived off the land, they also bought the comforts they required. For that, they needed goods to sell in Gunnison or farther east in Denver. Bear teeth were popular for jewelry, the nose and other parts, dried organs mostly, for medical potions.

The bear fell on its big belly with a thump, its limbs splayed. The men lowered their rifles and came in closer.

"Already looks like a coat," barrel-chested Liam McWilliams snorted.

"Except for the parts that are my shoes," said the short, wiry Alan DeLancy.

"Brain over brawn," observed the hulking Zebediah Tunney, oblivious to the irony in the remark. He was more like the bear than he was like the others, a Texan who used to fight bulls for pocket change.

As the others stood around, Pound slipped his

knife into the bear's mouth and began to remove the jaw. The teeth would come out later, with pliers, back at the cabin. Cuthbert took his Bowie to the animal's abdomen to empty the beast's torso.

The cold orbs above watched his grisly deed without judgment. It was impartial to the exposed red sinew, the still-warm intestines being carelessly tossed aside and sparkling with fake life. The meat and some of the edible viscera—the heart, the liver— would be harvested over the next hour. The paws, too, would be cut away for sale as candleholders. What was salvaged would be carried to the sprawling log cabin below, lower in the foothills. It would be carried by a thirteen-hand packhorse that always rode with them. The animal was standing mutely up-wind with the other horses, in a glade, after having carried the trap up the winding mountain trail.

Ironically, it was easier when they hunted men up here. It took only one or two members of the Red Hunters to do that. Men did not have the sharp instincts of beasts.

Save for Pound—who had learned all his lessons in bondage—that was something each of the men had relied on during the Civil War. The men had served under Colonel Patrick Moore. They had specialized in night raids on Union encampments: taking or scattering horses, stealing or disabling weapons, grabbing powder or food or clothing or uniforms, and killing whenever possible. Cutting a throat from behind or putting a knife in a man's back—anything that would have diminished enemy numbers and undermined morale. Their *carte de visite* had been a bloody palm print, left at the scene of the action.

The men had been barely twenty then. Moore had culled them from the ranks of outcast aristocrats: wealthy scions of great families who were gamblers, profligates, wags, womanizers. No drinkers, though: It would have been one thing if they had done something that had resulted in their own deaths. Moore could not allow one man to jeopardize the unit.

On the battlefield, the men had been filled with idealism and rage. They had gone from wayward colts to stallions ready to hurt you with both ends—biting, kicking, *attacking.* They had found their calling.

After the War, far from being spent, the men found themselves insatiably hungry. As Cuthbert had told the others around a campfire, while eyeing his Bowie knife, "Damn my eyes. I got nowhere to *put* it." It was a week after the dismal surrender at Appomattox Court House, and the men had still not gone home.

"To what?" their point man, Grady Ambrose Foxborough, had asked the departing Colonel Moore.

"To rebuild," the officer had replied. "There's not much else *to* do. Go back to your family in Canada."

It was good sense but spoken without conviction. When Moore had ridden off, the gaunt, narrow-faced, sandy-bearded Grady had spit at the idea of working on the family ferryboat. He had traveled south at fifteen to learn the tobacco trade. The only place he could do that now was Connecticut, and he would be damned if he would work for a *Yankee.*

The War had left most of their comrades tired and beaten. Like the colonel, they took Mr. Lincoln at his word, that there would be a general and kindly amnesty. Now that they had just learned he was dead, no one was particularly glad. No one knew what would happen next . . . especially with Andrew Johnson taking his place. He had been a fence-straddling Tennessee governor and senator who showed too little heartfelt affection for his native land. Less than Lincoln had, in fact.

The other reality was that four years ending in defeat had left them with humiliation and a hunger to destroy. They had talked about going north as bandits, living off the land and leading hapless Union soldiers into deadly ambushes.

But the focus of both the North and the South had shifted to the West, and the men decided to go that way. The wilderness held an appeal that the benighted North did not. So they packed their hate and gear and, unlike the James brothers, they did not strike at towns and institutions.

Instead, they withdrew. No longer guerrillas camping in the wild, they built themselves a fortress.

T HE SIX MEN were back at their cabin before the midnight owls had begun their nightly symphony. The meat and organs were placed, for now, in boxes that had been built and sealed with wax for that purpose, then set in the cold earth. Their cook, named Baker—Franz Baker, shortened from Diefenbach— would cut and cure the meat over the next two days, well before the snows came to their ledge and buried the crates. The bear would be for winter emergencies. Weather permitting, they would continue to kill smaller animals from squirrels to anything with feathers for food. When they needed something else, there were always settlers and frontiersmen, Indian parties and occasional military patrols, surveyors and wagons. The winter was easier on the plains below the foothills. There was never a lack of travelers.

The men did not hesitate to take what they required or just wanted—especially smoking tobacco and liquor—and, if necessary, killing to get it. Occasionally there were women with the mountain travelers. The Red Hunters did not kill them, though many died trying to get away.

The Red Hunters worked up here unmolested. The nearest law was in Buzzard Gulch, and gimpy Sheriff Tom Neal was not inclined to come after them.

Behind them, the remains of the black bear were already being scavenged by other predators—a scruffy, rogue red fox and an already emaciated raccoon, along with the insects the two mammals ignored. The feast would go on uninterrupted for days and would likely continue as wolves and foxes found and killed the family the bear had left behind.

And there was something else. Though the Red Hunters did not know it then, there was something ahead of them. Something they would not find so easy to snare as a bear.

CHAPTER TWO

THERE WERE THREE reasons why Dr. John Stockbridge had stuffed the newspapers against his chest, under his charcoal gray greatcoat.

One was warmth. Setting out from Gunnison three days previous—after a week of lying low, avoiding one Mr. Otis Burroughs—he found the air had turned seasonably cold. But not *this* cold. Folded in half, the dozen pages provided some insulation against the cold. Since it would take him a few days to make his way through the cold foothills of the Colorado Rockies, that was a major concern.

Another was sanitary. The absence of anything but brittle leaves was a reality this time of year—and those were uncomfortable against the skin of any man who intended to add to the moose chips and horse patties of the mountain pass.

The last reason was to start a fire. Dry grass was tough to bunch together; it broke easily and blew off even more easily. He couldn't ignite particles of grass.

But wrapping them in newsprint, he could place them on the ground and strike a flint, and then he'd be "off on a cloud," as his late wife used to say.

Stockbridge tensed as her round face and loving smile appeared vividly in his memory—and then transformed into the way he found her, bloodied and torn.

Don't! the man warned himself as his bare fingers dug into the hard earth on either side of him. "Do not!"

It took a moment for the tall, strong-jawed physician to settle back against the tree trunk. The image of Sarah Jane did not fade as quickly as the tightness in his chest or the longing in his heart. She and their children had been gone nearly ten years, but to the forty-five-year-old, the hurt was always there, always fresh.

He picked up the shotgun that lay by his side, the barrel rested on a small rock to keep it handy but off the ground. It was a customized double-barreled Parker Brothers heavyweight, loaded with buckshot called "co killer." It stayed lethal for up to fifty yards with a swath of nearly half that. The shells were kept in a gun belt that rarely took off. He would never again make the same mistake he had made that fateful day, entering his home unarmed.

"Never."

The weight and feel of the gun relaxed him, and after a full minute, Stockbridge set it back down. The dry newspaper against him crinkled loudly as he eased back once again, this time to stay. A hilt poked him in the side, and he adjusted it. Stockbridge also wore a serrated bread knife in a sheath on his belt. When grasses weren't available, like here on a ledge, he used that to cut kindling. It was easier to saw tree limbs than to hunt for patches of brush. There was a quality of self-protection to that knife as well. For one thing, the attention of his adversaries was invariably drawn to the shotgun he carried at all times. More than once he had used that distraction to reach and use his knife. For another, in close, most opponents would watch for a stabbing movement, alert for the cocking of the elbow followed by a thrust. Few would expect a lateral cut.

The fire danced fitfully at his feet, warming his toes and drying the boots that stood beside them. Stockbridge did not understand how the soles managed to suck in water even from dry ground, but they did.

"You don't realize how much your weight squeezes it from the earth, maybe," he muttered.

Stockbridge had managed to start a fire tonight without his paper, thanks to a piece of splintered plank he had found. The broken but dry board took the spark from the flint. He did not know how such a random item as this had made its way fifteen hundred or so feet up, but it had. Maybe it was part of a crate some settler had tossed to lighten a load to get up the mountain—or perhaps a piece of a wagon that had failed to make it up.

Beyond the blaze, his Tennessee Walker sat tethered to a tree. Behind the gray smoke curling from the fire, the horse was a vision, like something from a fable. More than twelve hands high, the white horse was an acquisition he had made before leaving Gunnison.

"New beginning, new horse," he had said to his dear friend Dr. Nehemiah Juran and his sister, Betty Newcombe.

The horse was named Pama, which had been his son's first word, a confusion of which parent was which. Pama had belonged to Asa Preston, aka Adam Piedmont, a monster who had mistaken his wife and children for the family of Jed Stockbridge, John's baby brother. Jed was a Wichita assayer who had refused to falsify a claim Piedmont had made on another man's silver mine. John Stockbridge was a Wichita doctor. The attack was Piedmont's payback. By the time John had arrived from delivering a baby, it was too late.

And Piedmont, that fiend who walked like a man, was unrepentant.

"This is a Stockbridge's doing however you portion it," the creature had spoken before leaving by the back door, the same through which he had snuck up on the sleeping mother and children. "You paid for him."

John Stockbridge hadn't been able to shoot the man, and he had not pursued him then. He was too busy trying to rescue whatever life remained in his blood-soaked family. But there was nothing his skill could accomplish, however battle-tested it had been. He buried them without a funeral, just a priest. He did not want further delay than that. Stockbridge had not even waited for his brother. He bore the man no malice, but he did not know what Jed's eyes would look like when they met his. As a doctor who had seen accidental shootings in combat, and drunken punches that killed in peace, he knew that guilt could be more devastating than sadness.

Stockbridge had not seen his brother since, nor read the letters he sent. Jed still had a family. Stockbridge could not pretend to be unaffected by that.

During the year that Stockbridge had looked for Piedmont, his fellow War medic Juran, along with Betty, had been his only friends and confidants. He would come and see them when he needed relief from the obsession that held him and from the awful loss that haunted him—

Don't!

The night was crisp and invigorating. Stockbridge had a high tolerance for cold and wasn't tired to begin with; it was the darkness that had stopped him from beginning his westward ride across the mountains. Bored and a little restless, he retrieved the newspaper in the hopes of wearying his eyes. It was a yellowish rag that Dr. Juran had given to him. It was not much, but it was something to try to occupy his mind, which had had only one occupation for a year.

A year.

The quest for the last man was over. Stockbridge had no idea now what would take its place. He wondered if he would find it farther west. That was the plan, anyway, vague as it was. He was still a doctor, and people were sure to be hurting anywhere he went.

Stockbridge suddenly realized that he was holding the newspaper without seeing it. His eyes had drifted up to the campfire beyond.

"I will miss Betty," he thought aloud.

Betty was not just Juran's sister; she was his nurse—a gentle, attentive soul. A War widow, she had been a friend to Stockbridge after the loss of his wife. They had shared warm times and challenging times. Both had wanted to share more, but as surely as if they had been gathered around Macbeth's feasting table, the ghost had refused to leave—

Don't!

Sitting by the brightly glowing flames, he glanced back at the wrinkled pulp paper. Stockbridge had grown closer to those two good people as a result of the horror that had been visited upon him. It had not been enough to make him believe in God, but that— and raw red hate—had been enough to keep him from turning the shotgun on himself.

Stockbridge turned his gaze to the newspaper, to a

story that began on the front page, and read the article that was the reason Nehemiah had given the paper to him. He grinned humorlessly as he read it.

"The story, Mr. Otis A. Burroughs, has been told as much as it's going to be," he said when he reached the conclusion. "Dr. Vengeance" was finished, done, and that was that. Stockbridge was still getting used to the fact that the year of training and tracking these men, and the effort it had taken to draw them out, were over. It was not the relief he had expected it to be. Love had been replaced by ferocious hate, which had been replaced by nothing.

Stockbridge was empty, his sense of purpose as brittle as the thing in his hand. He was lonely but he did not want to love again. Even caring about Betty had been a sweet ordeal. He was overly protective.

He tore out the article, leaned forward, and let the page catch fire. He dropped it and watched until the saga was ash. When it was gone, he stuffed the rest of the newspaper back against his chest.

A sudden sound stirred both Stockbridge and Pama. It was a muffled, echoing report that held the air too long to be thunder or a single gunshot.

"Rockslide?" he wondered aloud.

Avalanches were common out here, especially with people moving around where people had not moved around since the beginning of time. Or else sometimes such things just happened on their own.

That has to be it.

The sound had come from above, maybe a quarter mile up. He had not seen any settlers on his way up this path, the Peak Road, and had they been up there already, it was unlikely they would be hunting this late. The only Indians who raided here were war parties, and those were rare.

Nonetheless, Stockbridge rested his hand on the

shotgun, in case someone had slipped by and had un-
welcome designs on him or his horse.

Never again.

Pama relaxed before Stockbridge did. It was uncanny how this thing that felt so much a part of him
was something he had only taken up after the attack
on his home. He had carried a pistol during the War
but never anything this large or powerful. Mastering
it had taken some training, almost as much dedica-
tion as he had needed when he studied medicine in
Cincinnati's Medical College of Ohio.

Enough.

The man looked up through the puffs of cold
breath, beyond them through the bare trees at the
sky, impersonal and remote. The moon was somewhere behind a rise, but its light turned the treetops
into something like a picket—

"Protecting me from heaven's wrath?" he murmured. "Well, I leave it to God to judge whether Mr.
Burroughs is right about what he calls me."

And with the fire dancing warmly, a collection of
sticks and limbs nearby to replenish it, Stockbridge
fell quickly asleep.

D AWN CAME RUDELY early on the eastern slopes.
The fire was out, but the coat and the newspaper had kept Stockbridge warm, and he had not
awakened.

In the year he had spent mostly outside like this, the
first thing he did was listen. He could never be sure
whether it was the sun or a noise that had woken him.
There were only birds and hares stirring, and they
would not be calmly foraging if there were danger.

The second thing he did was make coffee. The
third, shave.

Stockbridge sat, picked up a stick to poke the fire. There were still some embers under the white ash, and he nursed them to life to make his morning brew. He still had half of what he had purchased in Gunnison. He would use the grounds again the next day, just to make them last.

Before the sun had risen an hour's worth, Stockbridge had eaten a stale raisin biscuit bought three days before—the last of them—and washed it down with the hot cupful. He shaved using a folding razor that glided across canteen water and a little soap, using the canteen as a mirror. Because he was headed to the higher elevations, he slipped Pama's Cheyenne blanket over his own shoulders for warmth, like a serape. Then he fixed a wide, flat-brimmed black Stetson on his head and, finally, retrieved the Parker Brothers shotgun and placed it under his right arm. After a year the gun not only felt like it belonged there; it felt like it was a part of him. He breathed easier when it was in place.

Finally tugging on leather gloves that Dr. Juran had made for him—being a surgeon had ancillary benefits—and mounting Pama, Stockbridge headed west along the trail. He let Pama take it easy, since they were still getting used to each other. The Walker was a little twitchy—a result, Stockbridge suspected, of Piedmont having driven him hard and sudden from place to place to place.

The rider had less than half a canteen of water left, but the owner of the Buzzard Gulch tavern where he had had his last meal—under the attentive eye of its imposing but eagerly solicitous Russian proprietor—told him that there was still running water at these low elevations if he listened for it.

Stockbridge had not gone more than a few dozen yards west and up when he heard a cry from somewhere below.

"Hold there," he cooed, and reined to a stop. This early, there should have only been crows and a lingering coyote making noise, and this was neither.

The sound came again, definitely a shout from lower and also southeast of him. It was a boy's voice, and he was calling to someone about something; Stockbridge couldn't make out exactly what. But it sounded urgent and Stockbridge was in no hurry to get wherever he was going. Turning the Walker around, he retraced his steps. He thought about removing the shotgun from under the blanket, but he did not hear any shooting below or cries of pain.

Better not to alarm whoever is there.

The sight of the grim-faced doctor and the polished weapon had been known to make the unsuspecting freeze, then thaw with a laugh with fright. How different, that, from the eager welcome he used to receive entering a place with his medical kit.

The ride down was a little faster, a little tougher than the ride up had been. With his right arm full of shotgun, Stockbridge had mastered the art of one-handed reining, with a gentle assist from his heels, but here and there along the incline, Pama's hooves dislodged rocks, compromising his footing. Stockbridge was constantly reassuring the horse that all was well. It was a skill he had mastered during the War, when not a single horse, ever, was happy to be riding into gunfire.

Cries continued to rise from ahead—now the boy, then a female, and occasionally a loudly snorting horse. Stockbridge could not quite make out what they were shouting, but it was clear they needed help. It was several minutes before he came to a level stretch of Peak Road, turned a bend, and was within sight of their distress. Stockbridge swore, nudged his horse in the ribs, and trotted ahead.

A fuzztail Paint was hitched to a wagon that had gone rear half off a cliff. There was a woman inside the cart section, and the struggling horse was losing ground. Two children were on the outside, on the nearer, driver's side of the wagon. Every time the woman moved forward to try to reach the outstretched hand of a boy, the wheels shifted, stones fell away, and the wagon inched back. The boy, holding the weathered boards on the side, was in danger of going over himself. The girl, a teenager, was struggling to hold the bridle by the noseband and keep the horse from panicking. She was not succeeding.

Stockbridge dismounted while he was still several yards away so as not to further spook their horse or his own. He tugged Pama along, their horseshoe-clattering approach causing the girl and the boy to turn at the same time.

"Mister!" the boy cried helplessly.

"Son, I'm here to help," Stockbridge said soothingly. "You've got to stay calm. All of you."

The girl's pretty, dust-covered face was lined with fear. Because of her position in front of the horse, she could not see how far over the wagon had gone. She only felt each little lurch; her terror came from the seemingly inevitable end. She looked back at Stockbridge with tears beginning to cut lines through the dirt.

"We're losing her!" she said quietly, almost mouthing it, as if she did not want the woman to hear.

She wasn't wrong, and Stockbridge was sorry that he hadn't brought a rope. Lariats were heavy and, frozen, weren't much good anyway. Playing the odds was a necessary evil when trekking through wilderness.

As he neared, Stockbridge could see the sharply angled wagon and the woman's right hand clutching the boards on the opposite side. She was on her knees inside, reaching up, trying not to add weight to the dropping tail end.

"Is that your ma?" Stockbridge asked the boy as he neared.

"Yes, sir!"

"What's her name?"

"Alice Keeler!" he said.

"Mrs. Keeler!" Stockbridge said slowly but firmly. "I'm going to walk my horse around, and we're going to get your hand onto his rein. Then we're going to help you out. Do you understand?"

"Yes!" he heard her muffled cry. "Please, God, hurry! The children—"

In his head, Stockbridge heard Sarah Jane. He gripped the shotgun and tried to redirect his mind.

"They will be fine," he said.

Stockbridge fought Pama with muscle, not big movements that might frighten the other horse. The Walker wisely wished to avoid what, through the metal on its hooves, would feel like an unstable section of ledge. The man saw listing old trees below. For how many decades, possibly centuries, he wondered, had they helped keep the cliff in place? Now several were surrendering to their last freeze and the jostling of the wagon, ready to join the husks and splinters of their countless forebears below.

Pama did not like the footing or the view. He fought harder, and Stockbridge finally gave up trying to pull him. They were about five or six feet from the cart. He sheathed his shotgun beside the saddle and stopped.

"What's your name, boy?" Stockbridge asked.

"Lenny."

"Lenny, I want you to put both of your hands on your ma's wrist. Just grab her, then dig in your heels like this."

Stockbridge kicked his right heel into the ground to show him.

"When you've done that, we're gonna pull your ma out with the help of you holding Pama. Understand?"

"Yes, sir," he said, then once more emphatically to convince himself, "Yes, sir."

The spindly young man did as he was told, leaning back and pushing down, his five thin fingers wrapping around Alice Keeler's bony wrist like an eaglet's talons. The woman, panting, her eyes searching for hope, did not yet release her desperate grip on the top panel.

"Stretch me your other hand, Lenny," Stockbridge instructed.

The boy did, his mouth set as he stood like Samson between the pillars at the Temple of Dagon. He was about a foot short of Pama's bridle.

"Sir, I can't *reach*!"

Stockbridge could see that. He also could not help since he had to be on the other side of the horse, his weight leaning in the opposite direction. And he couldn't ask for the girl's help. With every small slip of the wagon, her own animal fought harder to get away.

There was no time to discuss the matter with Pama or reason with him. They had, by Stockbridge's reckoning, only a few moments more before the boy lost his grip and the woman slid down to the rear and the wagon went over—with the horse and most likely with the struggling girl.

"Son, I don't want to put my weight on the ledge, so here's what I'm going to do. Join your free hand to the other and hold your ma tight. I'm gonna move to the left and do something to make the cart move forward. When it does, you get ready to pull your ma back toward the trail."

The boy was too busy grimacing and grunting and concentrating to speak. He nodded once.

Stockbridge dropped Pama's reins. The horse might run, but there was nowhere to go but up. The handsome mount was smart enough to stop when the threat was out of sight and hearing.

After Pama was released, he bucked up Peak Road and stopped, facing the other direction. Stockbridge paid him no further attention as he walked over to the hitch rail. He was facing Mrs. Keeler, with the girl behind him.

"Little lady," he said over his shoulder, "the horse is gonna bolt. You get out of the way when it does, y'hear?"

"Yes!"

As he spoke, Stockbridge had drawn his serrated knife. He extended his left arm, placed the jagged blade against the horse's rump, and drew it toward him. Just a small nick. The Paint neighed, loud, and jumped ahead. The wagon came with it, the rear wheels banging hard on the rocks but holding to the axle. Lenny did admirably as he had been instructed, pulling hard on his mother's wrist, and the woman came flying over the side. Stockbridge dropped the knife and, seeing that the girl had jumped clear, ran ahead. He threw out his arms as Alice Keeler came down, and swung to his right, hugging her to him. Had she landed on the ground, she would have been crushed by the rear wheels as the wagon rumbled by.

The woman was not screaming, only breathing hard, and he laid her gently on the road.

"Let me hear who's okay!" he shouted, less for information than to rally the children.

"I'm fine. How's Ma?" the girl cried from somewhere on the other side of the wagon. She had fallen, and Stockbridge could barely see her through the stirred dust.

"I'm all right. Thank God!" the woman cried.

"God—and this man," Lenny added. "He saved us, too. I'm . . . I'm fine, sir."

Leaving the family for a moment, Stockbridge hurried up the trail to grab Pama, this latest to-do sending him blindly toward a west-facing cliff. He did not bother trying to take Pama by the tail, since a horse was able to do harm from both ends. He risked an extra few steps and lurched for the reins, pulling back and half sitting like he was on a stool to turn Pama around.

It took a few seconds for the horse to quiet, more a result of the threat being instantly forgotten than by Stockbridge's weight beside him, pinning him to the spot.

The doctor recovered his shotgun and snuggled it under his arm.

He pulled the Walker toward the wagon.

"It's all right. You're fine. You're safe," he said.

Stockbridge was pleased when the young girl appeared at his side. Judging from the tears in her blouse and the dust that covered her, she had taken a hard fall.

The wagon horse being all right, the girl reached out the slender fingers of her right hand stroking Pama's forehead.

"I've got him," she said protectively.

"What's your name?" Stockbridge asked.

"Rachel."

"Then I leave him to you, Rachel," Stockbridge said, smiling.

Stockbridge turned and saw the woman standing a few feet away. She was leaning a little to the left, having taken a hit on her hip from something inside the wagon. But there was strength in the rest of her posture and in her resolute expression.

Behind her, the boy was climbing into the wagon. The hook on the back flap had held, but they were at a severe enough angle that some of their belongings might have slipped over the panel.

Stockbridge faced the three.

"Alice Keeler, Lenny, Rachel—I am Dr. John Stockbridge. I am happy to make your acquaintance."

"As are we," the woman said as gracious as she was grateful.

"I, uh— I was up the trail a way, headed west, when I heard the shouts. Glad I did."

He walked toward Rachel, who had fully calmed Pama.

"He is beautiful," she said.

"A little high-strung yet, but a trip over the Rockies should cure that."

"Where are you headed, Doctor?" Rachel asked. "Exactly, I mean?"

Stockbridge stopped. It was the first good look he had at the young woman. He put her at about fourteen or fifteen, thin but not gaunt. Pretty, though that was hidden somewhat by the smudges and the tangle of long blond hair that had fallen free of the bonnet that lay on the road. The doctor walked over and retrieved it for her. He swatted it against his hip out of view of the horses, then put it in the wagon.

"I don't know where I'm going, Miss Keeler."

"Where you coming from?" her mother asked.

"Gunnison."

"You took care of folks there?" Rachel asked.

"I did," Stockbridge answered, showing no expression. He turned his gaze toward Lenny. "How's it look back there?"

"Not so great. We lost the rifle."

"I know," Mrs. Keeler said. "I couldn't grab it."

"Also a few tins of beans went over, and the shovel was tied to the ax that Ma struck. Also my book—"

"Will we be able to go on?" Rachel asked, a little desperate and cutting her brother off.

"Sam Hill, I don't know!" Lenny said.

"Hush that," Mrs. Keeler cautioned.

This was not Stockbridge's concern. He had made it a habit, in his practice, of giving families time alone to discuss whatever diagnosis he had just given them. It kept him from getting too emotionally involved. With a woman, a daughter, and a son about the same ages as his own family, it was best to go.

He took Pama from Rachel, thanking her with a smile.

"If you're all right, then, I'll—"

"Dr. Stockbridge, we are not all right," Rachel said.

There was an urgency in her tone that surprised him.

"What's the problem?"

The girl looked at her mother. Mrs. Keeler limped forward and her son jumped down to lend a shoulder. She did not resist.

"Ma?" Rachel coaxed.

The woman seemed to be weighing not just the moment but whatever it was that had brought them up here—and near to death. She stopped by Stockbridge, her gray eyes turned toward him with a sense of sadness he had not noticed before.

"Doctor, my husband, Ben, is a fur trapper. He goes out from April to September, sometimes to October if the weather holds. He always comes up with a sledge full of all kinds of pelts. But he has never . . . never been out till now."

She paused and choked back tears. Rachel walked

over to her. She reached into a pocket and drew out a handkerchief.

"I'm okay," Alice Keeler said. She looked back at Stockbridge and smiled through tears. "That's been Ben's way since he and I were wed back in 'sixty-nine. He would go out in the spring, and then I would have him through the winter."

"It's hard weather up here," Lenny contributed. "Pa doesn't like for him or us to get snowed in down below."

"Where do you live?"

"On the homestead outside of Buzzard Gulch," Rachel told him.

"It's a cabin my pa and ma built," Lenny added.

Stockbridge smiled at the boy, but he held the shotgun tight at his side, along his leg. He felt his fingers trembling and his soul turning dark. *If you had been five minutes earlier!* he screamed inside.

"Maybe your pa thinks you're grown enough to take care of things," Stockbridge said.

Lenny grinned. "I can chop wood okay, though we just lost our ax."

"It's not us I'm worried about," Mrs. Keeler said. "My husband is strong and resourceful, but he has never wintered out here." She teared up. "He survived the War, though. He's a rugged man."

"Were you in the War?" Lenny asked.

"I served as a medic with the Fifty-first Ohio Infantry," Stockbridge said.

Mrs. Keeler seemed relieved to hear that. Even eighteen years after the armistice, people were touchy about what side someone had been on.

"My brother was with the First Pennsylvania Infantry Regiment, a sergeant with Company H. He died from typhoid. His wife tried to keep the millinery shop going. She died more slowly from a broken heart."

"I'm sorry, ma'am. A lot of men . . . boys . . . did not come home. And a lot of us still haven't reconciled the whys and wherefores of the whole thing."

"Pa sold her furs," Lenny said. "That's how they met."

Rachel had been shifting uneasily during the conversation. "Ma, you still haven't said if we're going on."

"I don't see as we have a choice," the woman replied. "Your pa may be held up somewhere."

"If he is, we lost the tools to help him," Rachel pointed out.

"This is your pa we're talking about, girl. We've got our hands, and there are limbs to leverage rocks. If he's hurt—well, those same branches can make splints." Mrs. Keeler gestured broadly ahead. "He may have made a crutch and is on his way back slowly. He may be around a turn just ahead."

"Or he may have fallen, as we almost did," Rachel said.

"Hush! The Lord God just saw fit to save us, and He did so for a *purpose*. If that purpose is to help your pa, we have no right to think otherwise."

"We—we lost your wedding Bible, too, Ma," Lenny said softly. "Pa's writing inside—"

"No matter. I carry our vows here," she said, placing a hand on her chest. "Besides, my Ben has his pocket Scriptures. When we find him, we will have that."

Lenny's eyes turned toward Stockbridge. "You're a doctor, sir."

It wasn't a request for Stockbridge to do anything; it wasn't a solicitation for help or advice. It was a boy seeking comfort. Again, Stockbridge heard the voice of Rance inside his skull—

"He is a doctor who helped us and has a place to go," Mrs. Keeler said.

The woman indicated for Lenny to stand aside. He did so reluctantly. The woman made her way to the side of the wagon, wincing with every step. There was obvious relief when she reached the side of the wagon and gripped the top board.

"Children, if you would help me back to my place, we'll go on."

Stockbridge looked at Rachel. "I take it you were driving."

"I was."

"Animals take to her kindly," Mrs. Keeler said.

"I saw that," Stockbridge said. "I'll tell you what. Since we both appear headed in the same direction, I would be happy to travel a bit with you—if you'll have me."

By their expressions, the children immediately embraced the idea. But they said nothing, deferring to their mother.

"As long as we do not take you out of your way, Doctor, we would be most grateful to have you."

"We're headed to Craggy Plains," Lenny said. "Do you know it?"

"Never heard of it," Stockbridge told him. "But the name makes it seem like a place a man should see."

"And we don't have to worry about being charged by a moose, do we, Dr. Stockbridge?" Lenny asked, looking at the shotgun.

"Boy, don't be melodramatic!" Mrs. Keeler said.

"He's not at all, ma'am," Stockbridge said. "He's being a boy." Peering out from beneath the Stetson, the dark eyes caught a spark of sun as they turned to Lenny. "You will not have to worry about moose or bear or anything else."

The boy's mouth smiled, all adult teeth and gaps.

"Lenny?" his mother said, turning toward their rig.

"Sorry, Ma." The boy had replied to his mother, but his eyes and attention were still on Dr. Stockbridge.

Leaving the boy and Rachel to help their mother into the wagon, Stockbridge mounted Pama. He crushed down his own reservations, the feelings this would draw like a well bucket. If his being here could provide a measure of solace, or help, he would stay—unless and until the scales tipped and his memories became too real.

As soon as the children had taken their places, Mrs. Keeler sat herself among two blankets that had been beneath her. The doctor realized, watching her, that the hip injury was not new. It was probably the reason she had been in the back. The springs under the buckboard were old and rusted and would have caused discomfort to bones that were equally set in their ways.

The small caravan headed west along the rocky Peak Road, Stockbridge in the lead. Based on what he had heard, he did not hold out much hope for the survival of Ben Keeler. If all things were equal, an injured man might survive for a while. There were water and small game. And a trapper would know how to catch it after his ammunition ran out. He would surely have the furs to keep warm. But there were other predators out here as well. Big cats, black bear, gray wolves, and birds of prey that might attack a man even if he weren't wearing the skin of a rabbit or a fox. The claws, teeth, talons—those were the real danger.

And gangrene. The green death had cost more lives than the loss of blood in his hospital tents.

Death. That is it, isn't it? he asked himself. Ben

Keeler had nothing to do with his being here. Stock-bridge had immediately felt protective of the family. That kind of connection was something he had avoided with Betty, swore to avoid for however long he lived. *Yet here you are.*

It was the last thought Stockbridge had before a loud report broke the peace.

CHAPTER THREE

Grady Ambrose Foxborough had not gotten much sleep after the bear hunt, but that did not matter to the sun. He woke with it, every day, even when it was hidden in a snow squall. The truth was, he loved being up alone, which was one reason he loved his job as point for the Red Hunters. Just being by himself had been what allowed him to come up with that name. The bounty wasn't wanted men. It was actual bounty: goods and pleasures.

There was tedium, yes. And risk: not just from always unpredictable human prey but from predators—those on four feet, those who flew, those who writhed on cold, scale-framed bellies. And there was the weather, which was rarely calm or accommodating. Even in the summer, the winds and floods up here were sudden and merciless.

But it was better than being in the crippled South, where he had grown up, loved, and fought. He had been a corporal, a scout in the War, sneaking right up to the Union pickets and reporting what he saw to Captain Cuthbert or field headquarters. Afterward, he had gone home to New Orleans where every street, every face was a reminder of the horrors that had been inflicted by the War and by Reconstruction. And also by the citizens themselves. The state had been torn by Lincoln's offer of amnesty during the War: Rejoin the Union and there'd be no hard feelings.

The people had argued, fought, and dueled over every topic from food spices to horse-trading, but none more than that topic.

When it was all over, the sundered population suffered from abusive carpetbaggers, vengeful men who had been slaves, Indians who did the dirty work of Northern politicians who wanted a reason to crush the Chickasaw, Shawnee, Cherokee, and Cheyenne. The poor, naive savages did not know they were being used, only that they were being paid in silver and alcohol.

Not just his native Louisiana, but the whole of the South was a swamp. So like so many in the fallen Confederacy, Foxborough had gone west. He had asked his fiancée to go with him. Flora, who had been betrothed to him before secession, chose to stay with her ailing father and their struggling crawfish business.

Foxborough had written to her, once, shortly after he had reconnected with Captain Cuthbert in Gunnison. That was fifteen years ago. He never heard back.

You make your choices; you live with them.

Foxborough liked it here, in what he called the "Wide Open." Even though the mountains closed them in, the skies were big and clear and blue. That was important as he waited for travelers to pass by. If they had something the Red Hunters could use or trade, he stopped them. Most agreed that living was more important than gold or food, boots or heirlooms. And sometimes there were women.

Man does not live by plunder alone, Foxborough knew.

Up here, women were not as cooperative as they were at Raspy Nikolaev's tavern—but they cost nothing and were a whole lot nearer.

Now, in the early morning, an hour after his arrival, lying on his belly, Foxborough saw coming up the Peak Road a bounty of possibilities. Two horses—one of them a beautiful Tennessee Walker—two women, a wagon that was not worth much but held what looked like blankets and sundries that were worth a closer look. The only resistance looked like it would come from the lone rider up front, though it would be easy enough to take care of him. The only reason for not shooting him outright was he had a nice Cheyenne blanket.

Shame to put buckshot in that.

There were some nice boots on the man, too, plus a canteen and what looked like some kind of shotgun. Foxborough did not want to ruin any of that if it wasn't necessary.

Carefully and quietly adjusting his lay, Foxborough aimed at a spot ten feet below, exhaled, and put the first and hopefully only shot into the ground between the two horses.

The cart horse reared, and the Walker up front whinnied and would have panicked if not for the strong hand of the rider. The people in the wagon all looked up. The man in the saddle did not. He turned the horse to the right, toward the shelter of the cliff abutting the trail.

A veteran, Foxborough thought. *Someone who knew to seek cover pronto.*

The girl with the reins fought to calm the horse. She was good, focused, strong. From here he could not tell how old she was. A teenager of some years, he hoped.

Foxborough remained on the ground, his chin just at the edge of the ledge.

"You folks in the wagon—y'all climb down with your hands up and no one gets harmed," he shouted down.

"Ben? Ben, is that you?" the woman in the back of the wagon cried up.

"Lady, didn't you hear me? You three step down."

"Do it," the man under the ledge told them.

"You come out, too, mister!" Foxborough called down.

"We're coming!" the woman in the back of the wagon told him. She rose and climbed out, helped by the boy sitting on the buckboard. He held her hand as she got down while the girl beside him tied the reins to the side rail. Then she got out, followed by the boy.

"Very good. Very smart," Foxborough said approvingly. "Now, you with the Walker, can you hear me?"

"I hear you."

"Good. You join the others with your hands up or I'll put a shot in you!"

"You might want to rethink this," Stockbridge cautioned.

Foxborough laughed. "You offering *terms* to the man with the rifle pointed at your family? What are you, loco?"

"We're not his family!" Mrs. Keeler cried.

"Shut up!" Foxborough yelled. "Mister, you coming out or am I putting the lady down like a tasty old deer?"

Foxborough waited, his heartbeat climbing in a way he had not felt since the War, a way he liked. The man in the saddle was silent. The horse was silent. A veteran for sure, probably *planning* something.

"Hey, is *everyone* here deaf? Mister, you come out where I can see you, or I put a shot in the lady."

"No!" Rachel shouted, and ran to a place between her mother and the man on the ledge.

Emboldened, the boy yelled, "Ma, get under the wagon!"

"Lady, you do that, and I target the clever lad," Foxborough said.

"Don't do that!" the man's voice called from under the ledge.

Foxborough chuckled. "I knew you had a breaking point, mister. Out, hands up!"

The onetime corporal continued to stare down the barrel of the rifle as he lay on the hard ground. His fingers, clad in deerskin, cradled the weapon and rested on the trigger. It was aimed just beyond the lip of the ledge where the rider had retreated. The scout was listening more than watching.

There, he thought with relief as he heard the hooves clop on the dirt of the dry, sunlit trail.

A few moments later, the horse and rider came from their place of sanctuary. The man was still mounted. The point had not expected that, not that it mattered. Most riders put the horse between themselves and him for protection. Not this man.

He cared. He was going to do whatever Foxborough wanted to protect the other three.

Just beyond the lip of rock, Foxborough saw a leather glove, then another, raised high. The man below was obviously a powerful rider, guiding the horse with his thighs, knees, and heels. The horse emerged fully from hiding, then out of the shadow of the cliff—

The saddle holster is empty, Foxborough thought just before the right-hand glove of the man below came apart in tatters, riding a storm of buckshot and fire. The air itself shook as though it had been punched from a wide circle around the explosion. But Foxborough heard and felt none of it. Also lost in the deafening explosion were the corporal's hat and the top of his skull.

Dropping his left hand, John Stockbridge scooped up the reins and steadied the once-more panicked horse as, like they were posing for a daguerreotype, the Keeler family momentarily stood motionless at the wagon. Only Rachel moved when, deciding the trail was not safe, the horse decided to try to turn back.

CHAPTER FOUR

STOCKBRIDGE KICKED HIS heels gently against
Pama, guiding him over to the wagon, where he
swung down beside the Keelers. His arrival seemed
to break the spell, and Alice Keeler began to cry.

"Lord, what have we done to *offend* you?"

The doctor dismounted and holstered the shotgun.
By then, Lenny had already put his arms around her.

"It's okay. We're all safe," he said.

"I'm very sorry," Stockbridge said earnestly. "There
was no other way."

Mrs. Keeler's right arm was outstretched and
grasping. Handing the horse's reins to Stockbridge,
Rachel went over and joined the embrace.

"If I'd shot the ledge, the rocks might have hit
you . . . hard," Stockbridge continued.

"I—I do not judge your tactics, Dr. Stockbridge,"
the woman said, breathing hard to calm herself. "You
saved us. The outlaw brought this on himself."

"In your glove," Lenny said, half turning at something just remembered. "You hid it in your glove!"

"Did you *know* him?" Stockbridge asked.

"No," Mrs. Keeler said.

"Should I go look to be sure?" Lenny asked.

"*No!*"

The woman relaxed a little, softened. "How do *you* feel, Doctor? A man of medicine forced to do . . . that."

Stockbridge picked what was left of the glove from his shotgun. "I feel like he left me no options."

"Did you ever have to doctor bad men?" Lenny asked.

"Sometimes. In the War, I treated Rebels who a minute before had been shooting at me. Humanity is a necessary thing."

"That's why we bless our meals," Mrs. Keeler said. "We were given dominion over animals, but it is unfortunate that they die so we may live."

"My pa and I fish," Lenny told Stockbridge. "I never like when they flop on the ground."

"That's enough talk," Mrs. Keeler said. She looked up at the cliff, suddenly remembering that it was a man who had died and not a salmon. The bandit's hand was hanging over the ledge, unmoving. The rifle had dropped to the ground.

Stockbridge noticed the gun and retrieved it, handing the carbine to Lenny.

"You know how to shoot, son?"

"Yes, sir."

"Watch your women," he said, turning to Pama. "I'll be going up there, see if I can find out who he was."

"Yes, *sir!*"

Stockbridge looked at the singed leather he'd tossed by his foot. "I also need his gloves."

"Do you think he had an accomplice—someone who may have heard the shot?" Rachel asked.

Stockbridge was impressed with the fur trapper's daughter. "That's another reason to go up and find out who he was, maybe where he came from."

"We're waiting for you, yes?" Mrs. Keeler asked.

"Against the cliff, out of the sun, I'd suggest."

"And safe from anyone else who may be up there," Lenny offered.

"You read my mind, son," Stockbridge said. "Would you mind watching Pama till I return?"

"That's his name?"

"That's his name," Stockbridge replied, turning before he had to explain it. He started out for a spot about thirty yards back where the slope looked as if he could climb it without much difficulty.

The spot he'd seen was the site of an old rockslide. The stones were still piled one atop the other, and he managed to make it up without dislodging any more. The climb was only two dozen feet or so. He found himself in an expanse of woods that ran into a sheer cliff several hundred feet high. Like some men Stockbridge had met on his long, strange journeys, the ridged, cleft face bore the scars of the years proudly.

Ducking low branches and listening for any distant sounds, Stockbridge made his way toward the ledge where the body still lay. He felt a little different about the man now that he was up here—no longer a threat eliminated but a corpse, like a battlefield casualty once the shooting had stopped.

The dead man was dressed in buckskins and fur boots, both weathered. They were about twenty miles from Buzzard Gulch, the nearest town, and the people there did not have much of a selection of anything. The shoes were not sturdy enough for long mountain walks. There had to be a horse somewhere.

He would look for it when he was done. Right now he had to work quickly.

Companions, if any, would have heard that shot. And they would have known that the loud report did not come from the carbine Stockbridge had recovered.

Squatting beside the man, the doctor turned him over, his head flopping grotesquely. It was gone above the forehead, the skin and skull ragged from the blast. His eyes were still in place, and staring, and Stockbridge shut them. He had never liked being stared at by dead men. It was an unflinching window to another world, one Stockbridge would get to know soon enough, as all men did.

His wife's eyes had been like that before—he thought while fighting back a scream that, had it started, would never have stopped—he had shut them.

The pockets had chewing tobacco and nothing else. There was nothing written, no indication of who this man had been or where he had lived. He did wear a set of bobcat teeth on a leather strap. The hide looked like it was from a smaller animal, possibly a fox, judging from its color and delicacy. Necklaces made from bison or bear tended to be thicker and used for bracelets. Stockbridge took it, not for himself but because men like the dead man did not make things—they took them.

From Ben Keeler?

There was no way he could take the time to bury the man. It would take too much time to haul rocks, and the ground was too hard—even if he had a shovel. A pick was needed.

"Sorry," Stockbridge said, yanking off the man's gloves before rising. "You belong to the land now."

The gloves were old and worn, but they fit. With a heartfelt sigh, the doctor walked to the ledge and tested the sturdiness before putting his full weight on it and leaning out. "Everyone okay down there?"

"We're well, Dr. Stockbridge," Mrs. Keeler replied.

"I'll be coming back down in a minute," he said. "I want to have a look around."

"Please be careful!" Rachel called up.

Careful?

That was a word he had ignored for most of his life. His War service, his move to Colorado with his young family, his pursuit of Piedmont. Nothing, ever, had been careful.

Turning and wending his way through the trees, his shotgun swinging like a clock pendulum ticking death for any accomplices, Stockbridge stalked toward the shadowy woodland beyond. It was the only place to conceal a horse that would not have been visible from the ledge. The grass was brittle and crushed in spots. Twigs were freshly snapped and hanging, too high for a buck but about the height of a man's shoulder. The dead man had come this way.

Sunlight and shadow played like a zoetrope that he had seen back in Gunnison, a spinning wheel of still images that seemed to move when viewed through a slit. The trees seemed to be in motion, bending north as though in obeisance to the mountain beyond. The ground was more level up here, then flat, and soon the trees gave way to an open field.

Stockbridge stopped suddenly. There was a horse ahead. There were no supplies and no packed saddle-bag, and the saddle was beside it. The horse had to belong to the dead man. Stockbridge jogged ahead. As he neared, there were disturbing signs about where the horse had come from.

This was not the kind of place Ben Keeler or any other trapper would have gone. There were no water and no fat trees or big rocks, no high grasses for predators or prey to hide in. No one but a bush-whacker like the dead man would have had reason to be here.

So what is the horse of a trapper doing tied to a tree up ahead?

As Stockbridge neared, he saw that it bore the marks of a sledge hitch on its brown-and-white-mottled hide. The marks were distinctive, the kind he had seen during the War. The carryalls were made of poplar or some other light, flexible wood, woven to carry considerable weight. There was no way that even the most careful trapper could have prevented the shifting and abrasion of such a conveyance.

Goddamn the man, he thought as he approached the quiet animal.

Stockbridge had had a feeling that the necklace hadn't belonged to the gunman. A man who would have bothered to make such a trophy in the first place would likely have killed the cat with a knife. He would not have fought a cat unless the cat had attacked him. And he would have cut out the teeth right there, a memento of a dangerous encounter he had survived.

Stockbridge felt hollow in his gut as he walked, heard the adornment clattering in his deep pocket. A trapper would have had the time and the reason to make such a thing. And not necessarily for himself, but for a son he loved and missed. Stockbridge had, with a lead ball he had removed from a famed Colorado lawman. His son had been wearing it on his belt buckle the day he died.

Nearing the horse, Stockbridge took care to look for signs of anyone approaching. He did not see dust kicked up anywhere against the clear sky to the east or the west of the looming peak. He did not hear anyone calling or hooves pounding. He moved cautiously, his shotgun loaded and ready. He saw the tracks the horse had made coming to this spot—from the west, higher up on the Peak Road.

This man did live here, then.

Finally reaching the horse, he heard nothing but wildlife and wind—

Until he heard Mrs. Keeler scream his name.

CHAPTER FIVE

IN THE PAST, one shot barely got the attention of the Red Hunters. It was usually a warning, fired by Foxborough. But two shots, especially one that boomed in a way a rifle did not, and fired some small time apart, suggested trouble.

Riding out from the compound built in the shadow of Tustine Peak, below the rich hunting grounds of Craggy Plains, Liam McWilliams and Woodrow Pound were prepared for trouble. With eagle eyes set in an aquiline face, his long brown hair in a ponytail, McWilliams had often ridden out to help Foxborough, when he had been trapped by Union soldiers, and he had usually been the man who rode out to check on his friend and help him with any booty. Pound rode out this time because the black man's weapons were blade and arrow, and danger sometimes called for stealth.

The men did not ride through the woodlands but

took the more direct route down the trail. McWilliams knew the spot where Foxborough hid. They slowed their approach as they neared the bend. Weapons ready, they came around the sharp turn.

Both men stopped when they saw the wagon tucked in the cold shadow below the cliff. It was situated right below one of Foxborough's lookout points along the trail. In the back appeared to be a woman and two children; the trail was too bright and the shade too deep to be sure. The new arrivals could not tell whether the others were armed. The men had to assume they were.

Slowly, the two men moved forward in a line, Woodrow Pound in front with an arrow in his bow. Behind him, McWilliams drew his carbine from the saddle holster. The gunman had a surer seat and was a better shot on horseback. He made sure the barrel caught the sunlight, suggesting to the folks ahead that it would be wise to adopt a civil manner. If Pound fell, McWilliams would fire.

The two men stopped again when they heard the woman cry a name. Liam rode up, inside of where Pound sat.

"Dr. Stockbridge?" the man with the carbine said, smiling crookedly. "Do you mean *Dr. Vengeance*? The killer with a ten-gauge against one shoulder and a chip on the other."

"I heard down at Raspy's it was double-barreled twelve," Pound said.

"That could be," McWilliams said. "Or it could be we were all drunk when we heard it." He adjusted his hat and looked around. "I don't see nobody."

"Nor hear 'im," Pound said.

"I think she's lying."

Pound's dark eyes were on the wagon. "Okay,

now—where's our friend Grady? You're here. He isn't. That suggests you know where he *went*. He take some stuff and go? Maybe a shotgun, test-fired it?"

As one, the Keelers did not answer. Lenny shifted dangerously, as threatening as a boy in single digits could be. A metallic point of light emerged from the darkness.

Pound's eyes narrowed. He rode forward a few paces. "Liam—is that Grady's carbine the kid's holding?"

McWilliams lowered the brim of his hat and peered ahead. "Damn. How'd you get that, boy?"

"Let's get back to the cabin, rouse the others," Pound said.

"Yeah," McWilliams agreed, his eyes searching the ledge for the hint of a shotgun.

Pound wheeled around but had not yet finished his turn when he stopped. He was staring at something behind them. He swore. McWilliams turned to Pound and saw where he was looking—

Grady's horse was standing in the middle of the trail to the west. The man in the saddle was not their point. He held a shotgun in his right hand. It rested against his shoulder, almost as though it were part of the arm.

"Ben!" Mrs. Keeler cried out.

"It's John, Mrs. Keeler," the rider said solemnly.

The sad cry that followed felt like a pistol shot in the heart. "But that's his horse!"

"I know. Stay where you are."

McWilliams was still holding his carbine but was facing the wrong way. Stockbridge's arm, his right arm, was pointed straight down his side. The Red Hunter was weighing his chances in a draw.

"I know what you want to do, Liam, but don't," Pound quietly cautioned his companion. He lowered his own bow and arrow.

"He won't shoot me in the back," McWilliams said. But he still did not move.

Stockbridge shouted past the men. "Rachel? Turn the wagon around and head back down the trail."

Mrs. Keeler was still sobbing. "But Ben?"

"He was not up there. I will join you presently. Leave Pama—he'll be fine there. I think he's getting used to me."

"Ma, please let's do what Dr. Stockbridge says," Rachel implored.

Without hesitation, Lenny urged her from her confused, frozen state. "You lie down. We have to go like Dr. Stockbridge said."

Rachel nodded and took her mother's arm. "Come on. It's not safe here."

Mrs. Keeler moved as if she were sleepwalking, allowing herself to be helped onto the blankets. Rachel hurried to the driver's seat of the buckboard.

With a lingering look at Dr. Stockbridge, the girl made a chucking sound to get the horse moving. The wheels sounded like a nest of crickets as she put the wagon through a tight turn and retreated to the east.

The two men of the Red Hunters watched in silence. Then they turned back to Stockbridge. Save for two daunting pinpoints of reflected sun, his eyes were lost in the dark beneath his Stetson. The shadow seemed almost like a mask, something the Red Hunters had once half jokingly said they should wear to instill fear and cooperation.

Stockbridge was not a joke.

McWilliams was sitting there, itchy and mad. Pound could see it in his little tics and twitches. The former slave wondered if Stockbridge could see it, too.

The answer was a shotgun blast into the air beside them. The two men and their horses jumped, the horses most of all. Stockbridge was right: Pama started but did not run. He had no trouble controlling the smaller, older Palomino he was astride.

Even before the echo of the shot had died, before a few pebbles unhappy with the sound had finished falling from the ledge, while McWilliams and Pound were still settling their mounts, Stockbridge was again composed and ready.

"What happened to the rider of this Palomino?" the new arrival demanded.

"To hell with you!" McWilliams cried.

"We don't know," Pound replied with a cooler voice. He glared at McWilliams, who snorted but settled some.

"I don't believe you," Stockbridge said back. "I'll ask it simpler. Is he alive or dead?"

"We don't know that either," Pound said. "That's the truth. This was Grady's horse."

"What happened to Grady?" McWilliams demanded.

"Grady is deceased. I didn't have time to bury him. If you are inclined to, he's right up top on the ledge."

The speaker's casual manner caused McWilliams to raise his rifle and start to turn. Pound moved between his companion and Stockbridge, one hand raised to show the doctor he meant no aggression.

"Not here, not now!" Pound said to the other through his teeth.

McWilliams hollered inarticulately at Stockbridge, a cry that seemed to start somewhere around his knees, but he did not raise the rifle higher or finish his turn.

Stockbridge relaxed but did not lower the shotgun. "I've shown you how easy it is to answer a question, so one more time. I am looking for the man whose horse this lawfully is."

"And I'm telling you, you killed the only man who could say," Pound replied.

"Then let's try this. Who are you two?"

"We're mountain men," Pound answered. "We like to live where it's clean and quiet."

"Wearing boots from an Eastern catalogue and a holster that's gunsmith leather and not stag hide? That's not the truth."

"It *is* the truth," Pound insisted.

"Your friend Grady was what we called a spotter during the War," Stockbridge said. "He picked off supply lines—in this case, your man picked off goods. I'm guessing you use what you need and sell what you don't. You probably live low enough in the mountains so you don't get too snowbound. How many of you are there and *where* are you?"

"You ask too many questions, Stockbridge," McWilliams said.

"Liam—," Pound said.

"No, the man runs off his mouth like he owns the place *and* us. Tell you what, Dr. Vengeance. We're through jawing. We won't go after the lady and her kin, but we *are* leaving. We're going to go collect our friend and comrade. You want to shoot us, shoot us. You want to tail us, tail us. Up to you. But the men up there"—he pointed—"they aren't gonna be happy when they learn what you done. I suggest that when you go after those folks below, you keep going—as fast as your big horse can take you."

"I'm still not satisfied with the progress of our conversation," Stockbridge said. "But you're right. That family needs seeing to, so I'll ask you something easy. Then we can all be on our way. Okay?"

McWilliams was still. Pound nodded.

"Where was Grady coming from, and when, first time he came in with this mount?"

"It was about two weeks ago or so," Pound told him. "He was still at the higher elevation then, the last time for the season."

"On the Craggy Plains?"

"No. Grady didn't go there."

"Oh?"

"Had problems with his wind. That's a little too high for him."

Stockbridge believed that. The man had had chewing tobacco instead of a pouch and fixings. "Where *would* he have been, then?"

"Eagle Lookout, west of where Oónâhe'e River turns. It's not far from the trail and convenient to watering horses."

"And ambushing trappers?" Stockbridge said with distaste.

"Grady swore he found that Palomino."

"I like to presume a man innocent, so we'll leave it there. But I'll be taking this horse back to the family that rightly owns him."

Stockbridge gave the horse a gentle nudge with his knees and started forward. The two other men stood where they were, even as Stockbridge passed by, presenting his back. It was not that Stockbridge was especially trusting of these two, particularly McWilliams. He did not need to be. If the Walker so much as whinnied or backed up a step, Stockbridge would duck low, turn, and blast everything behind him.

He didn't think the black man would permit that. Pound was the more rational of the two, as many former slaves tended to be. Bondage had taught them not only to do things silently but not to provoke anger.

Pama was calm, and when Stockbridge grabbed up the reins, the Walker followed on his own.

Eagle Lookout.

He knew the Oónâhe'e from maps he had studied

in Gunnison, when he was plotting his westward trip.
It meant "frog," and the river was named for the fact
that the Cheyenne had followed it up, carrying frogs
in baskets. As high as one of the animals could be
carried without freezing, that was how the Cheyenne
could settle what was safe for papooses.

The location was curious, though, if Pound had
been speaking the truth. It did not intercept where
Ben Keeler was supposed to have been. Craggy
Plains was to the west, and lower, separated by a wide
valley.

But there's the necklace.

It was a puzzle—one that required both identifica-
tion from Mrs. Keeler and some answers about what
else her husband might have been doing in the mountains, far from where a trapper going about his business might have been. . . .

CHAPTER SIX

THE RED HUNTERS called it a cabin, but their residence was substantially more than that. It was a compound, a combination of a long barracks and numerous outbuildings all nestled in a natural fortress.

The main building was made to endure time and relentless elements. It was constructed of logs and stone, put together by the men who lived there from trees they cut on the surrounding land. The squat, sure edifice was set in the middle of a stretch of flat land, far enough from the surrounding cliffs to survive an avalanche, should it come, and adjacent to a tributary of the Oónâhe'e River that ran clear to the lower foothills. The Red Hunters used it for washing and bathing. Many a Cheyenne or settler came to those tributaries looking to drink or bathe and found, instead, Grady Foxborough.

In addition to the cabin, there were a stable and, beside it, a barn. The former was entirely made of oak, which allowed the passage of wind and ventilation, while the barn was stone and tree, like the cabin. Three other structures completed the compound: a toolshed stocked mostly with items that had belonged to those passing through, a sturdy outhouse, and a large root cellar, which had meat, vegetables, and an ample supply of spirits. There was a stone well beside it, always rich with sweet mountain water. The underground waterway was extensive, stretching from the mountains to the plains, where it fed watering holes for miles around.

Every now and then, Franz Baker made half-hearted attempts to plant a vegetable garden, mostly for potatoes and carrots, but the lack of sun and the short growing season made the enterprise more trouble than it was worth. The scars of his failed efforts decorated the area out back like a patchwork quilt of dark brown fossilized mud. Also, the surrounding cliffs—which afforded the settlement protection from often battering winds—tended to keep the cold locked in place. It swept from above like an invisible waterfall carrying away seeds and plants along with the smell of the horses, pigs, and chickens. It wasn't easy lugging vegetables from Buzzard Gulch or the more distant but better-stocked Stackpole, but Baker had to do it only a few times a year. The root cellar kept food cold and unspoiled up here.

The cook actually did not mind the occasional trip for provisions. It was the only time he got out. Just like during the War, he had to stay by the mess wagon while the others fought and drank and found whatever women were to be found.

"The only female flesh I ever handle is dead," he had complained during the War. "And chicken or deer at that."

"At least you'll survive this damn thing," then-Captain Promise Cuthbert had said.

"Lest the Blues target the grub wagon, try to starve you gentlemen into surrender," he said. "I hear we had savages with flaming arrows do that to them."

"They ain't got the Indians *or* the smarts to do that," Sergeant Alan DeLancy had said.

"I think you're safe, Herr Baker." Cuthbert had grinned, slapping the cook on the shoulder.

So he was. They had all survived the War, every one of the Red Hunters. Promise Cuthbert had taken that as a sign that whenever and however the struggle ended, the core of them was meant to stay together. A new family to replace the flesh-and-blood family he had lost to fire and retribution. Since they had rejoined out here, they had looked after one another like the brothers they were—brothers at arms as well as brothers of the Deep South.

Except for Woodrow Pound, who typically kept to himself making new arrows or bows and reading. He had first taught himself to read, then spent his free time occasionally playing checkers with Baker or seeing the world without ever leaving the pages of the books he picked up on trips to Gunnison.

That was the other thing about the compound. It was not just a collection of walls and rooms, floors and handmade furniture. It was a state of mind. It had a name, which was emblazoned on a large wooden board that stood high atop two oak-sturdy posts: New Richmond. It was the small but assertive rebirth of a fallen civilization, transplanted to the West. There would not be any cotton or tobacco or peaches up here in the cold, sunless heights. The men could not even get an apple tree to grow here. But over cigars and drink, purchased from that Russian curiosity Raspy Nikolaev in Buzzard Gulch, the men would talk about ways the West could be shaped using the mistakes of the past.

"Without the leg-irons," Woodrow Pound would suggest as he cut new shafts or feathers or shaped new arrowheads. He never drank or smoked, not having had the chance to acquire a taste for doing so as a slave.

"That condition was the idea of our Northern brothers," Promise Cuthbert would answer back. "Importing you all, I mean. We had men here for those chores. The Indians."

Pound was not interested in debating men who believed that any soul should be enslaved. He had other reasons for staying here. The Red Hunters needed his skills, and he liked being the equal to men who could have been former masters. To him, New Richmond was a place where he could be the first man of his heritage to rise to Southern aristocracy.

His old friend, an elderly slave named Freddy Hat, would have found that amusing or uplifting or both. He could hear the dead man's voice in his ear.

"Woodrow Pound, Prince of New Richmond. I like the kick of that mule."

Right now, however, events were such that every filament of routine was rudely and suddenly torn and shredded.

The return of McWilliams and Pound had not been one of fellowship and celebration. For the first time since their founding, New Richmond and the Red Hunters had their first taste of grief—and, worse to some, of failure.

Wrapped in a bearskin cloak that was itself wrapped in the clinging smell of old grease, Baker was outside, sitting on a rickety stool, sitting over a pit used for collecting blood and guts. He was in the process of skinning three hares for stew, all of which he had shot himself. The open hole was far from the cabin and helpful keeping varmints like raccoons away from the residence.

When there got to be too many in that population, he sprinkled the pit with arsenic. He remembered the powder from when he had been a seven-year-old boy. The newspapers in Bonn told how an English confectioner accidentally put the stuff in sweets and poisoned more than two hundred people. That sounded like the kind of job he wanted. When he had been fourteen, he went to sea as a cabin boy, then worked in the galley for a dozen years before coming to these shores. He never did poison anyone, but it was nice knowing he could.

The offal pit was also far enough from the water table so that what they pulled from the well did not taste of blood.

Baker's oval, gray-bearded face took one look at the parcel the two men were bringing in, then a shorter, glancing look at the slumped shoulders of the men, then went back to work. He knew whom they were bringing back, and he did not want to be a direct part of what was sure to follow. He had served with the men in the War, but, as a recent immigrant, he had not been invested in their cause. Like Pound, he was an outsider on the inside.

DeLancy and Tunney came out when they heard the horses. They had the same immediate understanding as Baker, though their response was considerably less serene. Tunney swore loudly, and DeLancy said something in French that the others did not understand the meaning of—though they grasped the shock and disbelief.

Their cries brought Cuthbert out. The leader was smoking a cigar, and he stared through the smoke at the bundle of dead man still athwart McWilliams' horse. He threw the smoke aside out of respect.

"What happened?" he asked quietly—though his dark, ridged brow and scowling mouth were anything but gentle.

McWilliams dismounted and, in respectful tones, explained what had taken place on Peak Road. Pound remained silent. Since he was not one of the original Red Hunters, he did not offer intelligence and reconnaissance unless asked. It had nothing to do with his skin color but with the history the others had together. He accepted that as proper and natural.

When McWilliams had finished, Cuthbert was seethingly quiet for a long moment before he stepped over to look at the body.

He stood beside the corpse, which was draped over the back of McWilliams' horse. The head had been wrapped in the buckskin jacket the man had been wearing. It was thick with blood that was still *plip-plop*ping on the ground. There were scurrying sounds out by the entry and along the path, vermin already feeding on the blood that had spilled from the wound.

At last, Cuthbert spoke.

"One of us gone," he said mournfully, his face downturned, his voice falling onto the stones beneath his feet. "Lost in the line of duty. That's something. I always thought— Well, this being Grady, I always thought he would die over a card game. He would have liked knowing he went like a soldier." Cuthbert's eyes were red when they looked back at McWilliams. "What he would *not* have liked is that the coward who did this still lives—and was allowed to ride off on the horse that *belonged* to Grady!"

"Sir, this man Stockbridge believed it to be stolen from a fella name of Ben Keeler," McWilliams said softly.

Only Cuthbert's military training stopped him from slapping the speaker with open disgust. He moved to within inches of the man's cold breath. The captain spit a piece of cigar wrapping to the side. It landed on McWilliams' sleeve. He left it.

"I don't know or give a ripping damn who Ben Keeler is or was," Cuthbert hissed. "I *do* know that a Hunter is dead, and the man who killed him *isn't*. That will be fixed. Where did he go?"

"He left going south along the trail. I got the impression he was going to shadow the folks in the wagon in case we came after him."

"Which you should have done!" the captain said.

"I'll find him," McWilliams vowed. "I swear I'll find him. Grady was my friend, too."

DeLancy came forward. "Captain, I read about this man Stockbridge. Dr. Vengeance, they call him. Carries a double-barreled—"

"A double-barreled what?" Cuthbert turned on him. "I don't care if he's got a twelve-pound Howitzer strapped to his back! He is *one* man with *one* gun, and he's looking after a woman and children! How is that a problem for the bloody Red Hunters?"

The others stood in still, shamed silence.

Cuthbert laid a hand on Foxborough's dead shoulder as if it were a Bible and he was taking a vow. "I want the killer's body *right here*, living or lifeless, ready to feed to the wolves!"

DeLancy did not bother reciting what else he had read. He nodded to the captain and stepped back.

Cuthbert turned away from the horse and its dead rider. He looked at every face in turn, noted the grief in each, though with McWilliams it was mixed with abject shame.

"The name of the family he was with," Cuthbert said without looking at McWilliams or Pound, "it was Keeler?"

"Yes, sir," McWilliams answered.

"Fine. I was going to go and visit Molly for the night. I'll leave early, just as soon as we've seen to our fallen comrade. While I'm down there, I'll get a bead on the family and see what anyone has seen or heard of this Dr. Vengeance."

"You want I should come with you to town?" DeLancy asked.

"To do what? Take a bath?"

"No, sir. I was just thinking we could both ask around—"

"I can hunt a man with a double-barrel Parker Brothers by myself. Thank you," the former officer said. He snickered. "You see, Sergeant? I *do* read, sometimes."

"Captain, that man—he didn't face Grady," Pound said. "What we could tell, he snuck under him and blew off part of the ledge he was on."

"So he's a coward," Cuthbert said. "Maybe the newspaper lied about that showdown, dressed it up for the readers back east. So much the better."

"What I mean, sir, is he may come at you from hiding, or in the dark."

"I will not let him," Cuthbert said. He looked around again. "None of us will! We will be as vigilant as if we expected him to come riding right into New Richmond at any moment!"

Cuthbert's eyes returned to the black man.

"You, mister," he said, his eyes sliding to the other man, "and you, Corporal McWilliams, will be going nowhere today."

McWilliams stiffened and seemed to want to object but thought better of it. The other men seemed on Cuthbert's side, even Pound.

"After you bury Grady, you will stay out of my sight until I bring in the man who did this. Do you have any questions about those orders, *brothers*?"

"No, sir," both men replied as one, McWilliams without enthusiasm.

Cuthbert inhaled his grief and stood a moment

longer beside the body of his comrade. Flies were beginning to circle. The captain shooed them off and
then slowly, almost reluctantly, pressed his right palm
on a bloody section of the jacket. Walking back to the
cabin, stomping hard on the still smoldering cigar,
Cuthbert lingered at the threshold and pressed a red
handprint on the outside of the oak door.

"This is the first red patch of one of our own men,"
he said without turning. "There will not be another."

Then he went inside to prepare for his journey, a
trip that would take the better part of the afternoon.

Outside, the other men gathered around the horse
and its grisly cargo. Their cold breath, expressions
frozen in bereavement, and their drab winter colors
made them seem deader than Grady Foxborough.

"Wasn't there no way you could have shot him?"
vacant-eyed Tunney asked of McWilliams.

"Even if he took you down, where was your
honor?" DeLancy asked. It was an earnest question.
He truly did not understand.

"I wanted to fire! Lord Jesus, I almost did. But—
Woodrow, you saw; you warned me—that shotgun
would've cut me and Woodrow in half before I could
have shouldered the carbine."

DeLancy's eyes rolled toward the black man.
"That true?"

"Which part? Yeah, Liam was going to draw.
Yeah, I told him we'd both likely be shot off our
horses." The big man stepped forward, his hand on
the hilt of his knife. "I'm no coward, and I will gut
any man who says so," he said, and nodded toward
the cabin door. "But then you'd have three patches up
there and no idea who did it or where he went."

"Where did he go?" Tunney asked.

"We didn't see," McWilliams said. "He was behind us, damn it. He made us ride off."

Pound gave his companion a disapproving look. It wasn't the only one. As Baker joined the others, every eye, every tightly closed mouth, every fist said the same thing: *You should have died trying.*

All of them knew, without saying it, that the Red Hunters could have survived three deaths easier than two cowards.

Woodrow Pound broke the silence by heading toward the toolshed.

"Liam, let's take care of Grady," he said.

There was more than a touch of anger in his voice and in his posture as well. McWilliams had blamed him, the Red Hunters outsider, for the fact that they were both alive. They had survived the encounter because Pound had urged caution instead of stupid Southern pride and backbone.

You did that with Freddy, and Freddy didn't listen, he thought.

Freddy Hat had been named for the tattered straw hat he wore over his head in the field to keep out the sun and over his face at night to block the torchlight when he slept. He had no last name that he knew of. In the ledgers they just recorded "Freddy."

Freddy looked after his fellow Africans. He used to admonish Pound as he did all the male field slaves, *"Move careful, 'cause you don't get another chance in life."* Freddy was older by about ten years. Shortly before Pound was bought, Freddy had tried to escape while the slaves were bathing in a river. He was caught by whites and pulled down by dogs, and when the overseer caught up, he slashed Freddy's left hamstring on the spot. The slave had the choice of bleeding to death in the rushing waters or dragging himself back to the South Carolina cotton plantation.

He wanted to live. With his tattered shirt tied

tightly just above his ankle, he half stumbled, half crawled back.

Woodrow Pound, too, had wanted to live—even when he made the same escape on the same river in the same way. He did that for himself and for Freddy, who had died under the lash the week before. Freddy had really died on that river, his spirit crushed, but he had lived on for just over a year.

Pound had used that year to make a knife. He made it from a spike that had been used to hold a slave chain to a rock, working it out with a tenpenny nail. He had worked the iron out and over the next thirteen months rubbed it over and over on any stone he could find until it was deadly sharp. He killed the first dog that had caught him, then threw its dead carcass at the others in the pack. They all stopped to chew it up while he got away.

"Why'd you lie about where Stockbridge went?" Pound asked as they made their way to the shed.

"Got my reasons," McWilliams answered, and that was all he said. "Just shut up. You done enough talking."

"Me?"

"I wanted to shoot him. I should've took him."

"You didn't see you."

McWilliams glared at the other. "What the hell does that mean?"

"You sat there like a statue. You hadn't decided *nothing*."

McWilliams stopped and grabbed the front of the taller man's coat. "You saying I'm yellow?"

Pound slapped his large hands on those of the other man and pried them away. He held them tight so McWilliams had to stay where he was.

"I'm saying that you and the others with your Southern swagger—you're all ambush fighters. You never had to face a man with a whip or a dog whose leash he was eager to let go. I learned to pick my time. Back there on Peak Road? That wasn't it. Your life, *brother*? It was yours to spend if you wanted. What I didn't want to risk was my life on you outdrawing a man who carried that custom shotgun like it was part of him."

Pound released the other man and turned toward the shed. McWilliams stood there a moment, staring at the ground, seeing the moment again.

"No," he said softly.

But in his brain he said, *Yes*. He had been afraid to test himself against that man. To turn and raise the carbine and aim and fire—while facing those double barrels that had scattershot Grady Foxborough to the next world.

With the sudden weight of shame bowing his shoulders, McWilliams continued on to the shed.

The interment was slow and somber, with picks chewing up the hard earth and just McWilliams and Pound tending to the chore. The other men did not want to be around them. McWilliams muttered about being ashamed, and Pound told him to shut up.

"We ain't ever gonna be forgave," McWilliams said.

"By who? Them or you?"

McWilliams frowned. He had not thought of that. "Both."

"What d'you want to do, go hang yourself from the hayloft?"

"No," McWilliams said. "I got a different idea."

"Yeah? What?"

"That's my business. I had your advice enough for one day."

"Sure. I'll be quiet, with you the loser."

After the picks had loosened several feet of hard soil, the men used the shovels. With solemnity and respect, and all but Cuthbert watching from the windows, the men removed the body from McWilliams' horse and laid their dead brother in his grave. Only when the uneven, six-by-two hole had been covered and patted down did the others come out. There was complete silence in the circle until Cuthbert said words over the grave.

"Lord, we give you the remains of our beloved brother, and we vow to send your way the man who did this. It is our hope that you accept the soul of Grady Foxborough and consign the eternal spirit of the bastard who killed him to hell."

The leader of the Red Hunters was ready to go by then. He had his overnight grip, which included pearl-handled twin Colts in their holsters—worn guns upset delicate Molly—and his horse was saddled. He went to the stable and departed without comment, riding off with a fury the others had not seen in eighteen years—not in the War, but in the shameful peace, the news of which Colonel Moore had brought to them.

DeLancy, Tunney, and Baker went inside, followed by Pound. McWilliams stood by his horse, his hand on the bridle, his eyes on the ground.

"No, Woodrow," he said under his breath, "it will not be Liam McWilliams hanging from the hayloft."

Somber and decided, McWilliams climbed into the saddle. There was a reason he had not told Cuthbert that Dr. Vengeance Stockbridge had remained on the trail and headed east. He did not want Cuthbert to run off in pursuit. The captain was angry, but he was also a careful man. He used to plan their attacks after getting as much information as possible.

He would do that now. But because he was mad, he would hurry to do that now. He would take the fastest way down from the uplands, a turn to the north, headed higher, then a winding slope straight down. It was steeper and more dangerous but faster.

The route was prone to rockslides, rutted with run-off, and home to bobcats. It was not only faster, but it went around the hundreds of acres of homestead and would put him closer to Buzzard Gulch, the town where Molly worked. It was a place where Cuthbert could ask around about the Keelers and where they lived, maybe find out from Sheriff Neal something about the man with the shotgun.

McWilliams rode off. He did not look back to see if the others were watching. He did not care. Right now he was not a Red Hunter; he was Liam McWilliams with a stain on his name—a stain that could only be washed off with blood.

He would win back the respect of the captain and his brothers—even if it killed him.

CHAPTER SEVEN

JOHN STOCKBRIDGE AND the Keelers had reached the point where the foothills became a plain. They had been mostly silent on the passage down so that Stockbridge and Rachel could pay attention to their footing. It was an unseen fissure, hidden among weeds, that had spilled them before. Lenny helped, keeping a careful watch.

The only one who spoke was Mrs. Keeler.

"I want to go back for him," Mrs. Keeler murmured every now and then on the way down. "We must go back."

"We'll see to that presently," Stockbridge had replied, just once. "First, we've got to put some distance between us and those men."

The woman continued talking, as if she were in a trance. The others let her be.

They had stopped at the start of the level trail only long enough for Stockbridge to swap horses. Stockbridge wanted to be on his trusted mount in case there was pursuit. Having left the foothills behind, they were now on level ground with a clear view to about a mile back, where the path curved into the trees. They tied the Palomino to the back of the wagon, Mrs. Keeler eyeing it as if she expected her husband to appear magically.

They were riding among boulders and cacti, about the only things above ground level here. Stockbridge was riding a pace ahead of the buckboard, looking back at Lenny and Rachel—and their subdued mother, in the rear—but he was really keeping an eye on whatever might be behind them on the trail. He knew that if he kept turning around to check, it would make the Keelers nervous. This way was better.

With Ben's horse behind her, Mrs. Keeler started up again with a different cant.

"Where are you?" she said to the shadow in her mind. "Where could you be?"

Since she wasn't asking anyone other than herself, and since the question was unanswerable at present, the others said nothing.

"What book were you reading, son?" Stockbridge asked Lenny as cheerfully as he could muster. "The one that fell over the side?"

"I wasn't reading a book, Doctor," Lenny said, puffing his chest a little. "I was writing one."

"Oh?"

Rachel said, "My pa reads a lot to us when he's home. While he's gone, Ma schools us. She taught us how to read and write."

"Good things to know."

"I got bored just writing words, so I strung 'em together," Lenny said.

"Makes sense. What were you writing about?"

"A dog we had, Terrier Joe. He was killed fighting coyotes. I wrote about some of the adventures I'm sure he had in secret. All dogs do, I reckon. I drew pictures, too." He tapped his temple. "I remember most of it, though. I can do it again."

"Good lad."

"Did you ever have a dog, Dr. Stockbridge?" Rachel asked.

His voice was wistful when he said, "Once I did."

"Or maybe I should write about you, Doctor," Lenny said after some consideration.

"I see. But then it wouldn't be doggerel."

"Sir?"

Stockbridge smiled. "I was making a joke. That's what you call a kind of fun-loving story."

Rachel smiled. "And Lenny's story was *about* a dog. That's funny."

Mrs. Keeler crawled forward, bundled in the blankets. "Dr. Stockbridge?"

The doctor fell back a few paces. "Ma'am?"

"We should go back. We should find my Ben, alive or . . . or wherever he is."

"That will be done, Mrs. Keeler. You have my word. But you also have to think of yourself and the children now. You saw. There are men back there— the man who shot at you, who I killed, was their friend. They aren't going away."

"But I feel so helpless. Things—things were getting *better*."

"What do you mean?"

"The fur trade," she said. "Pelts were coming in from Canada, lower cost. The two other trappers from this region gave up. They went up to the Klondike, rumors of gold and all. Then President Arthur, the Lord bless, put on all these tariffs—and the demand rose again. Ben went out, full of hope for the first time in years." She smiled for the first time that

Stockbridge could recall. "Funny how a little thing so far away can change your spirits."

"Isn't it?"

"I thought—I *hoped* and still do—that he had stayed out longer just in case things changed again, like I read about them doing in Washington."

"As you say, that just may be what he's done," Stockbridge told her.

"But I don't feel it." Mrs. Keeler managed a thin smile. "I've known Ben for so long, and so close, it's as if a part of me is *gone*." She looked up at Stockbridge, her cheeks turning bright red. "I'm sorry. You've been so kind, and I shouldn't burden you. I barely know you."

"There's no need for apologies. I know that feeling all too well. And what I learned is that you have to let other people help you."

"Did you lose someone, Doctor?"

"Several someones, all of them dear. Mrs. Keeler, you took a bold, brave step coming out here. Now you have to take another by going back for the sake of the children. I have experience with people like those we met, and also with tracking. You'd be doing me a favor, and an honor, to let me see to this."

"Doctor, you *are* good. Me and Ben and the kids have never had anyone other than ourselves to rely on. It's a new feeling."

"I know that, too."

"Ben and me—we ran away when we were teenagers, my parents disapproving of Ben's trade. They had ambitions for me. They're the publishers of a newspaper, the *Colorado Line & Telegram*."

Stockbridge suppressed a snicker. "I know the publication. Did any part of you want that life?"

"Not really," she admitted. "I've always loved the

outdoors. The idea of a desk, ink, presses, type, counting out words for advertisers—it held no appeal."

"That could be where your boy gets his interest in writing and reporting."

"Maybe. He doesn't really know his grandparents."

"Perhaps this would be a good time to fix that."

Mrs. Keeler thought for a moment, then sighed. "That's too big a thought for right now. But thank you for giving me the thought, Dr. Stockbridge. You may be right."

Still riding beside the wagon, Stockbridge looked ahead. He saw nothing but more boulders, more cacti, and more dirt. "Will we reach your place before nightfall?"

"Maybe a little after," she said.

Stockbridge peered at the cacti that were the only things that grew here. They were clustered together around what were probably pockets of water close to the surface.

"Is there water nearby? The horses will need it."

She looked north, then south, then decided and pointed southeast. "There's a freshwater pond about two miles out of the way. We used to make it a day's outing, taking the children there to swim."

"It's a detour we'd best take," Stockbridge said.

Unlike on the trail, the plain to the southeast was dotted with hills so low, they barely merited the name. That was why the trail was where it was, pushing straight across the flatlands. Stockbridge suspected the region was laced with underground streams, something common to the land below the Rockies. Like the trail, the terrain would afford very little cover if they were attacked. Just the boulders, and he did not relish being pinned down behind one.

Mrs. Keeler seemed to read his mind. "Do you think those men are following us?"

"I don't know."

"Would you?"

"Probably, though not at once. Men make foolish errors when they don't take time to think. Either way, the animals need rest."

Mrs. Keeler nodded. "I wonder if we should have just given him the wagon."

"Forgive my asking, but you have an old injury, yes?"

"My leg. From a fall decorating a Christmas tree. It did not heal properly."

"Well, ma'am, you would not have survived the walk back," Stockbridge said, "and I don't think they would have left you your fuzztail."

"No, I suppose not."

"If you don't mind, when we reach the cabin, I'd like to look at your leg. Might be something that can be fixed."

"By cutting?"

"That would have to be a part of it, yes."

The woman shook her head. "Thank you, but I near bled to death having Rachel, and it seems that this is what God wanted for me. It hasn't held me back any."

"I can see that. Offer stands if you change your mind."

The woman smiled appreciatively before drifting into thoughts of her own—perhaps the past, perhaps the present, perhaps tomorrow. Stockbridge trotted to the front of the wagon and told Rachel the plan.

"I know the place," she said. "We always came to it from home, but I think I can find it this way."

"I could find it, too," Lenny said. "You see all the tracks in the ground? Lots of people probably come here."

Rachel frowned. "Lenny, there aren't 'lots' of people living in this part of Colorado. Plus, lookit—those are a lot of horse tracks, but each horse makes four of them."

"I didn't mean just *horses*, but other animals, too."

"You said 'people.'"

"I meant animals, too. Anything that's thirsty."

"Tell you what," Stockbridge said. "Rachel, why don't you follow your nose, and, Lenny, you follow the tracks? Let's see if they meet."

The dispute ended, Stockbridge fell back to cover the rear. He did not know if the men would pursue, but he did know one thing: The wagon was leaving tracks as well.

CHAPTER EIGHT

WHEN MOLLY HENSHAW was six years old, she had dreamed of becoming an actress on a big-city stage. She put on little plays for the chickens and cows on the family farm in Maryland, and memorized correspondence her parents received so she would have words to say. She gave soaring, dramatic readings of "due" notices and the "foreclosure."

When Molly Henshaw was seven, her father had been killed in the War, and her mother took to bed in their dark attic apartment in a home for destitute War widows, where she remained until she died. Still seven, Molly went to live in Pennsylvania with a relative on her mother's side, Aunt Eva Sommer. Aunt Eva was a seamstress who lived with her daughter, Thomasina, who was nine. Eva was still married to Izzy Sommer, but he had left three years earlier, and no one knew where he was.

When she was eight, and with Aunt Eva's approval, Molly learned a trade from Thomasina: picking pockets. When she was nine, Molly was beaten by a man who caught her in the act. Then she was beaten by Aunt Eva, not for the first time nor for the last. Still acting—only now to keep from crying—Molly liked to pretend that she was a great lady living in a fine house. It did not matter that the girl was just performing stories from newspapers she found in the streets. Eva thought she was being mocked and took a belt to the girl.

When she was twelve, Molly ran away to become an actress. She got as far as Ohio by hiding in trains and stealing food and clothes from luggage. When she was thirteen, Molly was already seven months on the job as a cleaning girl at the Hotel Cleveland. When she turned eighteen, and six hotels later— having moved farther south and west—the woman with blond curls and big brown eyes landed at the Poet and Puncher, a saloon in Buzzard Gulch. It was named for the fact that the men who ate and imbibed there either told one another their woes or beat the whiskers off one another. But that did not affect Molly. What did was that there, every Friday and Saturday night, there were performances by the White and Black Ladies—a mix of freed slave girls and poor Southern belles of once-grand plantations. And between those shows, Molly was allowed to take to the stage to read limericks that had been submitted during the week by patrons. It was not art and it was not even acting, unless wearing a bathing costume with the skirt and pleated blouse but no drawers and pretending to be warm was acting.

Promise Cuthbert had not known he had a love of verse until he'd heard it from the lips of Molly Henshaw. Molly did not like Cuthbert, but she did not mind him, which was more important. And being known as the girl of Captain Cuthbert was more important still. It made sure that locals and visitors alike let her be. Cuthbert did not like to share.

Every week, before going on, Molly would smoke one of her hand-rolled cigarettes in a tiny dressing room. She would stare at herself in the mirror and tell herself that this was an opportunity to learn how to tame a rowdy audience. And she did. Up there, in the flickering glow of the footlight candles, she could tease them, pose in ways that drove them loco, or use words they did not understand before introducing a limerick—*that* shut them up, and to cover their embarrassment, they threw coins at the stage. Everything they flung, she kept.

In short, she learned how to control men. The rest of the time, the other five days a week, she bathed many of those men at the adjoining Pap Hotel. That was all: just a bath, for two bits above the normal two-bit price. She split that money with the owner of both establishments, Raspy Nikolaev.

Raspy's real name was Rasputin. But with a throat worn to tree bark by the Balkan tobacco he smoked, everyone called him Raspy. He did not mind, as long as their money was not foreign or Confederate and they didn't abuse Molly or the other young bath girl, Doris. He lived a good life here, with a suite on the second floor—complete with a terrace for tea and breakfast, when it was warm—and a large surrey. Though Nikolaev did not have three friends to go riding with him, he liked the ostentation of the big buggy. It made him feel important. He had come to these shores to *be* important. Nikolaev had been part of a secret plot to annex California for Russia immediately after the Civil War. When that had blown up—unlike their explosives, which had failed to, allowing a local militia to cross a bridge and kill most of the foreigners—Nikolaev headed east with some of the Russian gold that was supposed to build a bigger, better stronghold. He got as far as Gunnison, where the question was: Use the rest of the money to go to the East Coast, or stay here and buy a saloon?

That had been thirteen years ago.

Nikolaev was very protective of his employees. It was an odd quirk in the otherwise sweaty, arrogant foreigner. Maybe Doris was right when she said, "He likes being a tsar, and a ruler needs devoted subjects."

Molly didn't care. It was the first time in her life someone had looked out for her.

Actually, there were two people who did that. Doris was too preoccupied with trying to find a husband, preferably a rancher. But never far from Molly's elbow was the linen girl and overall domestic Yi Huang, a tiny woman in her forties who was widowed and eager to work.

On most days, Molly was all right with her life. Rarely happy but not discontent. What helped was to take her own bath several times a week and, relaxing, to read magazines and newspapers. She liked stories about people. Their joys or sadness transported her, briefly, to a place that was sometimes better, sometimes worse than her own.

Rarely did one story do both. The article about Dr. John Stockbridge was one such. She read it after already having overheard talk about him at the bar. When she finally saw a copy of the *Colorado Line & Telegram*, the drawing was like something from a stage drama: one man falling backward, his hand on his wounded breast; the other tall, stalwart, legs in a wide stance, hat low, a large shotgun still smoking; and onlookers running away, with a horse rearing, its eyes wide with terror. The caption:

DR. VENGEANCE STRIKES
WITHOUT MERCY!

There was something awful but enchanting about the idea of a mysterious, fearless avenger. Molly was not one to follow the serial exploits of famous actresses or military heroes, the kind of thing that interested other women. Sarah Bernhardt, that new stage sensation Lillie Langtry, the fallen George Armstrong Custer. They were either self-promoters or, increasingly, a product of the press.

But this Dr. John Stockbridge—he was new. New and fascinating in a way that the figures in Scripture had once captivated her when she had acted their stories as a child. Sitting in the fast-cooling tub, she found long-unremembered words and phrases returned to her, and they made her smile.

"'Be strong and of a good courage. Fear not, nor be afraid of them: for the Lord thy God, He it is that doth go with thee; He will not fail thee, nor forsake thee!'"

"You need something?" Yi had said through the door of the bathroom, a small room with slanted windows that let in warm sun like into a painter's studio. There was even a small table with flowers in a vase.

"Yes, but not from you," Molly replied confusingly.

Yi walked away, muttering. Molly returned to the broadsheet. The report about the showdown was new, just three days old. And it was here—close enough, anyway. Gunnison was the better part of a day's ride. She did not know what Mr. Otis A. Burroughs had uncovered subsequent, but she was tantalized, then quickly obsessed, by the idea of making her own assessment of things.

A man so in love with his family that he sought to profane his own hands with the blood of the killer!

Asking Doris to fill in for her—which the other woman agreed to do, for two dollars—Molly persuaded Nikolaev to loan her his surrey, and she had ridden all the way to Gunnison in the hope of hearing of the deed from those who had witnessed it—or, if the fates were kind, actually laying eyes on this man.

She had achieved just one of those, but it was enough.

The encounter with Dr. John Stockbridge had occurred late in the day, entirely by chance, as she was passing by the Outfitting Depot of the Bartholomew Brothers. It was late afternoon, and Molly had intended only to ask the proprietor where she might find lodgings for the night. That was when a man on horseback, about to cross her path, had stopped to let her pass.

She did not. The woman, transfixed, stopped the surrey so fast, she actually lurched forward.

"Are you all right?" the deep voice asked.

"Yes—well, no . . . *yes*."

Her mouth had been uncertain but her eyes never left the figure before her. He was wearing a different coat—furs, not a duster—but the hat was the same, pulled down the same, and so was the shotgun. He held the reins with one hand, his left, and clutched the double-barrel shotgun along the inside of his right arm. His horse was packed as if for a journey.

Because it had been closing in on twilight, few people were about the dark street. Perhaps that was the reason the infamous figure was out now.

The two had remained in place for what seemed longer than it took to read that story. And it told her more, too. The man was a rock, but he was not unfeeling. She could sense it with a kind of animal awareness.

"Please, ma'am," the deep voice had said, "after you."

The words had not broken the spell but deepened it. Molly had lingered and smiled weakly, both for just a moment. Then she had urged her horse forward softly and rolled on to beneath the big sign that hung well out over the street.

Molly had watched as the man left town, headed west. He rode at a good clip, as if anxious to avoid pursuit—

Or to start over somewhere else? she had intuited.

Molly had not, herself, remained in Gunnison that night. She was suddenly not tired. Buying bread and cheese from the Bartholomews, she had turned around and gone back to Buzzard Gulch, the surrey's lantern guiding her way. She had gotten what she came for and wanted nothing more. It had been perfect—one of the few things in her life that ever had been. She memorialized it in verse she composed on the way home, seeking the words to express how right it had been. Even her boss had noticed, and she had finally confided to Raspy Nikolaev—no one else, not even Doris—about her daring pursuit and encounter.

"I think you are in love," Nikolaev had said after hearing her tale.

"I think you are right," Molly had replied. "That is why I am telling you. I would ask you to please watch out for me whenever the captain is here. He may think it is for him."

Molly did not mention her trip or her secret love to Cuthbert. She kept it to herself, in the locket of her heart. Whenever she opened it, she felt as though there were a guardian angel shining a strange, hopeful light on her.

Like so much of her life, it was silly but real.

That had been a week before, seven days in which

the power of the encounter had gone undiminished. What Molly did not know, when Cuthbert rode up to the Pap Hotel that night, was that the ephemeral relationship was about to take on another dimension: deadly.

CHAPTER NINE

LIAM MCWILLIAMS HAD no difficulty picking up the trail of Dr. Stockbridge. It had been ground into the earth by the Keeler wagon and Stockbridge's own—*Grady's* own—horse.

It was midafternoon, and the light was good. Not only were the tracks fresh, undusted by the temperate wind, but the rear wheels of the wagon had suffered nicks that left a distinctive pattern. It must have happened at a spot near where Grady had stopped them, since what remained of the tracks coming up Peak Road looked fine. Going down, every turn produced a jagged diagonal line.

The Red Hunter was tired. Not only had it been a late night getting the bear back to the compound, but his morning repose had been interrupted by the shooting. That, plus chopping and then digging in the solid earth had been a chore. Fortunately, he was enraged enough to stay sharp. It was not just Stockbridge—it was himself. He had listened to Pound, and he had let the captain down, and now he was set on recovering his battered honor.

Though McWilliams wanted to get this done, he did not gallop after the Keelers. The onetime corporal did not want to tire the horse, and he did not want to raise too much dust. A man like John Stockbridge, a physician with an eye for detail, he would be watching for that.

But he may also be looking for places where he can peel off and hide, McWilliams thought. Let the wagon roll on, with his horse, while he looked to ambush anyone who was coming after him. It was an old stunt, one he and his comrades had done themselves during the War when facing superior Union numbers. They would tie riderless horses together to leave tracks that suggest an army. Then, one by one, men would hop off—onto rocks, up trees, to the roofs of sheds, anywhere they would leave no footprints. Then they would wait to pick off men in pursuing units.

The ground was flat on the plains, without much opportunity for a man to seek cover. But there were boulders. Or maybe Stockbridge would not even try to hide. That story the newspaper had printed, it said he had faced that Adam Piedmont all proud and fearless. He might choose to plant himself and that Tennessee Walker between the wagon and anyone coming after it.

That would be welcome. That fancied-up Parker Brothers had breadth but McWilliams' carbine had range. He was prepared now to go shot for shot with that vile assassin and his cannon.

After nearly an hour of careful attention to the trail, McWilliams suddenly saw the tracks shift, wagon and horses both, from the weathered roadway to a well-worn path through the plains.

"Water," he realized with both clarity and satisfaction. Now he knew exactly where they were.

McWilliams stopped and dismounted. He let the horse graze on scrub as he considered his next step. To go to Stockbridge or to let Stockbridge come to him? That was the question. He looked at the trail ahead of the turnoff. Going up the mountain, the wheels had come this way. No doubt they would go back that way once the watering was done.

The thing about waiting, though, was that Captain Cuthbert might change his mind and decide to reach the plains and go west, come this way instead of going to Buzzard Gulch. He was angry, and after chewing on that, he might decide on immediate gratification. Cuthbert said he had once fought a duel before the War. This was that kind of affront.

If Cuthbert changed his plans, McWilliams wanted the captain to find Stockbridge slung sideways on the saddle of Grady's horse.

"Bastard's got that family to look out for," McWilliams reminded himself. "I only got me to watch."

That was it, then. McWilliams would go west up the trail a bit and circle toward the water from that direction. Stockbridge would be looking toward the cutoff, assuming pursuit was coming from the foothills . . . from the north, not from behind.

Mounting and setting off at a slow gallop, the Red Hunter decided to seek his prey with the sun full upon the killer, causing him to stand out from the rest of the dirt.

THE WIND MADE a fluttering sound as it came around the hills, like a big waving flag. Nearby the watering hole were three mounds, about twenty feet high on average, probably left there when the

earth had fallen in around them. That happened a lot
with underground water, as the underpinnings fell
away. The ground did not crack but sagged, as here.

The pond was only about ten feet across and protected from the wind by the northernmost of these
hills. The cutoff took a dogleg turn around it, like a
camel's hump, so as not to force a wagon to travel
over it. The outcropping blocked the wagon and its
occupants from anyone who might have been coming
from off the trail—and also made it difficult to see
anyone who might approach from that side.

Stockbridge had walked to the top of that rise and
squatted there, watching. He had instructed the Keelers to remain behind until the horses were done. Being horses, they were not greedy. They took only
what drink they needed, then fed on the brush a
while. The horse patties they left behind ensured that
more grass would grow, part of nature's brilliant if
malodorous design.

There were two things Stockbridge did not want.
One was to be caught here by hostile riders. The
other was to be stuck here at night. Predatory animals would come to use this water, and if they were
coyotes or bobcats, they would not hesitate to tackle
a horse or a boy. And a fire would be out of the question. It would tell the dead man's friends exactly
where they were.

It being somewhere around three o'clock, they
would have to start moving very soon. He had forgotten some of the patience he learned practicing medicine. He forgave himself, though, since the equation
had been altered. Lives were still at risk, though from
sudden, violent aggression. He wished that if anyone
was following, they would show themselves *now*.

As the horses finished up, Stockbridge went fifty
yards south to the pond. Sitting with her feet in the

water, Mrs. Keeler looked as though she wanted to ask again what she had asked before: Did he think those men were out there? She refrained, he suspected, because the children seemed relaxed, having spent several minutes splashing each other, and she did not want to worry them. Smiling, Stockbridge calmly addressed the others.

"I'm going to start back. You folks follow but don't try to catch up. I want some distance."

"Why is that?" Rachel asked.

"Shush," Mrs. Keeler insisted.

"Hey, Dr. Stockbridge, look!"

Lenny had been sloshing toward the edge of the pond. He was pointing toward the west, just north of one of the other little hills. There was a cottony cloud of dirt with a point of brown, like a stem, where it met the ground.

A rider and his dry, dusty trail. The man must have thought he was hidden by the low hill. Either that or he suddenly realized he wasn't. Either way, he was in a hurry.

"Lenny—get in the wagon and push your belongings to this side. Rachel, unhitch the horse. Mrs. Keeler, you help her. Then all of you get in the wagon and lie behind the water barrel and the other goods."

Stockbridge pointed to the western side of the wagon, the one facing the dust cloud. "Make sure everyone can lie flat behind it."

"Yes, sir," the boy said, jumping from the water and putting his young shoulders to work.

"Are we in danger?" Mrs. Keeler asked.

"Best to assume so," Stockbridge said.

"Do we tether the horses?" Rachel asked.

"No. If there are shots, we don't want them tugging the wagon around. They'll scatter to safety. Go *now*!"

Mrs. Keeler was suddenly about survival, like Stockbridge had seen mothers become at the approach of a tornado or an army. While the men ran plows and horses to safety, or took up arms, the women got their children into cellars or attics or hidden rooms. He could not help but think that people were all still animals in that regard, no different from a fox or a bear.

Stockbridge took a moment to look north, up the cutoff. He did not see anyone else in the direction of the trail, but that did not mean no one was waiting. The rider—he might be looking to flush them into a volley from that direction, like quail from the brush.

"Why don't you just shoot him, Dr. Stockbridge?" Lenny asked as he helped his mother up. Rachel was just finishing with the horse.

"I got power, but the carbines they were carrying have range," the doctor answered.

"We have that other man's rifle!" the boy reminded him, raising it high.

"Get down!" Mrs. Keeler shouted.

"*I* can shoot it!" Rachel insisted.

If Stockbridge fell, he worried that just one man, with a rifle, probably with side arms, might exact vengeance lower than killing. Blood was not always enough to satisfy a man's thirst.

"Stay sheltered," Stockbridge said. "If the attack gets past me, then you are to protect yourself, your family. Shoot the big target, the horse, then the man before he can get up. If it's me coming, I'll fire three shots. Do you understand?"

"Yes, Dr. Stockbridge," she answered.

Rachel lay in the wagon and found a slot between the boards to put the rifle, and Stockbridge strode to the pond, where, having supped and drunk, Pama stood at rest. Stockbridge looked out again. The rider was nearer, most likely the hothead who had held his fire back on the trail. In the mind of the Confederate, it was to be a joust, then, mounted champion against a hated emblem of the Union.

During the War, Stockbridge had seen too many heroic charges into the mouths of Union guns. Southern pride, the code of one who was or who fancied himself a gentleman. Then it had inevitably and ineffably resulted in gray coats spread across fields and valleys with patches of red crawling outward beneath the hot sun.

Such an action here was likely to result in Stockbridge's death. Up north, he had learned to be more practical about combat.

With that in mind, Stockbridge made his plan and his decision, both at the same time. The attacker was looking into the sun, and if the doctor did this right, he would undermine the advantage of range held by the Southerner. . . .

THE WIND WAS coming from the east, bringing grit and bits of dead grass with it. Riding directly into it caused bite and distraction. McWilliams slowed for a few moments in order to tie a bandanna neckerchief across the lower part of his face. He pulled down the brim of his ten-gallon hat with a rounded crown. It blocked his vision a little, but it kept the dirt from his eyes. He kicked his horse back to a gallop, then kicked it again for a little more speed. Someone was out there: Dark figures were moving in a blurry smudge on the horizon. He wanted to reach them before they fled.

McWilliams made out the figure of a horse and someone dark atop it. The rider was bent low, almost as if he was hiding behind the neck of the horse. The

Hunter smiled, his own hot breath warming his mouth behind the fabric.

"That's him. That's the devil!"

It was to be charge against charge. The carbine was still in its holster, and McWilliams yanked it out by the stock, tossed it up, and caught it as it dropped back down.

Though the horse was stirring up clouds that seemed to run with it, then ahead of it, then enveloped it, McWilliams caught flashes of the same coat he had seen on the trail.

"The diagnosis is *death*, Doctor!" he cried, raising the carbine above his head.

The horse was breathing hard beneath him as, with an experienced eye, McWilliams gauged the distance. They were about a quarter mile apart. He had shot a man dead at seventy-five yards. Not at a gallop, but then McWilliams did not intend to keep up this pace. He'd close the gap just a little more, take down the big target, the dark Walker, then dismount and send the ambusher to hell. The body would be a gift to Promise Cuthbert—an act of contrition, an offering, like a cat with a field mouse deposited at a doorstep.

The distance narrowed, and so, suddenly, did the eyes of the Red Hunter. The horse was not the Walker; it was the one the Yankee had been riding on the trail: Grady's horse.

"You stinking bastard! You figured some of me out!"

Stockbridge was flaunting his corrupt deed of horse thievery and daring Grady's friend to shoot it.

"I can't hit you clean," the man said into the warm vapor collecting on his neckerchief. The neck of the horse was still in the way. "I gotta wait till you're a little closer."

His own dust swirled round as McWilliams crossed

the dry plain. His eyes never left the target, especially as he neared the outside of his range. His palm held the carbine tightly, felt the weight of it, the power of the death it would bring to the hated Dr. Vengeance.

Now.

McWilliams reined and stopped and in the same motion dismounted to the left, the north side. He crouched, pushed up his brim with a thumb, then raised the gun and aimed. The shape of his target, the charging greatcoat, its tails flying, was hazy but visible within the tawny cloud. He did not blink, despite the pelting dust.

"Die!"

He fired.

McWilliams' own horse bolted, as expected, as did Grady's horse. The Palomino lowered its head, kicked, and flew off with Stockbridge still in the saddle. McWilliams rose and pumped two more shots into the man, into his side and back. The fringes of the greatcoat blew in the wind.

So did the empty sleeves. They had been tied around the neck of the horse before coming loose and sagging along the sides.

McWilliams lowered the rifle. "What the blazes?"

Shaking its head from side to side, Grady's horse ran to the south a bit before stopping. Perspiring beneath his own coat, McWilliams rose, still targeting the figure that held its seat before him. The dust had calmed and fallen. The wind kicked up some grains, stirred the tail of Grady's horse, and blew the garment, as a whole, this way and that on the animal's back.

McWilliams approached the animal, which was hazed by the dust of its retreat. He saw the holes he had made in the garment, but there wasn't any blood. It was then he noticed that the reins had been run through the sleeves.

He stiffened and glared to the east. The family had not left; he could still see the wagon. But Stockbridge had probably used this distraction, this delay, to get away, up the cutoff.

McWilliams ran back toward his horse, which was on his left. "You can't run, you coward!"

"I haven't," a deep voice informed him.

McWilliams looked across the saddle. Stockbridge was standing away from his own steed about fifty feet to the north. He was wearing a blanket over his shoulders. The double-barreled shotgun rested along the inner sleeve of his white shirt, like a splint. Stockbridge's finger was on the trigger. It was a formidable sight, reaching lower along his leg than his other arm.

"You damn coward!" McWilliams roared. "You circled round so you wouldn't have to face me."

"I'm facing you now. You've got your carbine—use it."

It was a stupid, reckless challenge, McWilliams thought. The shotgun was pointing down. McWilliams was holding the rifle across his chest, and he had the shield of the horse. All he had to do was swing the repeater over the saddle and fire.

The Red Hunter's move was not a thought but an impulse. He snapped his elbows to his side, the carbine was up and leveled, his eye behind it, his index finger in place—

Stockbridge barely raised the shotgun more than a few inches. He fired under the horse, between its legs. The scattershot peppered McWilliams' lower legs from feet to shins. He shrieked and crumpled at the same time as the carbine discharged into the air. The frightened horse ran, and then McWilliams hit the ground, moaning and bloody. He lay on his side, trying to bring the carbine around.

"Don't!" Stockbridge warned. "I can still fix you—"

"Go to hell!"

"Not me and not today."

McWilliams raised the gun and tried to aim on his trembling shoulders. Stockbridge blew the repeater away, along with the man's hands, with a second discharge. Pellets also struck the face, neck, and chest of the Red Hunter.

Liam McWilliams flopped back, still breathing, blood running from over a dozen holes at both ends of his body.

Stockbridge walked over and looked down at him. There was no saving him now. The doctor did not even try.

"If you can talk, I'll relay any messages you have."

But McWilliams could not talk. He just shook violently, then, suddenly, fell very still. Stockbridge exhaled through his nose. Once again, death had come for no mortal, earthly reason other than someone being stupid and rash.

Or maybe it was vanity with this one. Pride at having been humiliated on the trail and rushing out to prove himself.

In any case, it was a waste of something precious. Stockbridge felt sorry for him.

He decided to leave the body. The doctor did not want to believe of himself that he was leaving it as a warning—even if it was the truth. But there was something on the horse's saddle that alarmed him: the faded impression of a red hand at the rear of the kneepad. It had the look and feel of some kind of band—outlaws, mustered-out soldiers, he didn't know what. But there were likely more. He used dirt to scrub away the image so as not to alarm the Keelers.

He had other reasons, too, for leaving the man. He did not want to spend any more time out here than necessary. There was at least one other man, the black man with the bow and arrow. He did not want him to know where Stockbridge or the Keelers were; turning in a dead man, having an inquest, would surely tell them.

Stockbridge put on his greatcoat, which had two holes where his heart would have been. The man had been a good shot, if not a wise one. He picked up the carbine, collected both horses and his coat, and walked back to Pama. He fired three shots from the rifle, as he told Rachel he would so she would not accidentally shoot him when he returned.

After looking around and making certain that the man had come alone, the doctor mounted Pama and made his way slowly back to the watering hole, the two other horses trailing obediently behind.

CHAPTER TEN

For promise cuthbert, it was a relatively short ride into Buzzard Gulch.

Though the path he took was sloped and not generally traveled, it had one advantage. The sun did not turn its eye on this side of the mountain until late afternoon and the foliage was thick trunked and tall. As a result, the ground remained cold and hard, offering good footing. His horse, a strong Appaloosa, took the journey pretty much on his own. Which was a good thing. Cuthbert's mind was on Grady, on his two craven Hunters, and on his hatred for a man who would kill over a few *possessions*. Cuthbert and his men did not regard what they did as stealing; they saw it as reparation. Compared to what all of them had lost in the War—their homes torched and possessions stolen or destroyed—this was little enough compensation.

If there was any hint that the people Grady or the rest of them encountered were Southerners, they gen-

erally passed unmolested. The exception was men on
the run. Yellowbelly curs deserved to lose belongings, and probably much worse. During the War, if
they had met a deserter from either side, they would
tie him to a tree, cut him deep at the insides of his
elbows, and let him bleed to death, feeling and listening to the drip of his life going away.

That is what he wanted for John Stockbridge: an
irreversible injury that gave him time to contemplate
his sins.

Cuthbert arrived at the Pap Hotel several hours
before his reservation for the bath. He always booked
two hours, since he wanted to spend time with Molly.
Afterward, when she had finished whatever other ap-
pointments had been made, they would dine and retire to the room he had reserved.

To Cuthbert's disappointment, Molly was not
ready for him when he arrived. She had another client; a soft, middle-aged milksop named Spaulding
Doubleday, who had paid for a bath by himself and
then a brush scrub. He did not even mind if Molly
smoked while she bathed him. In fact, he said he kind
of liked it. Doubleday was always her most agreeable
client. But she was usually careful not to schedule
one of those while Cuthbert was in town. He knew
what she did, but he did not like to be near when she
washed another man.

Yi was hanging towels on the line when Cuthbert
arrived. It was chronically stuffy in the backyard.
The public stables were behind the hotel, with as
many mules as horses, and the Poet and Puncher was
beside it, with a large and growing compost heap out
back. Everyone from the small town seemed to dump
there, whether bidden to or not. To the right of the
hotel, there was a fenced-in section of chickens,
which provided eggs for the tavern. Doris was re-

sponsible for harvesting those. Passing directly over-
head, the sun baked the smells into an unventilated
stew.

Cuthbert rode in through the alley between the
stables and the pub, past the compost. He greeted the
Chinese woman with less than his usual smile.

"Hello, sir," she said only after he had acknowl-
edged her, little as he had.

Harry, a black boy, came over from the stable to
take the guest's horse. The owner, Festus—a one-
eyed veteran of the winning side—did not have to
coax the youngster. Cuthbert dismounted, took his
grip from the back, threw it over his shoulder, and
pressed a nickel into the boy's palm.

"Thank you, Mr. Cuthbert, sir," the boy said, and
walked off, flipping the coin into the air like he was a
Vanderbilt. Born free, Harry intended to own "a
herd of stables" before he was much older. He was
already well on his way to making a down payment
on a single stall here.

Cuthbert felt suddenly ornery and impatient as he
passed Yi. He stopped and dropped his grip.

"Go tell your mistress I'm here."

"Busy. Bath."

"Yeah, well, tell her to give the man his money
back. I'm coming up."

Yi hesitated.

"Go and tell her," Cuthbert insisted.

Yi smoothed her short graying hair like she was
calming a dog, then went through the back door.
There was no screen, just the heavy wood panel.

Cuthbert did not go through a servant's entrance
ever. He walked back through the alley and around
to the front. Raspy Nikolaev was just inside the front
door, waiting. The small lobby with its ornate wall
lanterns was empty, save for the liveried bellboy be-

side the registration counter. His uniform was an odd combination of Imperial Army whites and a black beaver hat.

"Hello, Captain," Nikolaev said in his heavy Slavic accent.

"Afternoon, Raspy."

The big Russian—nearly a full head taller than the other—put out an arm as Cuthbert attempted to pass. The captain turned to the man.

"I'm going up."

"I prevented Yi from delivering your message."

"You overwater carpetbagger, you what?"

Nikolaev looked over at the grandfather clock beside the counter. "Another twenty minutes, then he will be done."

"He's done when I say. Move your arm, mister."

"Only if it is your intention to sit in my gracious lobby. Please, Captain. Please understand. For Molly's sake."

The Southerner tilted his head toward Nikolaev's ear. "There is a derringer in my hand in my coat pocket. I will shoot your belly, Raspy—I swear on the Stars and Bars—if you do not lower your arm."

"That will not kill me, I think. But Yi will run for the sheriff, and I shall be forced to charge you for the bath . . . and the vest."

"The sheriff." Cuthbert snorted. "He'd take an hour just gimping over."

"Now you are just being ugly," Nikolaev huffed.

Cuthbert looked past the man at Yi. She was standing in the shadows in back, near the door that opened to the kitchen, which was in the back. She was rubbing her head as if she was trying to generate static electricity.

Dr. Vengeance, a Chink with nerves, and a fat Rus-

sian in my way, Cuthbert thought. *I'm in a damn circus.*

There is a time when events become so comical that they lose their fascination. His sense of purpose undermined, Cuthbert removed his hand from his pocket. The Russian lowered his arm as well.

"Will you have a drink with me next door?" Nikolaev asked.

Nikolaev stepped aside and gestured toward the door that connected his two establishments. Cuthbert plopped his grip on a wing chair, and the proprietor motioned for the bellboy to take it. Nikolaev did not like disorder, either human or in his decor.

"Leave it in the changing room by the bath," Nikolaev instructed.

The men entered the tavern, which was occupied by a spare, midafternoon collection of two prospectors, two cowboys, and a woodsman. The curtains were drawn on the small stage to the right. Cuthbert and Nikolaev made for the bar in the back.

Cuthbert sat, followed by the Russian. The former soldier slapped his hat on the counter. Dirt puffed in all directions. The Russian removed a silver case from the inside pocket of his vest and selected a prerolled cigarette. He put it in a cigarette holder, which he pulled from his vest pocket. The bartender brought him a match, and the Russian blew smoke.

"You look like your best friend died," the Russian said.

"Actually, Raspy, one of my men *did* get killed today. Grady."

The cigarette and holder sagged. "Captain, I'm sorry! My stupid tongue! An accident?"

"A cold-blooded murder."

"Do you know whose work it was?"

Cuthbert nodded as Nikolaev instructed the bartender to bring two beers.

"A lunatic from Gunnison, guy named Stockbridge. Paper calls him Dr. Vengeance."

Nikolaev's expression turned unhappy. "Have you informed the sheriff?"

"What for? Tom isn't going to hunt him down. And I got a posse bigger than he could possibly assemble."

"You're going after him?"

Cuthbert nodded as the beers arrived. He took a short swallow. "Nobody kills one of my people and survives, not even if he has a mortar in place of an arm and a cannonball for a head."

Nikolaev made a face at that image. He took a sip of his beer and wiped his mouth with the side of his thick hand.

"I have not myself seen this man but I have heard he is *moshchnyy*—tough or rough, I think you would say."

"So am I," Cuthbert said after another swallow.

"Yes, of course. I am thinking that, possibly, you should not discuss this with Molly."

"Why in hell not?"

"It . . . it might upset her. She knew Grady. From Friday nights, I mean."

"Better she should hear it from me than from a bare-skinned slob in the bathtub."

"Yes, but that will spoil your evening."

Cuthbert swiveled slightly in the stool. It wobbled and squeaked. "You're babbling, mister. You worried about me or her?"

"Both!" Nikolaev said quickly.

"You tub of guts—I hear what you're saying, but what *aren't* you saying? There's something. I can smell it."

"Don't be like that, Captain," Nikolaev laughed. "I swear there isn't anything."

"You're lying." Cuthbert's eyes narrowed. "Hold on. You only care about your damn business. Are you trying to tell me this killer was here for a bath? Did Molly actually *bathe* him?"

"No, that never happened!" Nikolaev said, no longer laughing. "My eyes have personally never even seen this person."

"Your eyes can barely see over your fat cheeks. Then *what*?"

"I think you should not wait here while he is out there." Nikolaev pointed toward the street. "What kind of time will you have with Molly?"

"So now you got a third story. Worried about Molly, worried about me, and now it's about justice."

"Is it not? To you?"

Cuthbert relaxed. He turned back to his beer. "Well, there's truth in that. Reason I even came to see Molly first was—she's caring, knew Grady. I wanted to be the one to tell her."

"Very thoughtful."

"She's also sociable, knows people. I wanted to find out about the people who Stockbridge was with when he killed Grady. He may still be with them."

"Who are they?"

"Family name of Keeler—a mother, a daughter, a son. Father is out in the mountains somewhere, doing the devil knows what. You ever hear of them?"

"No, but who do I hear of besides men who need to eat, drink, sleep, or bathe?"

Cuthbert was silent as he drank more of his beer. He thought through another gulp. "I got about ten minutes anyway. Might as well see gimpy Tom."

"A good idea, and consider pursuing your man before he moves on. Men who kill, run."

"Not this fella. Not what I've heard. He lost a family. Maybe he'll want to stay and endear himself to a ready-made one."

Nikolaev waited, smoking, sipping beer, as Cuthbert eased from the stool and walked out the front. He seemed to move like a drag-belly hog. When he was finally gone, the Russian pushed through the connecting door and hurried up the stairs.

His brain was storm tossed with possibilities, none of them favorable. Client or no, he had to let Molly know that the man with whom she was secretly smitten was the man her lover had come to kill.

CHAPTER ELEVEN

Sarah Jane Stockbridge had been a teacher, and she schooled her children. She especially loved arithmetic. She would have written her husband's mood on the slate as:

the weight of the day + the weight of life = melancholy

Add three murders to the equation? Stockbridge did not want to tote that sum.

How long can you work opposed to your nature and training before you turn the shotgun on yourself?

If, at the moment, his own actions on the plains did not give him pause, grief, or cheer, they unsettled some part of him that a decent family of two ladies and a boy could cheer the loud, violent demise of a human being. Not that he blamed them. It only made him sad that such was what the world had become.

Rachel was the first to spot the colorful Cheyenne blanket in the amber glare of the sinking sun. At

Mrs. Keeler's urging, they waited until she could make out, with her own searching eyes, that it was Stockbridge wearing the blanket.

But then tired of waiting, Lenny first, and Rachel second, leapt from the wagon and hugged the rider's legs. There was something akin to awe in the eyes of the boy. The man had ridden out with a plan to protect them, had tested it with his life, and had returned to them. Lenny had never felt unsafe, even when his father was away. But for the first time in his life, he had someone to look up to other than Benjamin Keeler and the elderly priest at the Buzzard Gulch church who sometimes came to see them, old Reverend Michaels. Lenny liked the preacher. He said gentle, peaceful prayers and told stories about a sister who was a sharpshooter out west.

Alice Keeler didn't believe those stories, always saying, after he'd gone, that it was an unlikely skill for a woman to have. But it was the reason Rachel had asked her father to teach her to shoot. The girl had her heroes, just like her brother.

Mrs. Keeler finally came over and took his rein hand between hers with gratitude in her heart and a smile. Stockbridge gave her a moment to thank him, then warned that they should move on.

"There may be a bunch of these men out there." He cocked his head toward the mountains. "We've inflicted a pair of wounds, and they won't be happy about that."

"What should we do?" the woman asked.

"Get you home, for one thing, and then I can go back to see about them and your husband."

"Dear God, Dr. Stockbridge. What have we brought you into?"

"Mrs. Keeler, there's no time or need for that. If you'd get back in the wagon . . . Lenny and Rachel, hitch these horses to the back. How much farther do we have?"

"About five miles that way," Lenny said, pointing to the northeast. "I read that on a map."

"Good man. We have to press on. It won't be safe out here, not when that one doesn't return." He indicated the plain where the dead man lay.

"Of course," Mrs. Keeler said.

With impressive skill and haste, the children tied the reins to the buckboard, and within a few minutes, they were headed back to the trail.

The passage was without event for most of the journey—until the left rear wheel snapped and dumped the wagon hard onto that side. The children managed to grab the buckboard side rails to keep from spilling over. Mrs. Keeler slid back but was unhurt, having fallen on one of the blankets that protected her from the growing cold.

The wagon was a loss, however. The one lantern they had brought was shattered and unsalvageable. Stockbridge cut away the ropes that held the backboard shut and tucked them into his coat pocket.

"Mount up and ride," Stockbridge said without hesitation. "Mrs. Keeler, your husband's horse is the gentlest. I suggest you ride him."

There was no debate, though Mrs. Keeler remarked, "This has been a most ill-omened journey."

"We're alive, thanks to Dr. Stockbridge," Rachel said. "I consider us fortunate."

"Yes, I'm sorry," Mrs. Keeler said with a trace of shame. "There is certainly that."

It was a bold remark for the girl to have made, contradicting her mother. But Mrs. Keeler was either too tired or suddenly aware of the ungrateful sentiment she had expressed to disagree. As they rode, and after the sun had set, she took to reciting Scripture—

such as she remembered. There was a certain poetry to hearing God's words as one of His most majestic earthly acts unfolded.

"Ma does that at the end of every day," Lenny confided to Stockbridge, who was riding alongside him. "That's why we had our Bible, the one we lost. She believes it helps God to find us."

"She may not be wrong," Stockbridge said.

"I hope she isn't," Rachel said. "I don't like to think of Pa alone out there with no one watching over him."

"I have a question. Maybe you can answer it," Stockbridge said. "Did your father ever do anything out here except trapping? Did he ever talk about doing something else?"

The children looked at each other in the last of the light. They shook their heads.

"He *talked* about how it would be nice to be home more," Rachel said, "but there were no jobs he could do in Buzzard Gulch. The Indians worked on whatever construction was needed. They got paid in liquor, which wouldn't have helped Pa."

"He didn't drink," Lenny offered.

Stockbridge nodded, but if the black man had told the truth—that, found or stolen, the horse had been at Eagle Lookout—it suggested something else was likely afoot.

It was necessary to stop about an hour out so that, with Rachel's help, Stockbridge could make and light a pair of torches. He used rope he had taken from the wagon, wrapping it tight around the tops of two branches and tying it there. It burned slow, long enough to get them where they were going.

The Keeler home was modest bordering on spare. Set beside a small patch of garden growing carrots and peas and protected by chicken wire, the house was a hodgepodge of log, stone, and thatch, suggesting that Ben Keeler would not have been hired to do construction even if there had been no Indians in the vicinity. But it was solid, and it retained heat, thanks to thick mud he had packed in to seal every seam. The long eaves, on every side, were supported by branches that helped to protect all four sides from rain. Not enough mud washed away to threaten the occupants with wind or leaking.

There was a slanting wood stable with two stalls. With Stockbridge holding the torch, Lenny and Rachel reintroduced their father's mount to his home, stabled the cart horse, then did their best to accommodate the new animal they had acquired. They left Pama out front, tied to the well. A habit Stockbridge had acquired during the War was to sleep near his horse, in case medical attention was needed in the field. He had also made it a practice to mark the trail in his head in the event of a nighttime retreat. He had done so now. If the men came after them, Stockbridge would be ready with his mount and a knowledge of the terrain that newcomers would not possess.

As soon as she was inside, Mrs. Keeler was comfortably in charge. She lit a fire in the modest hearth—the only illumination—dispatched Lenny to the well for water, and sent Rachel for the sewing box so the woman could repair Stockbridge's coat after dinner.

"The wind out here—Ben always said . . . *says* . . . you don't want it running up your spine," Mrs. Keeler told him.

"Ma'am, there is nothing out there I welcome along my spine," Stockbridge said.

Everyone laughed at that, and it was enough to break the dreary mood that had settled upon them all.

"Ma sews real good," Lenny said. "She made all our clothes."

"One must be resourceful," the woman said. In that was the weight of months, years she had spent husbandless in this small cabin.

Rachel prepared a pot of oatmeal and set tin plates on the table along with biscuits. Feeling that they were safe for the present, Stockbridge went to the only bedroom. He shut the door and stood there for a moment. The shotgun seemed welded to his right arm. He did not want to put it down.

Now is not then, he told himself. *You are here to help if they need it.*

It was not modesty that had brought him in here. He would adjust his shirt and trousers to make the Keelers think that. He was here because he did not want them to see him falter. Stockbridge's fingers were on the barrel. He coaxed them to loosen. . . . They hurt as they opened, so tightly had they been closed for the better part of the ride. Reaching across his chest with his steadier left hand, he took the gun and leaned it against the foot of the bed so he could remove his coat. He trembled as he did that. He felt both lighter and afraid.

You can take it with you, he thought. *Just set it somewhere nearby, like you were taking off your boots.* Which he would not do, in case he had to run out.

That moment he had entered his house—it would never let him go; he knew that. The best he could do was handle the feelings that kept returning.

Stockbridge tucked in his shirt, fixed his belt, settled his cuffs above his boots, then picked up the shotgun and coat and returned to the main room, the only other room.

Mrs. Keeler was waiting for the garment and hung it on a wall peg. The sewing kit was on a stool beneath it. While the food was brought from the hearth by Rachel and her brother, Stockbridge took in the room. There were the stool, a rocking chair covered with a bear hide, four chairs with soft deer cushions around a rickety table, and two piles of assorted furs, where he assumed the children slept. Buffalo skins hung on the windows, a large, beaten-up leather trunk below one of them. They kept out the cold though they did little to stifle the roar of the wind. With nothing around it but open lowlands, the Keeler home took the full force of the evening westerlies that swept from the mountains.

"Heated and dipped, you won't notice the biscuits were made two days ago," Rachel half apologized as she set out the meal.

"Never damaged any of us," Mrs. Keeler said.

"I'm sure I won't mind," Stockbridge replied.

"Just don't drop one on your foot," Lenny dared, leaning over conspiratorially.

Supper was preceded by a prayer and followed with tea. The leaves were weak from overuse, the brew poured from a pot that had seen happier times. But as timber was not lacking out here, the fire was bright and warm and, while she sewed, Mrs. Keeler did not bother to stop the children from recalling the events of the day with giggly relief. The two never stopped working all the while, putting the tableware in a big metal bucket in the corner and then wiping the table and sweeping the floor around it. Rachel and Lenny were slope shouldered by the time they had nearly finished, as the steam they had run on during the long day ran out.

Stockbridge was tired, too, and had pulled one of the dinner chairs close to Mrs. Keeler and sat.

"You and your husband raised good, strong, dutiful children," he remarked.

"Thank you, Dr. Stockbridge. They have made

this a family, and the family made this a home." She broke off, turning slightly and sobbing. "I don't— I can't think of—"

"It's best not to," Stockbridge said quietly.

"No. You're right. I mustn't. The Lord will do what He thinks is best."

The doctor informed Mrs. Keeler that he would rest a bit and then set out before dawn.

"There are the furs," she said, nodding toward the beds. "The children can stay with me."

"There's no need to go to any trouble. The rocker will suit me fine."

"Sitting? How will you ever—"

"I'm used to it. Actually, I've come to prefer it. During the War, I always slept in small bites with my back to a tree. Made me feel safe, one less side to be shot."

"A quilt, then. I'll get—"

"I'll stoke the fire and put on my mended coat, and I'll be quite warm," he said. "You ought to rest, too."

"Just as soon as I'm done here."

Stockbridge rocked for a moment, hoping to make what he was about to say sound less important than it might have been.

"Mrs. Keeler, there are two things I want to ask you if I may."

"Anything, Doctor."

It was barely perceptible, but her eyes grew guarded, and her mouth tightened. She appeared to be bracing for bad news.

"The first— Well, I have something to show you."

The woman stopped sewing as Stockbridge reached into the pocket of the coat she was repairing. He withdrew the necklace he had taken from Grady.

"I wondered what was rattling in there," she said.

"Do you recognize this?"

"Yes. That belongs to Jacob!"

"Who?"

"Jacob Wallingham—a traveling salesman. Ben gave that to him. Jacob comes around twice a year or so, trades goods for pelts, Indian jewelry, anything he can hang from the big chuck wagon he ran for the Union Pacific."

"When was the last time he was here?"

"Summer. Where did you find that?"

"On the neck of the man Grady," Stockbridge told her.

Mrs. Keeler's expression relaxed into sadness. "Lord, I hope he wasn't harmed."

"Maybe Jacob just traded it," Stockbridge said without entirely believing that. He put the necklace on the table. "You can return it to him. I've been told that your husband's horse was found at Eagle Lookout, higher in the mountains. Did Ben ever mention that name?"

"In stories he told," the woman said. "Never anything serious."

"What kind of stories?"

"Indian legends," she replied. "He used to tell them to the children."

"I remember them, Mama!" Lenny shouted from across the room. He and Rachel were taking shifts bringing well water to the dish bucket and the washbasin.

"You're not supposed to be listening to adult conversation," the woman reproached him.

"Sorry."

"Tell me about these stories, Mrs. Keeler," Stockbridge said.

"Oh, they were silly, flighty things that he heard from other trappers who heard it from some prospectors. Those men," she laughed thinly. "They try to out-tale each other when they're in the woods or mountains. Or at the Poet and Puncher Tavern. A lot of them spin fables there."

"Such as?"

"Secret tunnels, treasures, great animals with fur like snow and a stride like Goliath's. Fables. Just fables, Dr. Stockbridge."

"I've talked to businessmen, Cheyenne, and no one has ever spoken of silver, gold, copper, or anything worth mining up there. Certainly not at Eagle Lookout. Did Ben ever talk about any of those?"

"Never."

"What— Was there anything that came up over and over?"

She stopped sewing for a moment and looked wistfully into the past. "One name. Ute Mountain."

"I'm not familiar with it," Stockbridge said.

"It's supposed to lie somewhere in the southwest, a great many miles and peaks from here."

"Pa talked about Ute Mountain and Ute Indians a lot," Lenny blurted, completing his last trip. "He showed it to me on one of the maps."

Mrs. Keeler scowled at her son a second time. "The legends Ben talked about were of underground caves that went clear into the middle of the earth. I honestly didn't like how he scared the children with his tales of wicked men in the passages, either guarding ancient treasure or making magic potions."

"Aw, I was never scared," Lenny said—mostly to himself to avoid a third chastisement.

"What *are* those little men called?" Mrs. Keeler wondered aloud. "The ones in Ireland?"

"Leprechauns," Rachel said.

Mrs. Keeler frowned at her daughter. Rachel went back to adjusting the dishes for a soak.

"Leprechauns," Mrs. Keeler repeated. She looked

at Stockbridge, who was listening intently. She leaned a little closer. "Doctor, my Ben has been all through those mountains, and he never came back with anything but pelts or injuries. I know he wanted more than anything to find magic or treasure or something that would improve our lives by making him famous."

The fire seemed to cackle. Mrs. Keeler settled back and resumed her sewing.

"He talked about getting us a place made of wood, with stairs, with chamber pots, with walls that didn't howl. But riches just aren't out there, Doctor. They just aren't."

"But he didn't believe that."

"Ben? No. He's a dreamer. But he's also practical, when he wants to be. To go ranging around that region for something, in terrain he didn't know, would mean leaving his traps untended. And nothing was more important to him than providing for us. And why now? He's known about those stories since before we even owned a cradle."

"A man does things at a certain age that he wouldn't consider before."

"Is that you?"

"Some men are forced. Some men, like Ben, they go more willingly."

Mrs. Keeler gave him a look of sympathy for whatever it was he carried in his heart, whatever hurt so deep that he did not even want to say its name.

"Whether he believed those stories or did not, Eagle Lookout is where his horse was found, and it seems a good place to start when I leave here." Stockbridge looked over at Lenny. "Son, you said there are maps?"

"Uh-huh!"

"Respectful language!" his mother said.

"Sorry. Yes, sir," he said, and went to the old trunk

in the corner. Stockbridge guessed that it was where the family kept their most precious items. Many families did that across the Mississippi in case they had to leave in a hurry due to weather or savages.

The boy carefully removed a pony carved from stone, a golden eagle feather, and other knickknacks. He hurried over with several hides bundled in his arms. They were black-ink maps, his father's record of years of trapping and travels.

"Thank you," Stockbridge said when the boy handed them over. There weren't many and only one that showed Eagle Lookout. "May I borrow this?"

"Of course, sir. They were made to be used."

Stockbridge smiled at that. The boy smiled back, proud to have been of assistance. When Mrs. Keeler was finished with his coat, Stockbridge folded the pelt inside a deep side pocket.

Rachel went out for water and filled the washbasin while Lenny spread the furs. They were stacked in the corner so the family would not walk all over them in the small living area. Stockbridge took the opportunity to go out back and select a few logs for the fire. He settled them in, then poked the fire to set them ablaze. The room glowed with renewed heat and light. Good nights were said along with prayers, after which Mrs. Keeler retired to her room. The children fell asleep quickly. The wind quieted as the night deepened. Save for the crackling fire, the children breathing, and the baying of distant coyotes, it was quiet—and, for Stockbridge, expectedly mournful. It reminded him of his own married home and all he had lost.

The doctor turned the rocker so that the back was to the hearth, his eyes to the window facing east. As he drifted into sleep, he wondered about the red handprint on the dead man's saddle and the greedy, murderous men out there who would soon learn of the latest killing. Other than the former slave, Stockbridge knew nothing of their numbers or their identities.

Not that that mattered.

His last thought as he fell asleep was both frank and bracing: *Come the dawn, they will be looking for me.*

CHAPTER TWELVE

Promise Cuthbert knew that his meeting with the sheriff would be a squandered ten minutes.

Tom Neal was a former Texas Ranger who, three years previous, had suffered a mishap with a gun and his big toe during a wild pursuit through San Antonio. As a result, he'd had to leave that beloved institution and seek employment elsewhere. He still had enough heft in his big arms and skill with a revolver to land this post in a town that was not really going anywhere. And the reason it wasn't going anywhere was the same reason that Neal was a moderately effective sheriff: Buzzard Gulch was not on a route anyone took from east to west. Passage was farther south, from Fremont to Montrose. It was so quiet here that the previous law, Goodman Peake, had gone for a ride one day, his pearl-handled six-shooters shining in the summer sun, and kept on going.

"The Keelers?" Neal said in answer to Cuthbert's question. Sitting back in his chair, near the warm

stove, he looked out from under bushy white eye-
brows that matched his woolly mustache. "They live
about three miles outta town, west, foot of the homestead area. Well, nearly west. A little northerly, in the
lowlands."

The men were seated in his small office, Neal's
right foot on the desk, Cuthbert sitting on the edge,
trying not to look at the hole cut in the top of the boot
for the twisted nub of the shattered toe. There were
wanted posters on a board behind him and a spit-
toon beside him. Neal was not smoking at the moment. He had run out of tobacco and so had the
general store. A rider had gone to Gunnison for more
but was overdue.

The sheriff's office did not have a jail cell. That
was out back: a brick structure with bars, a door that
closed over them—to keep out the cold, though
barely—and a bucket and a stool inside. It had never
been occupied by anyone more dangerous than a
drunk. The way people drank in Buzzard Gulch, that
usually meant the prisoner was passed out. It was
likely, Neal thought, that the tobacco-fetching rider,
a souse who had been released from that very cell,
had gotten drunk on Gunnison rye and was drying
out in a much nicer cell.

"Have you been to the Keeler place?" Cuthbert
asked.

"No cause. I see them now and then when they
come to town for essentials or on Sundays, for
church." Neal looked up through watery blue eyes.
"Why are you interested in them, Captain?"

"I'm not. I'm interested in the man who was riding
with them this morning and killed one of my men."

Neal eased his foot to the ground and sat up
straight. "Hold on there! Who got it?"

"Grady Foxborough."

"Who shot him?"

"Man name of John Stockbridge."

"The one from the *Line & Telegram*?"

"Selfsame."

"How do you know?"

"Two of my men came upon them."

"They saw him do it?"

"No. All they saw was Stockbridge riding Grady's horse after blowing the top of his head to beef."

Neal's mouth twisted. "That won't raise Judge Wilson's flag. He likes witnesses and bodies. One without the other—"

"I know. Fortunately, Sheriff, I did not come here to discuss the law. I just wanted to find out about the Keelers."

Neal absently reached into a pocket for tobacco fixings he knew weren't there. His thick fingers moved among the fabric for a moment before his body sagged.

"Goddamn town," he said. "Captain, listen. I'd be careful around this Stockbridge fella. I had a drink with a deputy from Gunnison who came looking for a new job. He saw the showdown, said the man was fearless and lethal."

"Then it's a good thing I'm not asking you to go after him."

"For what? Tell me, Captain—and I say this with no disrespect intended to you or to the deceased—but how do you know Grady didn't start whatever it was?"

Cuthbert rose. He'd had enough of Neal. "I don't care who started what. All I know is my friend is dead and someone's to blame. My men say it's John Stockbridge and that the Keelers were there, so we start there. If that's all you can tell me, I'll be on my way."

"That's all I got, other than to suggest that you bring an army if you're tackling that one."

"Thanks. I intend to."

"And that you don't do any killing. You just pre-confessed your intentions, which is like Old Glory itself to Judge Wilson."

Cuthbert left in a hurry. It hadn't been just a waste of ten minutes; it had been a waste of ten minutes plus a lecture from someone who felt like threatening him with the state's general statutes. Annoyed with Tom Neal, with himself, and with Raspy Nikolaev for having pushed him, Cuthbert returned to the Pap Hotel. Nikolaev was behind the counter. The captain ignored him, crossing the Persian style carpet and heading up the stairs.

"Captain Cuthbert!"

"Shut up, Raspy."

"Sir, there's no point going up."

Cuthbert stopped. "Why not?"

The Russian came around the counter, tugging the hem of his vest, a man of property in authority. He was not only in charge of this establishment; he had the answer to Cuthbert's question. He delayed giving it to make that point to the bully.

"Molly is gone," Nikolaev said.

"What the *hell* are you talking about?"

"Do not shout, sir."

Cuthbert looked around the lobby. The bellboy was the only other person there. The Russian had grown some brass in the last few minutes.

"I'm sorry," Cuthbert said in a mockingly quieter tone. "Where has Molly gone, Mr. Nikolaev, the man who failed to build an empire?"

The Russian stiffened. "We have both failed at that, have we not?"

It took a moment for Cuthbert to realize that not

only had the man insulted him, he had maligned the Confederacy. The captain walked back down, his gaze grown sinister.

"All right, mister, what's your game? What's got you suddenly all puffed like a general?"

"You do, Captain. What has me outranking you, suddenly, is that I can prove you killed Sheriff Peake. You remember Sheriff Peake?"

Cuthbert half turned toward the wing chair where he had left his grip . . . the bag that seemed a lot thinner without the pearl-handled six-shooters.

"The belt is right there," Nikolaev said, pointing to a package shelf behind him. "I'd noticed the guns before, of course. In my business, you miss nothing. But I never had any reason to remark about them. I remember how you didn't like him wondering about the currency you always seemed to have, you and your men, even though you never worked. Oh, yes"— Nikolaev wagged a cautioning finger—"he talked when he drank. 'How did the captain and his men come here with Confederate money? They don't work, but they have all these greenbacks? Why do folks come here asking about missing people?' He was going out that morning to ask you those questions, Captain."

Cuthbert thrust his hand in his pocket, gripped the derringer.

Nikolaev's finger, still upraised, rotated toward the back of the lobby. Yi stood there with one of the Colts gripped in her two tiny hands.

"I said the belt was there, not the guns. I have the other behind the counter. Poor Yi. The recoil will knock her back if she fires, but she *will* fire. How do you think she became a widow?"

Cuthbert was angry, but more at himself than at Nikolaev. He was always so careful when he went on a ride. But this time his mind had been red with rage and cloudy with being unrested.

Once again, the former Confederate released the derringer. There was enough of a soldier and a gentleman left in him to know when he'd been outmaneuvered.

"All right, Raspy. All right. You made a move. You *want* something. What?"

The Russian knocked his heels together and bowed, like the old-world aristocrat he still wished he was.

"Let Molly be. She went to the church. To pray for Grady."

"I thought I was supposed to tell her."

"*You* said that, not I. She came down with our guest, and she could see from my face that something was wrong. I could not lie. I told her what happened, and she ran out, her red shawl trailing like woven tears."

Cuthbert did not know if Nikolaev was still taunting him or not. This was the longest amount of talking the two had spoken since the man first came to Colorado. But the Russian wasn't the issue.

"Church," Cuthbert said. "Molly hasn't said a word to God since she learned to talk."

"Perhaps she was secretly devout."

Cuthbert shook his head. "Raspy, you are just a big envelope of hot, wordy gas today. I don't know what game you're playing, but you'd best stop."

"Playing games is not my intention." He put a pudgy hand on his heart as if that would add to his sincerity. "We are, after all, a small community that depends on one another."

There was a hint of retreat in the Russian's voice. He was a smarter man than he let on.

"Church," Cuthbert repeated. "You swear she's gone there?"

"On the tsar's all-seeing eyes."

Cuthbert looked from Nikolaev to Yi and back to the Russian. "You give me back my guns?"

Nikolaev pretended to consider the request. He had already decided. "One, no belt. I need insurance. And you promise not to get rough with Molly. I do not want to forbid you from ever returning."

"With what my men and I spend? You'd go broke in a fortnight."

"Nonetheless—"

"Fine, Raspy. You win the bluff."

Nikolaev waved his fingers at Yi. Watching the captain with eyes like little machines, she walked over, put the gun on the counter, and left.

With an annoyed huff, Cuthbert tucked the weapon into his belt, turned, and went back out into the growing sunset.

CHAPTER THIRTEEN

JUAN JUAREZ SAT in the mouth of the cave, listening.
Small fires burned to the right and to the left of
him, in large pits he had hacked from the solid rock
when he first arrived in this remote region. He used
them for warmth against the frigid night but also to
keep eagles from coming after him or his scraps. He
always tossed the remains of his meals over the cliff,
but bits of flesh remained. It could not be helped.
Though he was just forty-seven years old, life up here
was hard. Gratifying, private, and beautiful, but never
easy. The skin cracked, small bones broken here and
there and more than once, his lean, cold fingers were
not as supple as they had been. Meat fell, and he left it
for the bugs. Eating that, they stayed out of the old
skins that were wrapped around his bony form.

His eyes were hollow but they reflected contentment. His face tended to be gaunt though the bushy
beard and spiky mustache concealed that fact. He

whistled a lot, partly to entertain himself, partly to keep his lips from cracking in the often bitter cold.

Deeper in the cave were a pottery wheel he had built himself, the handmade spears used for hunting and fishing, and the furs he had taken from animals smaller than a bear and less feral than a wolf. He used them for clothes and blankets, and he had even used a fox skin to make a flag. With a burning stick, he had seared the words *El mundo de Juan* on the tanned side. It had been draped along the entrance for over two years until a blizzard carried it off. He wondered if God had been cross with him for his vanity, or maybe it was the angry spirit of the fox. The Cheyenne had years ago warned him of the animal spirits in the mountains. Juan was a Catholic who, with the blessings of Padre Alvarez, had left the constant wars in Mexico to come here. He departed on foot with a wooden cross that was being replaced with a gold one in their little church.

Juarez sat and Juarez waited and Juarez listened. Since the visit by the man named Grady Foxborough, listening had become an obsession. Juarez was afraid—not of Grady, but of the man whose horse had been taken. More specifically, the ghost of the *dead* man whose horse had been taken. He believed in a Holy Ghost, so why not an unholy one?

To those he met while heading north, Juarez had alternately called himself a prospector, a hunter, a trapper, a missionary—all things he had been during the two years of his journey. Now he just had the hollow-cheeked, sunken-eyed, scruffy-bearded look of a mountain man—a hermit.

His cave was located a rough hundred-foot climb below Eagle Lookout—rough because there was an overhang that was impossible to surmount for someone not a ghost. The only way to get up there, from his abode, was to spiral around the mountain—a journey that could take the better part of a day, depending on snow, wind, and cold.

So Juan Juarez rarely went up there, and save for one occasion, he did so only in the spring, to collect eagle eggs for his meals. Sometimes the eagles built nests low enough to make that possible.

The exception was over a week before when Juan had heard noises from above.

It was just before sunset, and it had sounded like there was a horse stomping on his head. Since those animals, not even the boldest mustangs, did not run wild up here, and riders rarely went above the high trail that wound around the peak—there was no higher trail beyond that, just mountainside—Juarez could not imagine who was up there.

When he woke the next morning, there were no sounds. Then he heard rumbling. Landslides were not uncommon—but landslides and whinnying horses together, above, were.

Fearful, but concerned that he was soon to have a neighbor—especially one who was tearing things apart—Juarez had decided to investigate. He had pulled on his patchwork of furs, grabbed his old rifle—which was little more than a walking stick, since it had not been fired since the previous winter when he ran out of bullets—and made his way around the cliff.

On the way, Juan had been surprised to meet a man who was coming up the high trail on horseback. This could not have been the horse Juarez heard. He had already gone a quarter mile to the east, too far to hear anything from above. But good Lord Jesus, he hoped this was not an invasion. That was why he had *left* Mexico.

But there was, his sharp eyes had noted, a reason

to not be entirely rude. The stranger had had guns and, more important, a well-stocked saddlebag that might contain a needle and thread. Juarez's garments needed repair, and he was tired of sewing with thistle and vines.

"Hola!" Juarez had said affably.

"Howdy," Grady Foxborough had responded. "Speak English?"

"Sí," the man responded, then shook his head. "Learn a little from gringos on way here."

"What's your name?" the newcomer asked. "I'm Grady Foxborough."

"Juan Juarez."

"Hello, Juan. You must have strong lungs, *amigo.* Where'd all the air go?"

"God blow it away. This His place," Juan said.

"You could be right. Well, Juan and"—he looked up reverently—"and God, Your Highness, I'm looking for a man who was following this trail up. Came through about two days ago. You see such a fella?"

"Maybe. I hear horses."

"Where?"

"Señor, you have—to sew?"

"So?"

Juarez had made a motion with his pinched fingers.

"You mean a needle?"

"Sí, sí!"

"I don't have that, *muchos* sorry."

Juan had scowled. The man's carbine looked like a twelve gauge, not a ten gauge. He could not even trade his help for bullets.

Bundled against the wind in a heavy sheepskin, Foxborough looked around at the gray cliff to one side and a precipice on the other. "Mister—Juan—do you *live* up here?"

"*Si.* Not a nice place. You would not like."

"I can see that. I wasn't thinking of moving here." Juan's temper relaxed a bit.

"Listen, Juan—where are *you* headed?"

"Heard a horse. No horses up here. I usual no hear anybody, except me."

"It wasn't my horse, was it?"

Juarez shook his head.

"Do you mind if I come along to where you were going? To where you heard the horse?"

Juarez spit—and the stranger's hand slapped down to his gun belt.

"No!" Juan said, holding up one hand and pulling at his lips with the other. "Fur from collar blow in mouth!"

Foxborough snorted. "That gun of yours—it even work?"

Juarez shook his head yes . . . then no.

"Tell you what. You help me, and if we find a gun up there, it's yours. Deal?"

Juarez had not even thought of that. He did not dislike the man, and as long as he was not going to settle here—

"Okay, you can follow. But I don't know why anybody would come up here. There is nothing."

"Well, I ask you, Juan: Why would somebody come up here searching for nothing?"

"You are," Juarez said.

Foxborough laughed. "Maybe you're correct. But this friend of mine, a trapper, is kind of loco."

"Come," the Mexican said, and trudged past Foxborough. "Cold here."

The Southerner followed.

The trip had taken nearly three more hard, leg-wearying hours. A low cloud layer had gathered around them, adding chill and obscuring their view, and there was increasingly icy ground caused by condensation from those clouds. In addition, the trip was made hazardous by a narrowing path that became little more than a rock-strewn band some five feet wide.

If Juarez was not exactly a stranger in a strange land, he felt like Moses on Sinai, with his rifle staff and blowing cloak of black bear.

The path had finally broadened as it led to a ledge about the size of the small cemetery back in Chihuahua, the one with just nine departed. This was Eagle Lookout. There was a horse away from the ledge, by a cliff—a restless and unhappy animal with its reins tied around a rock. Juarez could see the beginnings of its ribs. What he could not see was a rifle. The man must have taken it with him.

"That's why the horse make noise," Juarez said, walking over and stroking the animal's side. The horse flinched. There were bird droppings on its back. "He scared and hungry."

"He's also still saddled," Foxborough observed.

"Is this the trapper's horse?"

Foxborough nodded. "He obviously did not intend to stay away this long."

The Southerner dismounted and looked up, squinting through the shrouding clouds. He could dimly see, and also hear, the nests on outcroppings above. But there was nowhere a man could just disappear. The trapper, or whoever had been riding the horse, had not fallen over the ledge. There was a faint coating of undisturbed ice particles and intact eagle droppings on the overlapping slabs of slate. Except where the horse had stepped, all around the rock, or licked at the ice underfoot, nothing had been disturbed.

That was when Foxborough spotted a few dislodged chips of rock around the horse. He had looked up as far as the clouds permitted, some ten feet above.

"Damn. He had to have gone that way."

"*Sí.* Nowhere else."

"Do you know what's on top?"

"Just mountain, I think. But I have never been there. The trail, it ends here."

"Then he had to have gone up the mountain—and here, since that's where he left the horse. May have even used the saddle for a boost up."

"Maybe a rope? The rock is slippery—the birds."

"Yeah, I didn't see one on the horse. But to throw it up there in this wind—it wouldn't get him very far." Foxborough shook his head. "Keeler, you lunatic. What were you thinking? Juan, you know what's on the north face?"

"More rock. More eagles. You can see it from the lower trail."

"No openings?"

"I never see one." He shrugged. "But then I never look."

"Does it ever clear up here? Can't make out very much."

"*Sí.* Weather changes pretty fast. But—you could start climbing, it's clear. Before you go ten feet . . . it's not."

Foxborough slapped his reins in the Mexican's hand like he was a stable boy. *Now* Juarez disliked him. The Southerner stepped back as far as he dared, and Juarez did not care if he fell. Eagle Lookout had a slight slope toward the abyss where there was a mix of peaks, ledges, and, below that, tall pines. If a strong wind came around the slope, it would be easy to tumble over.

Foxborough turned his face up and put his hands on the sides of his mouth and shouted, his voice echoing. "Hey! Hey, you with the Palomino!"

"Not so loud!" Juarez said with urgent hand motions. "You bring this wall down."

"Good point, old man."

You are idiot, young man, Juarez thought.

The two men fell silent then, listening through the wind. There was no reply, no sound of movement above.

After a minute of not moving, Juarez was looking down when he noticed something beneath his furry boots, something that concerned him.

"We should not stay too long," the Mexican said.

"Why not?"

He pointed down. "There is blood under the ice."

Foxborough went over and looked around at the ground, more carefully than before. "What do you think did that?"

"Eagles bring food to the nest. It bleeds. Come dark, maybe they think *we* are food."

"It's been a couple of days, maybe a week—they haven't attacked the horse."

"Horse is too big to carry. My feet and hands, they look like foxes. Your cap, a raccoon."

Foxborough sighed. "You may have a point. Anyway, it doesn't look like ole Keeler is anywhere near." Foxborough came back then and took the reins. Of both horses.

"We should not leave horse?" Juarez asked.

"To die? No. That would be cruel."

"Man may die when he come back."

"*If* he comes back," Foxborough had said. "For all we know, he went up and fell from there. Anyway, he can make it down on foot just as okay. You got up here."

"I wasn't hungry or thirsty. Or tired. Or maybe lost."

"Look, Juan, I admire your compassion, but Ben Keeler is probably beyond hearing," Foxborough said. "If he isn't, then he'll find you, or maybe he'll find me, and when he does, I'll give him back his horse."

Foxborough noticed then a necklace made of cat's teeth draped over the pommel. He took it off, slipped it over his head. "You see him, you give him food. He'll know we were looking after his interests."

Juarez did not care for that idea. But if this Keeler was lost or had fallen, it was true that the horse would die. He did not want to see that either. He also wanted this Grady to leave now, before it grew dark, so he made no protest. Not that the man would have listened. He was a stiff-necked one—the kind of aristocrat the Mexican had wanted to leave behind when he came up here.

The two men and the two horses reversed course, Juarez in the lead, on foot, Foxborough riding his horse and pulling the Palomino behind. It was slow going, since the downward slope made the men want to speed up—which would have put them right off any number of sharp turns in the cliff.

They made it back to Juarez's level without incident, and the other man and his horses stayed on the trail to head home.

"Sorry you didn't get the rifle," Foxborough said. "But I tell you what. You still stand a chance to make some profit. If you see Ben Keeler, bring him to me on the lower trail, at the last rise. I'll give him his horse and you a rifle. Okay?"

"I will tell him," Juarez promised, then added quietly, "either in person or in my prayers."

Now, more than a week after that journey, Juarez sat by his twin campfires and watched as the sun disappeared somewhere behind his mountain. The clouds had remained, snow had fallen, and then the clouds had started to break. As he sat there, a misty white puff was all that remained. A sunset wind came along and pushed at it, and the cloud flew off like an angel.

Ordinarily, the vision would have made him smile.

This day, it made him uneasy, afraid of the unwelcomed dark. He had come up here to be alone. Now there would always be the ghost of a mysterious man named Keeler haunting his ledge and his cave and his soul. . . .

CHAPTER FOURTEEN

I<small>T WAS A</small> bad day and night for Molly Henshaw.

When her employer, Raspy Nikolaev, informed her that her boyfriend, Promise Cuthbert, was gunning for her hero, Dr. John Stockbridge, her first thought was to ride out, find Stockbridge, and warn the man who had made such a strong impression on her in Gunnison. Over her many years of engaging with the public, Molly had acquired a strong first sense about the bad ones and the good ones. Cuthbert was somewhere in between, leaning toward bad, though not enough so that she hated being with him. But Stockbridge—

He's better than good, she thought as she ran from the Pap, uncertain where she was going other than to get away. In their brief, brief encounter, Dr. Stockbridge had not permitted his profound personal misfortune to touch her. He had been like a knight. Promise Cuthbert? He was a coyote whose only asset was that he wasn't as bad as all the other barking, pawing, ravenous coyotes.

You did not cross a man like Promise Cuthbert. But at peril of your heart and soul, you did not betray such a man as John Stockbridge or allow him to be betrayed.

So she ran out after finishing with Spaulding Doubleday and turned north, toward the plain and the small church with its steeple, which was dirty on one side, the side that was exposed to the buffeting western winds. The priest, Reverend Michaels, did not intrude on her devotions. If the solace of the place was all a parishioner needed, the pastor was happily content with that.

It was not prayer, though, that had guided Molly's feet and folded her hands in prayer. It was sanctuary. It was fear. It was dread of what Promise Cuthbert would do if he learned what was in her heart.

She had not been there more than a few minutes, on her knees in a pew, when the door opened, flushing the somber darkness with light before closing again with a slam. She recognized the beat on the wooden floor, Cuthbert's heavy stride caused by the ramrod posture. She could picture, could almost hear the to-and-fro swing of his shoulders.

He sidled into the row behind her and sat heavily. She heard his breath, fast and angry. When she did not turn, he leaned forward. She felt his stubble brush her jaw, felt the heat of his mouth near her right ear.

"I hear you're mourning Grady Foxborough."

She did not respond.

"You barely knew him, Molly. Why are you here instead of washing my back?"

She did not want to answer him but nonetheless fell into the same, rutted pattern that had helped her to survive for so many years, in town after town, in this lopsided world of men.

She lied. She said what she thought would appease him.

"I am . . . I'm praying for you, Promise."

"For me? Why? What do you think is going to happen to me?"

"You will seek the man who killed Grady."

"Ambushed."

"I'm sorry?"

"Grady was shot from below while he was facing another way."

"What—what was Grady doing?"

"Hunting."

"Hunting who?"

Molly did not regret saying it, even when Cuthbert leaned over the pew and glared at her sideways.

"You forget yourself, girl."

"Do I? And *you* forget where we are."

Cuthbert regarded her curiously, then said with disapproval, "You're suddenly bold."

"Am I?"

"And toying with me. Why?"

"Maybe I just wanted some time alone."

"To pray for Grady. And me."

"That's right."

Cuthbert changed suddenly, as was his tendency. He kissed her earlobe. "Come back to the hotel with me. Let me remind you what kind of man Promise Cuthbert is so you won't be afraid for his safety."

"I need to finish praying."

"No, Molly. What you have to do is get off your well-worn knees and come with me."

Molly did not move. Now she *would* not move. She could not be in the arms of this man ever again; she knew that now.

When the woman did not rise as ordered, Cuthbert grabbed her right arm, rose, and started pulling her with him.

"Leave her be!"

The voice echoed through the small, dark church. It did not cause Cuthbert to release the woman, but he did stand very still.

"Who's there?" the captain demanded.

"God's servant."

Though the old, diminutive, white-haired Reverend Michaels was only ten feet away, behind the pulpit, he was barely visible in the shadows.

The former Confederate captain snorted. "You were addressing me, Padre?"

"None other."

"How about, instead, you mind your own business and God's business and leave me and the lady alone!"

"Within these walls, you do not give instructions."

"Well, forgive the hell outta me," Cuthbert said. "But I'm taking her out, and you're not stopping me."

The pastor stepped from behind the pulpit and walked toward them. Cuthbert gave Molly's arm a tug. She refused to move. He tried again, and she grunted her resistance.

The much smaller reverend, dressed in a black cassock, stepped up to the pew. "You will release the lady, or you will be forced to strike me down."

"You think I won't?" Cuthbert snickered. "Padre, your rank means *nothing* to me!"

"You may be cavalier about the house of God, but there are many in this village, in this region, who are not. They may overlook a brute who manhandles women, but they will not think kindly of one who would strike the clergy."

Cuthbert released Molly and moved into the aisle,

stopping with his face inches from that of the preacher. Reverend Michaels did not flinch or lose his serene but firm disposition.

"You are pushing the wrong man," the former soldier said.

"You are the one doing the pulling and pushing. I am merely standing with a member of the family of Jesus Christ."

Cuthbert sneered and waved dismissively at the man. "You're an empty frock," he snarled, and then looked hotly at Molly. "I am going to take my own bath. I will deal with you later."

With that, the Confederate stalked away, kicking the next pew and causing it to scrape against the floor as he left the row. When the man was gone, Molly erupted in tears and sat heavily, her pale face in her hands, her blond curls falling over her sleeves.

Reverend Michaels sat beside her.

"Thank you," she said into her hands. "Thank you."

"Thank God," he replied.

She lifted her tear-filled eyes to the modest wooden cross that hung on the front wall. Her lips moved in grateful silence.

"If you need to continue your prayer, I will go. If you need to talk, I am here. And if you need to leave without being seen, there is a back door."

Molly was so surprised by the pastor's understanding that she threw herself against him and wept into his shoulder and accepted the light, comforting touch of his hands upon her shoulders.

She was also pleased with the courage she had shown Promise Cuthbert. Molly was certain she would need more of that before this business was through.

*   *   *

A QUARTER HOUR later, watching through the stained glass window in the front of the church, Molly saw the curtains draw shut in the bathroom. With a gift of bread and cheese tied in a white cloth, and a skin filled with water the priest personally drew from the well, she hurried across the street to the stable to get her horse.

Under cover of the falling twilight, she slipped from Buzzard Gulch and turned her horse west. That was where the homesteaders all lived and where she was likely to find Dr. Stockbridge.

Unfortunately, what she found was Promise Cuthbert. The man had lured her out by telling Raspy Nikolaev to prepare the bathroom for him alone. Then he had gotten his horse and waited behind Tom Neal's jail, where he had a view of the front and the back of the church. When she left, he galloped ahead. There was nothing but Gunnison more than a day's ride to the east. She would not be going there, dressed as she was.

As soon as she neared the sheriff's office, the last building in town, Cuthbert trotted forward. She stopped, and the two stood with their horses facing on the cold, windy plain. She was cold, despite the seasonal shawl she had pulled on. He looked ominous in his dark, granite posture against the sinking sun.

"Where you going, Molly?"

"For a ride."

"This hour? Dressed like that, with no coat?"

"I know how to make a fire, and Reverend Michaels gave me food—I just want to be alone for a while."

"Where? On the plains?"

"That's right. To clear my thoughts."

He laughed. "Girl, you must think me the biggest jackass this side of the Mississippi. I don't know what you're up to, but I want you to go to the hotel with me."

"Not tonight."

"That was not me requesting. I'm telling you. There's something not right, and I want to find out what it is."

While Molly was frozen, considering what other options there might be, Cuthbert rode forward a few paces and grabbed the bridle of her horse. Being bold was one thing; being reckless was something else altogether. There was no choice then, as she had already come to realize.

The two returned to the hotel and went upstairs. Nikolaev was surprised and saddened to see Molly. She gave him a look that said she was all right, for now. Cuthbert took his bath and Molly soaped and scrubbed him—considering and dismissing the idea of running when he was naked and in the water. For the safety of Molly and Yi, there was no lock on the door. But Cuthbert put his six-shooter on the floor beside the big tin tub. Given the man's threadbare patience with her, Molly did not want to risk angering him further.

Not before she had a plan for getting away.

Until the confrontation in the church, Molly had not thought about doing anything other than somehow getting word to Dr. Stockbridge that there were men searching for him. She did not for a moment believe the doctor had "ambushed" Grady Foxborough. Cuthbert and his men were not cowards, but they did not play fair either. Now, partly from a young woman's infatuation and from fearing for her safety, she wanted to do more. Short of provoking Cuthbert to a rage and shooting him with his own handgun, she wanted to help Dr. Stockbridge in any way possible.

And in so doing, help herself. She could no longer be beholden to this man.

The opportunity to escape presented itself when Cuthbert finished bathing and called Yi to fetch a bottle of whiskey. He was not about to send Molly on the mission and have her run off again.

Some men, especially those who intended to take advantage of being alone with a woman, would enter this room and idly look into drawers and under wash-cloths for weapons. Nikolaev expected his woman to endure liberties—to a point. At the same time, he did not want his clients shot nor stabbed. However, since some men wanted a shave, he agreed with Molly and Doris that a straight-edge razor could be left on the nearby wooden washing stand, sitting innocuously among the soap powder, mug, and brush . . . hidden under a folded towel.

Molly intended to use that razor, if necessary. However, unknown to the woman, Cuthbert had confiscated it—innocently enough, his back to Molly as he removed his boot and tucked the straight-edge razor deep inside when he arrived, stuffing his socks on top of it.

Molly had noticed the blade missing as the man stepped into the tub. When she called to Yi for a bottle of whiskey, she asked for one from Nikolaev's special store.

Cuthbert did not know that mentioning Nikolaev's special store was the ladies' signal to lace the bottle with sodium bromide. Even if Cuthbert did not fall asleep, it would make him groggy. Nikolaev could always blame the liquor. Since Molly would make sure to spill whatever was left, the Southerner would not be able to force the proprietor to drink from the bottle.

"Feeling apologetic?" the man in the tub asked when Molly made the request.

"I want this to be a pleasant night," Molly replied, sounding earnest. And she was, though not for the reasons Cuthbert might have imagined.

"I'm glad you've come around, Molly," he said. "I didn't want to hurt you back in the chapel. I'm upset over Grady, need a clear head."

She did not answer. Of course he wanted to hurt her. He *had* hurt her.

The captain did not immediately turn to the bottle. With the neck of the bottle tight in one fist, the gun in the other—he was taken to his room by Molly.

The bathroom was on the second of three floors. Cuthbert's room was on the third, overlooking the street. He did not want to overlook the stable.

"Yi got my clothes?" he asked as they left.

"She'll get them."

Yi never gave them a full washing. She would just beat the dust from them out back, on the line, then iron them. Otherwise, they would not be ready when Cuthbert wanted to go to the bar. Tonight, by mistake, they went in the wash barrel to soak.

Molly used her passkey to open the door. Once inside, she lit the lantern on the dresser while Cuthbert went to the window and drew the curtains. The room was cold, and he pulled the bed quilt around his bare shoulders. He warmed himself further by pulling Molly to him. He held her under the quilt, his strong arms tightly wrapped around her. It was not a loving embrace. He had on a cruel expression as he looked down into her eyes, his skin a pale orange in the light.

"You're still not *with* me, Molly. You're not looking at me. You're hardly talking to me. Why? What aren't you and that fat Russian telling me?"

"I told you. It's Grady . . . violence."

"You told me, yeah. Only I don't believe you."

"I've never lied to you, Captain."

"That's what makes the lie stand out." Cuthbert shifted his grip to the backs of her arms and squeezed. "You've been with him, haven't you?"

"Who?"

"Stockbridge. He's *been* here!"

"Never! Please, Captain. Let me go!"

"When you tell me the truth. And don't bother calling Raspy. He comes in here, I'll kick him out the window."

"Don't!" she said. Then she suddenly stopped resisting. "All right. Let me—let me have a drink, and I'll tell you."

"You admit it, then? Lying?"

She nodded.

Cuthbert relaxed his grip. "That's more like it. Yeah, go and have a drink. Help yourself."

"Do you want one, too?"

"Not yet, sugar. I'll wait to hear what you have to say. Then maybe we'll have something to toast."

Unscrewing the cap, she put the bottle to her lips and drank deeply. Far, far deeper than usual.

"Hold on there, girl!" Cuthbert cried. He rushed over.

She kept drinking. If the whiskey enough wasn't sufficient to knock her legs out, the sleeping powder was. Before a quarter of the bottle was gone, before the captain could smack it away, she had already begun to see circles swirling behind her eyes, like the colorful Mexican spinning toys she had seen one New Year's Eve. Within a moment, she felt herself dropping.

I T WAS MORNING before Molly woke.

She was in her own bed on the second floor, and there was a washcloth on her head. It was still slightly damp and quite cold. She removed it, wincing from the effort of raising her arm.

Someone took the cloth from her fingers.

"Th-thanks, Yi," Molly said, squinting up. Yi shared the bedroom with her. The only other employees who lived here, besides Doris, were Bertram the bellboy and the handyman-janitor, Iron Jaw, a former rail worker who could bend nails with his teeth.

"You welcome. You drink on purpose, yes?"

Molly nodded.

Yi smiled. "Good thinking. Cuthbert not here. Hit boss."

"I'm sorry."

"It okay. Sheriff was at bar. Arrest Cuthbert for assaulting. Boss happy."

"Is the captain still in jail?"

"Yes. Hit sheriff, too."

Molly's first thought was that the bastard deserved worse. Her second thought was that she had wasted the cover of night. She had to find Dr. Stockbridge before the Red Hunters did.

"How late is it?"

"Eight." Yi added proudly, "I finish laundry and breakfast dishes already. Doris take morning bath men. We help you."

"You're both angels," Molly told her. "But I have to get up. I have to go before Cuthbert is released."

"Boss say you been kicked by mule—need rest."

"What I need is to move," Molly replied.

Yi knew better than to argue with the woman when her mind was set. Instead, she took both of Molly's hands and, leaning back, helped her to sit, very slowly, on the edge of the bed.

Molly shut her eyes and sat there, wavering to and fro, fighting the quick, stabbing pain that punched her forehead from the inside out, then recoiled to the back of her skull. At the same time, her ears were throbbing sideways. She remained very still, waiting until the pain subsided before opening her eyes.

Yi had magically transformed into Nikolaev. The big Russian was standing beside the bed, smiling down. The left side of his jaw was swollen.

"I wonder which of us feels worse," Molly said.

"You. For me, it was worth the blow to take some strut out of that man. And to put some iron into the sheriff." He raised and shook a fist in emphasis. "This is the first ruffian in Cuthbert's group Neal has ever arrested—and it is Cuthbert himself! Is that not delightful?"

"It is. But I still have to go. Now."

"To find your knight."

She smiled thinly. "To do what's right."

"As you say," Nikolaev replied.

Molly extended her right hand, and Nikolaev offered his forearm. He held it firm as she removed the quilt and slowly, very slowly eased her legs onto the floor. It was cold—everything was cold—but she stood and waited while the Russian took her robe from a hook behind the door.

"Do you want Yi?" he asked.

"Thank you, no. She has more work . . . because of me."

"You know it makes her happy to help you. How you feel about Stockbridge is how she feels about you."

"She is a dear."

That was all the conversation Molly could muster at the moment. Nikolaev left, telling her he would have Iron Jaw ready his surrey for her. He did not want her riding a saddle horse.

With the pain in her head softened by the gratitude in her heart, Molly Henshaw went to the stool, where Yi had sweetly left her folded clothes, and began to dress. When she was finished, she pulled on her leather riding gloves and headed downstairs.

Nikolaev was behind the counter. Cuthbert's six-shooters were on it.

"Do you want one of these?" the Russian asked. "Perhaps my derringer?"

"Thank you, no," Molly said, moving by.

"It might be prudent."

The woman accepted the small gun, smiled gravely, then turned her squinting eyes from the bright day as she opened the door. She looked back at her boss.

"Killing men is something I'd better not commence," she said.

With that, she left the hotel.

CHAPTER FIFTEEN

Dᴏᴡɴ ᴏɴ ᴛʜᴇ homestead, the sun rose on cottony
clouds that held no threat of snow. They were
drifting slowly east, into the dawn. Like little brushes,
they painted a canopy of red, then yellow, then blue
behind them.

Stockbridge had slept well. The room and the setting turned to deep silence when the animals had fed
and none of the Keelers stirred. He did not imagine
that any of them had the strength to move. It had
been a difficult day, physically as well as emotionally.

Stockbridge had left the buffalo-hide shade open
a slice so the first of the sun would strike him. He was
on Pama's back and riding through purple sage before the great, ruddy orb was half risen.

The doctor's brain picked up where it had left off
the night before. He could not think of a reason for
Ben Keeler's absence, other than it having to do with
the men he had met, so he planned to return to that
spot. It could be that, with Grady gone, another man

would be up there, perhaps the black man with the bow and arrow. Stockbridge would approach with caution, expecting that if anyone was there, he would shoot the man on sight.

Especially if they already discovered that the one who came after us didn't come home.

He was hesitant to leave the Keelers unprotected, but felt that if anyone came gunning for him, they would either see him on the trail or figure out that he was not there.

What a world it was. There was no war, yet people were still galloping hard to their deaths. Was there ever to be an end?

The morning sun did little to kill the cold, and Stockbridge was glad Mrs. Keeler had mended his coat. There was not much wind, but the chill tried to creep under the garment as he moved rhythmically up and down in the saddle.

Chewing jerky from a pouch Betty Newcombe had prepared for him, Stockbridge reached the trail in two hours. Peak Road was untraveled at most times, but even less so in the early morning. There wasn't sight or sound of another rider, of cart-wheel tracks, of discarded apple cores or chicken bones or coffee grounds. He followed the trail past where they had lost the wagon, the poor conveyance sitting, a lopsided wreck, already home to small plains animals. He approached the turnoff to the watering hole. He looked south and saw buzzards coming and going from where he had left his attacker.

The man's comrade—or comrades—has not found him. Otherwise, he would not have been left there as carrion.

At this distance, the dead man was indistinguishable from a bison or an elk. But that did not mean anyone looking for him would not check on it up close.

Which gave him an idea.

Searching for the dead man, others would spot the birds just as he had. Why ride to them when they would come to him?

Stockbridge stopped Pama and weighed the notion of lying in wait. But then another possibility occurred to him, equally sinister.

What if they had already found the body and left it. That would make the killer think he was safe from ambush.

I'm expecting it in the mountains, not on the open plain.

Stockbridge looked at the terrain ahead. There were boulders, some more than man high, on both sides of the trail. They had likely rolled there from the mountains in some distant age. The big rocks were too far apart for anyone to set up an effective cross fire. And riding forward, he would be able to see all but the eastern side. They did not present much of a hiding place for a man or, more important, his horse. He did not see one, hear one, or smell one. There were no hoofprints that he could discern.

Stockbridge urged Pama on, his hat pulled low in the sun, his eyes on the trail immediately ahead, his ears listening everywhere else. He neared the first boulder, a shoulder-high mass that was wider than it was tall and rounded on top. There was no one up there. Possibly behind. There was enough room for a man beside a horse. He listened carefully. Pama did not seem perturbed, suggesting there was neither man nor animal out there.

Stockbridge did not suspect the bear trap until its ragged iron teeth clamped shut on Pama. The horse simultaneously cried out and buckled forward. Stockbridge went over the animal's long neck, dropping to the left, by the rock, and landing hard on his back. He lost his breath and his hat. The shotgun had been under his right arm; it dropped on its stock and landed between Stockbridge and the horse. To the other side of the man was the chain that had been hammered to the ground just under the boulder. The powerful links had been unearthed by the horse's futile struggles to get away, to stand.

Stockbridge grabbed the shotgun and immediately looked around. No one came by—not immediately. They did not have to. The doctor would not be going far.

As Pama whinnied and fought, Stockbridge managed to push from the dirt. He sat, saw the bloody foreleg nearly torn clean and about to be ripped away by the animal's pitiful struggles. Without hesitation, he put a single shot in the Walker's skull. The head blew out the other side, the side to which Pama fell. The horse landed with a dusty thud, blood pouring onto the trail in a long, pumping, nasty stream.

Stockbridge crawled to the boulder and put his back to it for protection. He did a quick self-diagnosis. No broken limbs or ribs. No bleeding. Except for bruising, he would be all right.

He looked to the east. The point where the trail turned up into the mountains, the nearest peaks, was about a half mile distant. There was no one on the horizon, as far as he could tell. Unless they were buried like the trap had been, waiting for him to walk by, the immediate coast seemed clear. Feeling relatively safe, Stockbridge put a palm against the rock and stood. When no one fired from the other side, from the south, he moved from the rock toward the dead horse. He retrieved his deerskin water pouch and the wax paper containing the rest of the jerky.

There's enough food and water till you reach the foothills, he thought as he hurried back to the boulder. *How are you set for patience?*

Once again, his thinking turned to staying put. Whoever had set this so near to the remains of the dead man obviously wanted Stockbridge. Sooner or later, he would come looking. Stockbridge dismissed the idea of going back to the homestead. He did not want to put the Keelers in jeopardy.

The buzzards migrated over almost at once. They had finished with the man lying to the south and were flocking to the horse. They were a mass of knobbed heads, wings like black pirate sails full of the wind, and big, dark, gore-streaked feathers.

He did not bother to shoot them or shoo them. He had seen angry buzzards turn on trespassing humans. And killing a few would only attract multiples to feed on their dead flesh. To these creatures, like most of nature's predators, meat was meat.

After considering his options, Stockbridge decided to make for the mountains. Before nightfall, he could likely get as far as the point where he had met the Keelers. He could go back to the ledge where Grady Foxborough had lain and build a fire, secure that come nightfall anyone approaching would need a lantern. They would step on branches or leaves or rocks. He would see them, or he would hear them.

And if someone up ahead was lying in wait to snipe at him, he would watch for flashes of light. In another couple of hours, when he reached as far as he could now see, they would be facing into the sun.

Recovering his hat, Stockbridge tipped it to Pama.

"I apologize most earnestly for what I am about to do," he said, then went over and used his bread knife to saw away the tendon that barely held the animal's rent foreleg in place. There were no branches around, and he was concerned that there might be other traps. He needed a cane of some kind to go before him, tapping the dirt. His generous mount was helping him to the last, though Stockbridge could not imagine what any travelers would think, seeing the track of a one-legged horse.

CHAPTER SIXTEEN

W OODROW POUND WATCHED the trail with attention that matched any he had displayed during
his daring escape from servitude. Back then, his life
and freedom were at risk. Today, it was his honor as
a man and a brother.

The qualities were no less equal, in his mind. And
now, as then, he was counting on his natural skill and
cunning to see the matter through.

The preferred weapons of the former slave were
the knife and the bow and arrow. During his years of
slavery, Pound had always been able to find sticks in
the field. Secreting them in his trouser leg, he would
practice thrusting and stabbing. If he ever had the
opportunity to steal a knife, if one of the house slaves
could slip one to him, he would not only feel safer,
more able to protect his fellow slaves, but he would
feel as though he had some command over his des-
tiny. If that poor slave Freddy Hat had owned a knife,

he might have been able to make good his escape that fateful, long-ago day.

Pound had been good with a stick, then good with a sharpened stick, and when he finally secured a knife from a white Southerner who attacked him after the War, he had instantly been good with that, too.

The bow and arrow came later. Shortly after falling in with Cuthbert, Pound had traded a bear paw to a Cheyenne with the unfitting name of Strong Elk. The Indian was something of a failure as a brave and needed a gift, powerful medicine, to present to the father of a squaw he fancied. The first thing Strong Elk did after making the trade was to have Pound rake his back with the purchase. Back at the settlement, the brave would be asked to sit at the campfire and recite the tale of his adventure. Since he could not have inflicted those scars himself, the story would seem more creditable. Pound often wondered what had become of Strong Elk and his woman.

The bow and arrow came naturally to Pound. He made a quiver from wolfskin and filled it with arrows he cut and whittled from spruce trees. He fitted them with granite arrowheads he chipped himself. The fletching was from game birds they ate for dinner. Pound had been born on the slave ship that brought him to these shores. His father was sold elsewhere, and his mother died when he was still a young boy. He knew nothing of his tribal background. But the skill came so well and so easily, he wondered, often, if his people in Africa had known this weapon. He had seen a picture in a book, once, that suggested spears.

"I believe they musta been good with anything that came from the treed earth of the savannah," Freddy Hat once said. *"You'll see, little brother. One day the*

land will be barren 'cause we will refuse to make the cotton grow."

The day before, back at New Richmond, Pound had been concerned when McWilliams charged off in pursuit of a very dangerous man. Pound had not wanted to shame his friend by riding in pursuit. To begin with, McWilliams would only have turned on his brother, accused him of trying once again to turn him yellow. McWilliams would have been adamant about not listening, not even stopping. Beyond that, when a man lost the respect of his own self, the last thing he wanted was someone to help him recover it. That had to be done by the man who had been injured, or it only deepened the shame.

Instead, Pound had taken time to eat before setting off on McWilliams' trail. Even if he hadn't known where the other man was going, it was not difficult to follow the hard-riding prints he left behind.

Pound had been too far to hear more than the distant report of the shot that took down his friend. It was dark when, by the smell of the gored body and defecating animals surrounding it, he found Liam McWilliams. Pound had come as close as he dared— one did not interrupt a pack of coyotes when they were feeding or buzzards when they were circling, awaiting their turn—but a struck match confirmed that it was McWilliams being torn apart on the dry earth.

Riding a little farther on along the trail, he came upon the abandoned Keeler wagon and the tracks leading from it. He knew that Stockbridge had gone with them, and he knew something else. Either that night or early the following morning, once he got the family safely home, the devil would return. Stockbridge knew there was at least one other man, someone he could not afford to leave alive to seek revenge.

Pound turned around and rode dangerously up the mountain trail in the dark. He did not need to rush. He had at least all night, he reckoned. As he headed back to New Richmond, he formulated a plan to outwit and destroy John Stockbridge. Pound did not even have the time or energy to hate the man. One did not hate during War; one acted and survived. He came up with a plan that required the bear trap the Red Hunters had used so effectively just the previous night, along with other items at the cabin.

The Red Hunter member made it to the compound and back without resting, taking the road slowly because he dared not carry a torch. Carried on a strong oak sledge, the bear trap was easy enough to transport and then to hide and set. At sunrise, Pound looked for any telltale signs of digging, then brushed them over with a bouquet made of dried grass. The wind would do the rest. It was blowing from the east, and he piled dirt high on that side, not only by the trap pit but near his footprints. It would slowly cover any sign that he had been there. The next trap was more challenging. If Stockbridge survived the bear trap, he would be looking for more of the same and might decide to walk off-trail.

Burying the sledge behind a nearby rock, Pound set about arranging the next part of his snare. The black man had little experience with guns and was not much of a marksman. He had no intention of shooting it out with a man who toted a powerful shotgun. Fortunately, there was no need. It was called a *Hó'öhtöhená'e* by the Cheyenne: the Cane Woman. It would seem harmless, if someone walking past noticed it at all. The Cane Woman was a cactus invisibly rigged to kill. Indians would steal kerosene from settlers or outposts, then pour it through a slit made in the highly absorptive plant. When the liquid inside was ignited with a flaming arrow, the heat caused the plant to burst in a white fireball, sending its burning meat and thistles in all directions. The Cane Woman was used to maim and frighten horses and also to temporarily blind anyone standing nearby. This allowed the targeted individuals to be captured and used for a long night of bloody entertainment. Their remains were tapestries of unimaginable suffering, left in plain view to warn others from Indian lands.

Pound had hitched his horse to a large cactus behind a small rise where it would not be seen. He had chosen a spot he knew well from regular visits to the Poet and Puncher, where he was allowed to sit in the small "Indians Only" section. It was a spot with a triangle of cacti—two on the north side of the trail, one well to the south. Passing anywhere nearby, Stockbridge would be struck by projectiles from one or more of the Cane Women. And Pound would make sure Stockbridge went exactly where he wanted the other man. There was a large upright rock near enough for Pound to hide behind. When the target came within view, Pound would light a fire. Stockbridge would see the smoke and approach cautiously. Hidden, Pound would nonetheless hear his steps. If Stockbridge decided to circle the boulder from the south, Pound would be ready with an arrow. Stockbridge's left side would show first—and take a shaft. If Stockbridge came along the trail then, without being seen, Pound would launch arrows to set one, then another, then another of the cacti aflame. Within moments, on foot, Stockbridge would be injured or dead.

Only hurt, Pound hoped. He wanted to have the satisfaction of looking down into the demon's eyes as he put a blade into his black heart.

Pound had prepared the firepit with grass and

some meat he found clinging to the bones of an old, dead buzzard. Burning that would make the smoke dark and oily. It couldn't fail to be seen and smelled. Then he had waited on his belly, behind the rock, until he heard the jaws of the trap close, the horse cry out, the bullet crack to end its life. Pound peered around the rock at the figure approaching in the bright morning light.

It was Stockbridge. He was holding something— possibly a stick to check the road for traps.

A sensible precaution, Pound thought. Devils were known to be clever.

The black man withdrew, waited a little longer until he could hear the crunch of the man's approach. Stockbridge was coming straight down the trail—a perfect path, from the Red Hunter's point of view. Pound struck a match and touched flame to grass. The blaze took quickly and thick smoke billowed up, catching the wind and blowing toward Stockbridge. Squatting, Pound pulled an arrow from his quiver. He fixed the notch on the string. The shaft seemed like an extension of his arm, his hand, his fingers. It was reaching out to work his will.

His heart racing—more with anticipation than fear—the black man remained crouched, listening and waiting. . . .

M AKING HIS WAY west along the trail, Stockbridge was still quite a distance from the cacti when he noticed that the air had a tartness to it. It smelled as if someone had slit one of the plants for water. Maybe they had, though there was no one around, and the odor—and, thus, the slice—was relatively fresh.

Instantly on guard, Stockbridge stopped when he

saw the first wisps of smoke rise from behind the rock. It appeared that he was not only expected; he was being invited in.

Whoever had started the blaze felt damn confident. Possibly the black man who had been with the others up on the trail. He had been carrying a bow and arrow.

He would have to step out pretty far to shoot me square, Stockbridge thought. *Maybe if I talk to him—*

"Nobody has to die here!" Stockbridge shouted. "I assume you got a horse. I take him, we're square."

The answer was immediate.

"You left my friend for the buzzards. *You* have to die."

It was the same man from the high trail. He had probably ridden down the night before, looking for his companion. He would have had water with him; there was no need to carve up a cactus. Stockbridge crouched, looked at the dirt around the three plants. There were damp spots that rippled the air above them. They had more substance than water.

An ambush, remotely triggered. Down low he could smell it now, faintly, on the wind. Something unctuous and heavy, creeping along the ground.

"Last chance to come out before I come in," Stockbridge said, rising. "There's been enough killing."

"Not yet," the man shouted. "Not until I see your heart."

The man's voice had come from dead center behind the rock. The would-be assassin could not see Stockbridge without standing. He was depending on the sound of his boots on the stones of the trail to give Stockbridge away.

Stockbridge was still carrying Pama's foreleg. Laying it quietly on the ground, he raised the shotgun and aimed at the cacti that stood together on the right side of the road, farthest from him. He fired at the one nearest to him. Even as it erupted in a hissing plume of yellow, green, and red, Stockbridge was running to the left. Realizing that Stockbridge probably intended to circle the rock, Pound lit and loaded another arrow, intending either to hit the doctor or else take him down by igniting the last cactus. The black man rose and aimed where he thought Stockbridge would be. But the doctor had stopped, hard, and was aiming directly at Pound.

"Lower it!" Stockbridge shouted.

Pound swung the arrow toward him. Stockbridge fired.

The discharge hit the black man hard in the upper chest, knocking him over backward. Released by a limp hand, the arrow flew a few feet up before coming down on the rock. Sparks from the burning shaft flew, one of them catching the last cactus and setting it afire with a long, sibilant cry. In fate's last irony, the cactus spines did not spray in Stockbridge's direction but peppered the unfeeling boulder.

Another needless death, he thought unhappily. *Another grisly find to bind to the legend of Dr. Vengeance.*

All of that was now beyond his control. He'd tried to reason with the man. With the charred and shattered cacti snapping and bursting behind him, Stockbridge made his way around the rock toward the rise. He had heard the horse neighing at the first blast and immediately took to comforting the big brown mustang. Except for riding him, there was no surer way to make friends with a horse than by calming him in a panic.

Once the horse had settled down, Stockbridge left him tied to the cactus. He searched the saddlebag for any sign of who the man was or where he'd come from. There was nothing, not even food. That meant the dead men probably lived very close by.

If there were others, they would probably see the smoke. They might spot a new flock of buzzards. And like this poor avenger, they would probably come looking for the man who had cut down their comrade.

"We'd best put some height between us and them," he said to the horse.

Without looking back at the bloody, smoking carnage he had created, Stockbridge turned the mustang toward the trail. He rode purposefully along the trail to do what he'd set out to accomplish: to find out what had happened to Ben Keeler.

CHAPTER SEVENTEEN

MOLLY WAS IN no condition to drive the surrey, but that did not stop her determination to try.

On her way down, Molly received a hug from Doris and another, in the main lobby, from Nikolaev. Her employer reached two fingers into his vest pocket and pressed his derringer into her palm.

"I told Iron Jaw to ready the surrey." He dipped his chin toward the gun. "I hope this is not needed."

She was as grateful for the sentiment as she was for the gun. It would have been too much effort, just then, to get up on her toes and kiss his beefy cheek. Averting her gaze from the bright light at the front of the lobby, she went next door to the Poet and Puncher and borrowed a sunbonnet from the small costume closet, something with a high ruffled front to protect her eyes. It was the same hat she wore when she read the limericks, her eyes wide and long lashes aflutter. Then the hat completed the portrait of maidenly innocence to contrast with the words she spoke. Now it was essential to ease her pulsing forehead.

The woman was not even sure where she was going. She stopped to ask Pete—that was the entirety of his name—the white-haired bartender, if he knew the Keelers. Pete was a tireless, spindly man with the longest fingers she had ever seen. He could hold a bottle fully around the base with room left to tuck in several utensils. The man was up early, cleaning glasses. He had very few teeth and those clacked when he said he thought the Keelers were out on the range with the other homesteaders.

"Y'know, where else would they be?" Pete asked.

He described the horse he had seen Ben Keeler ride to town, a Palomino. Pete had a memory for such things.

"You heard where Captain Cuthbert is?" he added.

"I have."

"He won't be happy when he gets out."

"I imagine not."

He reached for a Colt .45 single-action revolver he kept by the cash register.

"Take this, honey."

"The boss gave me his derringer just now."

Pete *pshaw*ed. "That won't kill a dog, just annoy him. You need something that'll scare the heels off a man's boots."

"A scared man's likely to fire back without thinking," she said. "I'll stick with what I have."

"I see your logic, if not your sense. Good luck, muffin."

Molly thanked him, and wrapping her shawl around her shoulders, she went out back to the stable. The surrey was hitched and ready.

"I'm sorry," she said to the stable boy. "I don't have any money—"

"That's all right," Harry replied. "Yi, she gave me a penny."

Molly was almost overcome. She smiled, climbed in, and allowed the youth to lead the horse through the narrow alley to the street. She faced the surrey in that direction and, for the moment, let the horse have his own say in how fast they would go. She only looked up as they passed the sheriff's office. She wanted to glimpse the place, the temporary home of Promise Cuthbert, the man whose presence and pursuit were suddenly so objectionable that she preferred alcohol, a sedative, and oblivion to his company.

At least her plan had helped her get away. That, and her beloved allies. The question now was whether she would ever be able to go back. Promise Cuthbert was not a forgiving man.

The clean air and sun actually had an analgesic effect. The drumming in her cranium subsided by half. For some reason, snatches of limericks she had recited at the Poet and Puncher returned unbidden.

She actually smiled, as if she were not the star but standing in the wings, listening. There was one that came back in full, one she had composed on the ride back from Gunnison. It came back as easily now:

> *There was a physician named John*
> *Who loved his wife, daughter, and son.*
> *They were taken away*
> *On a tragical day.*
> *Now the man who had done that is gone.*

Molly was happy to be away, and the horse seemed pleased to be freed from captivity, trotting on its own. As the pain in Molly's skull ebbed even more, she took to looking out at the countryside. She did not typically come this way. Whenever she rode out it was east, toward Gunnison and occasionally to Denver.

She saw a ruined wagon, wondered what had become of the occupants. The west was full of unfinished stories like that. Then she saw something else, a blotch on the southern plain, black and red and torn. It looked like it might have been a man, once—and fairly recently, given the sunlight glistening in tiny shards off the ruddy patches. A little farther on, to the east, she drove past the dead horse.

"No," she uttered aloud.

Molly knew that horse from Gunnison, and her heart began to ache. She was in a daze as the surrey pressed on to even greater carnage. It looked as if lightning had struck three cacti but she could not tell what had happened to the man behind the rock. He was covered with feathers, a rolling, bobbing sea of buzzards. She began to sob, fearing that Stockbridge was under that seething mob.

Then she saw a patch of uneaten ankle and part of a foot on the corpse. The skin was that of a black man.

Molly exhaled. At once, she turned her eyes back to the trail. The wind was not strong, but it was steady. The only tracks remaining were faint. The shape of the hooves suggested someone had ridden to this spot from the west, from the foothills. And there were fresher tracks headed the same way.

Up to where Cuthbert and the Red Hunters had their cabin.

Dr. Stockbridge survived and took this man's horse, Molly concluded—more hopeful than certain.

Taking the surrey whip in hand for the first time, Molly urged the contentedly lazy horse to greater speed and made for the lower peaks.

* * *

THE RED HUNTERS did not need a rooster. They had Franz Baker.

Because the compound was in shadow most of the morning and the men were often up late—here, in Buzzard Gulch, or hunting—they did not rise with the sun. They rose with the smell of cooking.

Today, Alan DeLancy rose with the distant sound of gunfire.

After pulling on his boots and coat and using the privy, he came back and noticed that the doors to the rooms of Liam McWilliams and Woodrow Pound were open, the beds empty. DeLancy made for the kitchen.

"That may not be hot yet," Baker said, nodding at the coffee. "I just started the flame."

"Hotter than cold is fine," DeLancy said. "Hey, you seen Liam or Woodrow?"

Baker shook his head, then began mixing batter for flapjacks.

Zebediah Tunney shuffled heavily into the living area from his room just then. He passed through like a winter storm in his white nightshirt and matching long johns, visited the outhouse, then returned with a look of simple contentment.

"Others asleep?"

"They're not here," DeLancy told him.

The big, dull face showed confusion. "What do you mean?"

"I mean they're gone."

"You check the stable?"

"Coffee first."

"You wouldn't say that if the captain was here."

"They would *be* here if the captain wasn't with Molly."

Not disagreeing, Tunney went back out the rear door, oblivious to the cold on his bare feet and wide body. He lumbered back less than a minute later, pounding his big feet on the floor to circulate the blood.

"They're gone, all right. To see the captain, you think?"

"Why would they do that? He didn't give no such instructions."

"Yeah. No," Tunney said, pouring coffee and sitting across from DeLancy at the big oak table.

"I'm thinking they went after that killer Stockbridge," DeLancy said.

Tunney laughed from his belly. "They will come back with his paws and nose."

DeLancy looked over at the sizzling griddle cakes as he finished his coffee. "I wonder why they didn't ask us to come with them."

"That doctor hurt them, they hurt him," Tunney said.

"But—remember that story Liam told us, about the hens he saw gang up and kill the fox that came into their coop?"

Tunney guffawed. "An Irish lie. Even the chickens are tough there."

"Sure, maybe. But the idea is sound—the more you are, the more you stand to win. The captain believes that. He said we learned it from U. S. Grant pouring men on us."

"You saying we should go after them?" Tunney asked. "They are probably eating his heart by now."

They wouldn't be doing that, but the impressionable hulk had heard about Indians doing such a thing. He liked the idea, and it had stayed with him. DeLancy believed if the other Red Hunters ever left him alone with a kill, he would try it.

"I am saying that," DeLancy said. "We should eat quick and ride out, show them we got their action covered."

Tunney nodded as he took a hard roll from the bread box. He ripped off a piece and stuffed it in his mouth. DeLancy joined him presently, though he ate with uncommon haste as a sense of urgency warmed his part-Cajun blood more than the coffee could. . . .

Y OU'RE GONNA WEAR out your palms before you wear out my bars."

Tom Neal was neither sympathetic nor apologetic to the man who was winding and unwinding and turning and churning his fingers around the iron that kept him inside the cell.

Promise Cuthbert was cold, having just his clothes and a tattered, foul-smelling wool blanket to warm him. He ignored the coffee the sheriff had offered him, preferring to grip the bars and wind his fingers around them. It kept his hands warm and his temper venting.

"I'll have your ears over my mantel," Cuthbert vowed.

Neal drank the coffee himself. "Doesn't help your desperate situation threatening a lawman, Captain Cuthbert."

"A lawman. You're a gimpy goat with a badge."

"Also not a help."

Cuthbert squeezed the bars until his fingers were white, his face nearly against the rusted iron. "I'm in jail because I hit Raspy Nikolaev. That Cossack slob tried to overthrow the federal government, and he owns two establishments. What kind of justice is that?"

"What you did is within the jurisdiction of Buzzard Gulch. The other ain't."

"All right, fine. I won't do it again. I won't *go* there again. Just let me out of here. Hell, I won't come back to this map stain."

"That's my home and bailiwick you're insulting."

"Jesus, Sheriff—just open the damn door!"

"Can't do that, Captain. Nikolaev hasn't finished considering whether he'll lodge charges against you."

"Christ," Cuthbert sighed, his hands once more in motion. "Jesus Christ. What does he want—an apology? He can have it. I'll even write it out. Money? I'll give him that, too."

"I'll go find out in a bit, which I was going to do anyhow."

"I can't stay here. I can't. There's something I have to do!"

"Me, too, which is where I was planning to go after offering you morning coffee and victuals."

Neal turned back to the office, and Cuthbert rattled the bars in rage, but that did nothing but make noise. With an oath, he turned and flopped on the cot that stretched the entire length of the jail cell.

"Raspy Nikolaev, you're going to get beat raw," Cuthbert said through his teeth. "Molly Henshaw, you're going to get it worse. I'll take you to the cabin, where you'll be passed around like a butter plate. And Dr. John Stockbridge—you're still going to die, but staked cold to the ground up high where you can freeze while you're pecked at by anything with a beak or teeth."

Warming himself with those thoughts, and relaxing at the same time, Cuthbert lay there and waited to do whatever he had to, say whatever was needed, to get out of here.

CHAPTER EIGHTEEN

I T SEEMED LIKE more than a day since Stockbridge had passed this spot. When he considered how much had happened, it both uplifted and saddened him.

He had killed three men. During the War, he had lost that many in surgery every quarter hour. Both were needless losses though this was the result of greed and hotheaded stupidity on the part of the dead men.

But Stockbridge had also made new friends. He had, he believed, inspired Lenny Keeler to be his best young self in this difficult situation, and he saw what looked like increasing grit from Rachel. In just a few hours, as her mother struggled, something seemed to rise and blossom in her.

And Mrs. Keeler was in his debt. Not just because he had helped them out of several fixes, but because the absence of her husband had weakened the woman. She had not been willing to lean on Rachel, but she had taken the doctor's help without reserve. She was further in his debt because he had gone back out for Ben. That had given her both strength and hope. Empty hope, perhaps, but that was better than the fear she'd had when he met them.

All of this came up like a remembered dream as Stockbridge reached and then passed the spot where they had met. The scrapes of the wheels on the ledge were still there, the tracks that marked as far as the Keelers had gone. They had outlived the men who had tried to waylay them.

Stockbridge did not linger here, but he did not hurry. For one thing, he did not know this horse very well. It did not seem to mind him. If the big animal noticed the lesser weight of the new rider, that was in no way evident. Nonetheless, Stockbridge let the animal set its own pace. But there was another reason for caution. There had been a bear trap hidden below; there might be one or more above. He did not know where the men lived, and they might have arranged snares or pitfalls anywhere along the way—not just for him but for any person or animal that came by.

At least it was quiet up here. The trees creaked, and rocks occasionally slid, and the wind had its own voice that, just now, was humming very low. That was how he was able to hear the clatter of something moving regularly, rhythmically on stone coming from somewhere below. He held up at a spot that overlooked the plain as well as the lower levels of the trail. Though there were several points like that on the way up, the trees were thicker lower down, and they blocked noises from below. Up here, closing in on two thousand feet, there was just open ledge and treetops.

He saw no one. Turning, he faced a hundred-yard stretch of the trail that emerged from around the mountain to the north and came straight up, in a gentle but narrow slope, before disappearing back into the north.

The sound grew louder. There was one set of hooves, no talking. The clatter was pretty lively, suggesting there was not a lot weighing the conveyance down, either goods or people. It was probably an empty cart with one passenger, possibly having delivered pelts or firewood to the homesteaders. If it had gone farther, to Buzzard Gulch, it would not be coming back empty but loaded with goods.

The new arrival surprised Stockbridge. He had not guessed it might be a woman alone, let alone one in a flatlands surrey. And on top of that, a woman who, upon seeing him, stopped the surrey and just stared for a moment.

"I'm not going to hurt you!" he assured the woman.

"I know!" she replied. "Dear God, I know!"

That, too, was a surprise. Most of the time, people saw him and either turned away or backed off, sometimes both.

Seeing no weapon or anyone behind her, Stockbridge started forward. "I am Dr. John Stockbridge," he announced. "But you seem to know that."

"Yes. I am Miss Molly Henshaw. I work at the Pap Hotel. In Buzzard Gulch."

"I've never been there."

"No. I would have seen you."

It was a strange conversation to be having, but then Stockbridge had had several of those since appearing in the *Line & Telegram*.

Stockbridge stopped his mount a few feet in front of the surrey horse. Both animals seemed skittish to meet each other. He waited for them to settle.

"This is an out-of-the-way place to go riding," Stockbridge said, "especially in a buggy built for Sundays after church."

"It was all I could borrow. It was important that I find you."

"Why?"

"Not for anything bad, not . . . not like the others."
She nodded slightly back toward the plains.

"What makes you think I had anything to do with
that?"

"They were Promise Cuthbert's men. They came
after you because of Grady Foxborough. You're going after the rest of them, I assume."

"The rest?"

She regarded him. "You're going to New Richmond."

"Ma'am, everything you're saying is new to me.
How many are there?"

"Four more," she told him. "You're telling me the
truth. You really *don't* know."

"Truly, I do not."

She pulled her cloak tighter. "Dr. Stockbridge, if
we could talk while we ride? It's chilly just sitting
here."

"Of course, forgive me." He started to turn around.
"Just one more question. You say you came looking for
me—why?"

"To help. I know a little about you, something more
about these people and the man who leads them."

"You read about me?" Stockbridge asked.

"That, and also—I met you briefly in Gunnison.
You kindly gave way on a road so I could pass."

Stockbridge thought back. He remembered the
surrey and, now, the bright face that had looked up at
him in the twilight.

"I recall it," he said. "It was brief—"

"It was enough."

"For you to risk your life?"

"Dr. Stockbridge, I am here because I wish to be.
And frankly, you could use an extra set of eyes and
ears, could you not?"

She was not wrong on either count, though Stockbridge also did not want to be distracted looking after those eyes and ears. Still, he knew from treating patients when there was no point arguing with them. Nodding, he finished turning the horse around.

With Stockbridge riding on the outside of the narrow pass, and amidst the accenting clop of hooves and clack of wheels on stony earth, Molly told him the story of her relationship with Promise Cuthbert and his operation up in the mountains. She revealed how she was able to get away and that when she left Cuthbert had still been in prison. Nikolaev had promised not to forgive him until she'd had time to get to the mountain and hopefully find the man she was looking for.

Her narrative filled in the gaps in Stockbridge's knowledge, and he was grateful to know who else might be hunting him. When Molly was finished, she said, "I've had my say. Now, tell me. If you're not looking for *them*, why are you here?"

"I'm searching for someone else, Miss Henshaw. Ben Keeler, a trapper who has gone missing."

"Keeler," she repeated. "The captain was looking for a family by that name in order to find you."

"That's the family I helped a little ways back—"

"And why Grady Foxborough is dead," she said.

"Do you think that's still this captain's plan? To find them?"

"I don't know. When he's this agitated, it's impossible to say what he will do."

"These other men of his. Where exactly are they?"

"Not far," she said, gesturing ahead. "About a quarter mile up the trail."

He motioned her to stop and reined up beside her. "Are they likely to see us?"

"The cabin is set back a ways from a cutoff, which

is itself about two, three hundred yards off Peak Road. Unless they're waiting for you, they aren't likely to hear. Where do you plan to look for Ben Keeler?"

"A place called Eagle Lookout, Miss Henshaw." He pulled the map from his pocket, handed it over. "Have you heard of it?"

She looked at the map and shook her head.

"Looks like we have to make our way to the Oónâhe'e River, then travel west from the bend. That's where Grady found Ben Keeler's horse, at least according to the black fella who was part of the group."

"Woodrow Pound," Molly said. She made no expression though her mind returned to the gory tableau she had seen below. "The other man was Liam McWilliams."

"You saw them back there," he suddenly realized. She nodded.

"Sorry, ma'am. There was no time to—"

"There's another ridge," she said, looking at the map. "Right below where the horse was found."

"I know. I thought I'd go there first. If there's a way up, saves a lot of riding."

"Eagle Lookout," she said, changing the subject and returning the map. "It sounds fresh. Clean. Better than the town I've left behind. I'm eager to see it."

With that, Stockbridge put his heels gently against the ribs of the horse, and they started back up the trail.

The ride was cold but scenic and marked by an absence of contact with any of the Red Hunters. When they passed, Stockbridge saw the path that branched from the main trail and the big, brash sign that announced New Richmond. Trees had been hewn to make the cutoff, their stumps manfully pulled out, and there were more rocks that way than this. The path wound up more steeply through a wooded area only to be lost behind a large, striated wall of rock.

It was a perfect place for a hideout, an ideal warren for weasels.

Stockbridge looked up the steeper, bolder trail. It had occurred to him that by riding up the path now and unleashing the shotgun he carried under his arm, he could very well end the threat from the men who wanted him dead. A surprise attack, rather than being surprised himself. But he had never done anything prophylactically except in medicine. He would not take a life because someone might have been or even probably was after him.

Molly seemed to read the mind of the man riding beside her.

"Yi Huang," Molly said. "She's a Chinese woman who works with me at the hotel. She has told me a little about the religion she follows. Taoism. And there's an idea she believes in more than any other, one that I especially like. She said, 'Whatever your goal, if you break the harmony of the universe, you have already lost.' I thought that was beautiful."

"Whenever I ministered to the sick, I would almost always hear them pray to their own god. White people, red men, black folks, yellow—it didn't matter what they called Him or how they saw Him. It was always the same. They had a humble, *very* humble manner. They were fearful of judgment. They were sad at the thought of maybe being called to leave this life. I always wondered if Sarah . . . ," he said, his voice choking and then trailing off. "Sorry," he said.

"Your wife?" Molly asked quietly.

He nodded.

The woman did not press him to continue. In the

context of that story she had read, Molly understood now, most forcefully, that he would do anything necessary to prevent others from suffering such a loss.

With New Richmond falling well behind, they rode in silent reflection about that goal and none other.

J UAN JUAREZ FELT as though his land, his home, was being invaded.

In his years of being a mountain man, he had never found himself so popular . . . or so annoyed. It was at times like these that he felt he should make a second flag, one with *El mundo de Juan* and the skull and crossbones he had seen in a book about pirates. He would fly it below with a warning to keep away.

The latest clanking, squeaking, clomping intruders were a man and a woman.

He saw them as they came around the bend. He did not mind the lady. It had been at least five years since Juan had seen or smelled one, and this woman was lovely on both accounts. She smelled—clean, like flowers—and was even prettier than that wicked she-cat Maria, who had chosen Esteban over him. This one was paler than he had remembered women to be, but better dressed and not so cross. And her hair was not like a raven but like sunshine.

The man approached with bullet-hard eyes pinning Juan where he stood holding a wooden bowl with a late lunch of stew—fox meat in melted snow, cooked in a clay pot he had made himself. He faced the newcomers with his wooden spoon in one hand, steam from the bowl blowing to the west, off the cliff, like a little version of the clouds above.

"Hello, friend," said the man on horseback.

Juarez just stared.

"I'm Dr. John Stockbridge. This is Miss Molly Henshaw."

"How do you do?" Molly asked.

Juarez put down the bowl and spoon and took off his fur cap. She smiled appreciatively.

"I am Juan Juarez," he said.

Without shifting his dark eyes, Stockbridge noticed the rifle leaning against the wall just inside the cave. He did not think the man would go for it. Or that it would fire if he did, the barrel being rusted and the stock splintered. He did not see any ammunition nearby.

"Sorry to interrupt your meal, Juan. We are on our way to Eagle Lookout. We would not have stopped except—we thought this might be a quicker way up, which I can see that it's not."

"You are correct," Juan said. "You looking for man?"

"Yes," said Stockbridge. "A man named Ben Keeler. Do you know him?"

"No." Juarez raised a finger above his head. "Man came looking for him. Eagle Lookout."

"A man named Grady?" Stockbridge asked.

"*Sí, sí*, that was his name."

"And the lost man was a fur trapper?"

"I think yes. This lost man, he had a horse tied to rock. The other man, Grady, he looked around, took it."

"Tell me, were there any other signs of Ben Keeler? A fire, a cigarette, food scraps, tracks—anything?"

Juarez shook his head. "Grady shout. No one answer. We think the man climb *up* from Eagle Lookout. But the clouds, they do not let us see where."

"And if he had come down, that path is the only way."

"That way—or this." Juan tilted his head toward the edge of the ridge, the one that fell into the forest below. He pulled at the jagged hairs of his mustache.

"Would you have heard him on the trail?" Stockbridge asked.

"No. Not on foot."

"I see. You've been a big help, Juan. I'm going to leave my horse, too, if you don't mind—"

"*Señor*, I tell you what," Juarez said, his eyes still on Molly. "I will go with you. Show you where we were. Maybe help the lady. The ice up there, it can be very unfriendly."

Molly smiled her thanks.

Juan finally looked away, turning his eyes to the shotgun. "One thing, though. If you are thinking to fire that up there—I would not. The rocks like to make a loud noise, but they do not like to hear one."

"I understand," Stockbridge said. "We appreciate everything you're doing."

Juarez put the bowl back in the cave and covered it with a wooden lid. Then he collected his walking-stick rifle and pulled a heavy bearskin from the wall.

"This is quite a place you've made for yourself," Molly said admiringly. Curious, she had followed him just a little. "Large, roomy."

"You know, it is *nicer* than what I have in Mexico. Colder, *sí*, but a better view."

"And privacy," she said longingly. "Quiet."

Stockbridge had come up behind Molly. "I know what you said. But are you still sure you want to come? I don't think Juan would mind you resting here."

"No, she make it friendlier," Juarez agreed.

"Thank you both," Molly said. "But we should be starting out. According to the map, we've got a bit of a walk to make before nightfall."

Juarez shrugged, and Stockbridge kneed the horse,

turning it in a tight circle. Molly snapped the reins and transited the front of the cave, backing in carefully in order to turn. The unlikely party was in motion, in search of quarry that was no less improbable—a fur trapper who had gone hunting for something other than fur.

CHAPTER NINETEEN

ALAN DELANCY AND Zebediah Tunney did not feel a special sense of urgency when they finally came down the mountain. They saw no clouds of dirt rising from the plain, suggesting neither travelers nor a dust devil, and no one dwelt between them and the homesteaders. Their ride was leisurely; they half expected to stop and turn around when they encountered McWilliams or Pound or the two of them together coming the other way with their prisoner.

That did not happen, and the longer they rode, the more concerned they became. It was possible the men had not found the man they pursued. It was possible they had gone on to see what Captain Cuthbert had learned. What was not possible was what the two riders actually encountered.

Riding along the trail below the foothills, they saw the buzzards flocked on the plain and figured that a deer or a bear was beneath them. Nothing smaller would have accommodated so many birds without them squawking and biting at one another.

Then they saw the bow and arrow.

The men stopped and sat transfixed by the impossible.

"Woodrow," DeLancy finally whispered.

He drew the Colt from his holster and put six rounds into four birds. The rest of the flock took wing, hovering. The four dead creatures spilled their blood onto what was left of Woodrow Pound, a sight worse than any the men had ever seen on the battlefield.

The men dismounted and tied their horses to the charred, broken cacti on the north side of the trail. They knew at once what Pound had done.

As they searched for rocks and began piling them on their dead friend—shooting birds that insisted on trying to return—the men knew that Pound's target had survived. There were hoofprints headed up to the mountain and away from the mountain. The ones going up seemed fresher.

It couldn't have been McWilliams. They would have seen him. It had to be Stockbridge. But there were also wagon wheels. It might just be a traveler. That thought offended the men deeper, thinking that this was how Woodrow Pound would be remembered by whoever had passed—a mass of chewed-up skin and gut.

What the tracks did not tell them was where McWilliams might be.

It was only after burying Pound, and saying a heartfelt farewell, that they noticed the discarded horse leg. Tunney squatted and examined the protruding bone.

"Bear trap," he said with certainty.

"I don't recognize the color," DeLancy said, indicating the leg. "Could be Stockbridge's."

"Why would he carry it *with* him?" Tunney asked with disbelief.

"We'll find that out when we find him," DeLancy said.

The men rose, Tunney angrily flinging the leg like a boomerang, out toward the foothills.

"He didn't go north, so I say we continue east, see if Liam's out there."

Tunney did not disagree, and after mounting up, the men continued along the trail. Almost immediately they came upon the horse. It was spread across the trail with both sides athwart, having been tugged this way and that by four-legged predators. Coyotes, most likely, since the thing had been chewed apart in small pieces.

The men did not stop long. It was only a few minutes later that they saw what looked like another body off to the south, in the direction of the watering hole.

"Shit no," DeLancy said.

"Liam or Stockbridge?" Tunney wondered.

The men galloped over. There were no buzzards surrounding the picked-bare bones and clothes that were all that was left of Liam McWilliams. They knew it was him from the bloody fur and the gray shirt. The bloody knobs of his anklebones still stuck out from his shoes. Mice were inside, trying to work out the meat.

DeLancy—who had witnessed horrors on the battlefield, such as maggots writhing in the eye sockets of fellow Rebels—looked away. Tunney could not turn from the sight.

The white bones, spotted and streaked with little

bits of sinew and blood, caused him to grow empty in the gut and sick in the chest. It became even clearer now, what had happened.

McWilliams had ridden out earlier—probably the night before, which was when Pound had said he was just out for a ride, thinking. He had been killed here, possibly when he had gone to water the horse . . . or seen Stockbridge watering his. Pound had gotten concerned by his absence and ridden after him. Rather than ride after Stockbridge in the dark, he had gone back to the cabin and planned a trap.

A good one. One that would have done the Red Hunters proud.

It was easy to put McWilliams in a temporary tomb of rock. There was less of him to cover than with Pound. If the Red Hunters did not use this water themselves from time to time, they would have gone back and roped the horse carcass, dragged it over, and tossed it in, poisoning the water for all the wretched settlers and officers of the so-called law who came through here, through *their* domain, a home that seven heroes of adversity had established in this forsaken land.

"What do we do now?" Tunney asked when they were done. "Captain's going to be real angry."

DeLancy was silent as he finished a short prayer.

"We have to go to the Gulch to tell him, let him decide," the former sergeant said. He could not even bring himself to say the full name of the town. DeLancy had had enough of buzzards for one day.

"Yeah, I guess that makes sense. The three of us together, we can sure take this son of a bitch."

"Brother, let us not underestimate that madman," DeLancy said. He took a moment to flex his fingers, which were swollen and sore from carrying rocks.

"We do not want to make the same mistake the others made."

Tunney grunted his agreement, and after mounting, the men turned north, headed back to the trail.

R ASPUTIN NIKOLAEV APPROACHED the stand-alone jail as if he owned it and the land it sat on. He often thought that if things had gone right, he would have. The tsar had not given him enough men or money to rally Indians, Mexicans, and unhappy fortune seekers against faraway Washington.

Ah, well, he also thought often. Life in Buzzard Gulch was not a dream, but it was better than returning to frozen Moscow, where he was a respected chief of gendarmes, charged with keeping peasants and workers from expressing their grievances directly to government functionaries. Because of his family, Nikolaev was a favorite at the court of Alexander III. Because he was a favorite, he had been sent on the mission to California. Because he failed, he was no longer a favorite.

Nikolaev was wearing a beaver hat and a matching coat, buttoned and tight around his wide girth. His shoes were polished. They had gotten a little dirty on the walk over, but he had taken time to spit on them and wipe them with his handkerchief before entering the sheriff's office.

Nikolaev wished to be the very image of prosperity when he faced the man who had given him a black, blue, and swollen jaw. A prisoner whose fate was now in the Russian's fleshy, gloved hands.

Nikolaev collected the sheriff, and they went through the back door. They approached the bars and the slightly more worn-out occupant. Cuthbert was lying in the bunk, unshaven, disheveled, obviously not having slept and out of energy.

The Southerner rose at once and gripped the bars as though they were an adversary's throat.

"I'll give you two some privacy," Neal said.

"Thank you, your excellency," the Russian said. He just stared at Cuthbert, and Cuthbert at him, until the back door of the office clicked shut.

"Caged like a mad dog," Nikolaev said.

Cuthbert growled and thrust a clutching hand through the bars. The ruddy-faced visitor had anticipated that and stepped back.

"See? Mad! You would attack the only man who can get you out of here."

Cuthbert withdrew his arm and backed away from the bars. He drew his shoulders back.

"I would rather stay in jail than beg you."

"A sentiment worthy of Dostoevsky!" the Russian said. "Have you read *Crime and Punishment*? You should. You may have the time."

"Gloat! My men will hunt you and her down if you don't get me out of here."

"They may try. You forget that John Stockbridge is not in a prison. And he is not as helpless as a woman or a simple hotelier."

"You will *all* die," Cuthbert said.

"Eventually." Nikolaev moved in closer. "The question here, now, is whether *you* go free or stand before Judge Wilson when he comes to town. You know, he was a respected judge up north before coming west. I am told, by men who drink in my establishment—men who were guests at the Colorado State Penitentiary—that it is a quite unwelcoming place."

Cuthbert's jaw shifted back and forth. He said

nothing. After a moment, he turned. It was not a defiant move but a grab for a moment's privacy.

"Despite the insult and hurt you inflicted, Mr. Cuthbert, you have been a good customer, and I would like to see you leave here."

The prisoner turned his head slightly. "At what price?"

"To begin with, leave Molly alone. She is a good worker. She is liked by the customers and by the staff. You may hire her for baths if you wish, but then you leave her alone. There are women at the tavern you can . . . woo."

"What else?" Cuthbert asked.

"I wish to buy more land in Buzzard Gulch. You will pay me a share of your earnings, the same as the other men."

"You reptile."

"Coming from a common highwayman, that fails to sting. Think about it, Mr. Cuthbert. The bigger our town becomes, the more people will arrive, and the richer your Red Hunters will be."

Cuthbert was not surprised that Nikolaev knew about that. He was observant and the other Southerners, when they drank, talked too much.

"I don't much like the idea of making deals with you, Raspy," Cuthbert sneered.

"We have that much in common."

"You got this foreign swagger I do not care for, something you did not earn like the rest of us."

"Earn?" The Russian moved closer. "My family earned their prosperity on the bent backs of serfs the way you did on the scarred backs of slaves."

"Don't you dare mention my family—!"

"Poor, wounded *aristokraticheskiy*!" he said, using the word mockingly. "The only things either of us 'earned' are what we have now. So. You've said what you think. I don't care about any of it. Do we have an arrangement, or do we not? Do you get out of here or not?"

Cuthbert took just a moment to decide. "Get the sheriff."

With a satisfied sigh, Nikolaev went back inside to inform the lawman that he had decided not to press charges. As he was so informing Sheriff Neal, two figures on horseback appeared through a western-facing window. The two were riding hard and thundered to a stop just outside the sheriff's office. They threw their reins over the hitching rail and hurried inside. Nikolaev recognized big, dumb Tunney and oily little DeLancy from the Poet and Puncher.

"Sheriff, we heard, at the hotel, that the captain isn't there but here," DeLancy said. "We need to talk to him—and to you, too, Sheriff."

"What's the trouble?"

"It's bad. Where's Cuthbert? He's got to hear this."

Neal had never seen DeLancy so agitated, and even Tunney looked like he had run his face into a fence post. It was easier to go out back and get the captain rather than argue. The sheriff returned less than a minute later, holding the door for Cuthbert to go in first. Sheriff Neal did not bother telling the prisoner just then that there was a release paper to sign. Cuthbert's eyes fastened on his men.

"What is it, Sergeant?"

"McWilliams and Pound are both dead," DeLancy revealed. "Woody out by the trail, Liam near the watering hole. Buzzards got them good before we could."

It took a moment before Cuthbert had fully absorbed what they had said. "Stockbridge?"

"Looks like he did it— We, uh . . . we found a leg of what looks like his horse nearby."

"A *leg*?" the sheriff interjected.

"One of Woody's bear traps did it. His horse is gone, and so's McWilliams' mount." DeLancy looked at the sheriff. "Murder *and* horse thievery."

"Yeah, I heard that."

"*Where's* Stockbridge?" Cuthbert demanded.

"His trail leads to the mountain. Maybe he went looking for the rest of us—I don't know."

"I need my guns," Cuthbert said, glaring at nothing in particular but seeing the newspaper image of John Stockbridge—burning.

"On the horse," DeLancy said, jerking a thumb. He looked at Nikolaev. "I saw them at the hotel, had to threaten your bellboy a little."

"He is not managerial material."

The sheriff had limped forward and looked down at the smaller Southerners. "Gentlemen, if you go off gunning for Stockbridge, and you succeed, then you'll be right back here."

"Did you not hear about my men being *murdered*?" Cuthbert roared.

"Every last word, but that's for me, not for you, to investigate."

"Stay out of this, Sheriff. This is a matter of honor!"

The sheriff went to his desk. "Sign this release form, Captain. I'll fill it in later."

His mind elsewhere, Cuthbert took the pen proffered by the sheriff, dipped it in the inkwell, and leaned over the desk.

"Where is Molly?" Cuthbert asked as he signed.

"I don't know," Nikolaev replied. "And that's the truth. She rode out for some private purpose. That's all I know."

"What the hell is a 'private purpose'?"

"Something she didn't share," Nikolaev answered.

"Where can I find the Keelers?" Cuthbert asked.

"What do you want them for?" the sheriff asked.

"That's who Stockbridge was with when he killed Grady Foxborough. They may know where he went."

"They've got to be out on the homestead," DeLancy suggested.

"How many Keelers are there?"

"There're a man, wife, two kids," Neal said. "You molest any of them, I'm coming after you with a posse. Seems to me, three men down, you can't stand up to them like you said you once could."

Cuthbert reacted as though a lit torch had been shoved under his face. It contorted into something feral.

"Try me!" Cuthbert said. He tossed the pen on the floor and spit on the document.

"I hope I won't have to," said Neal.

Cuthbert turned and stalked to the door, wincing as he walked into the bright sunlight. His men followed.

Nikolaev and Neal looked at each other.

"Are you going to ride out to the homestead?" the Russian asked.

"What for? There's nothing gained by that. Those three'll outrun *and* outgun me. And by the time I could assemble a posse *at* the homestead, it would be too late."

"This is not an efficient system," Nikolaev observed.

"No, it ain't, which is why, speaking plain, men like Stockbridge are needed. If I could, I'd deputize him. Liam McWilliams and Woodrow Pound—they were tough, especially Pound."

"Well, I hope you will forgive the sentiment, Sheriff, but I hope Cuthbert and his men survive. I cannot afford to lose so many customers."

"There's the contradiction, ain't it?" Neal re-marked. "I sell justice. You sell vice. One can't sur-vive without the other."

Stepping to the window, he watched as DeLancy and Tunney watered the horses while Cuthbert re-trieved his from the stable.

A few minutes later, they were headed north, for the homesteads.

Neal shook his head. "What a stinking town this is."

CHAPTER TWENTY

THE SKIES DIRECTLY above Eagle Lookout were as
cloudy as they had been the last time Juan Juarez
was up here. The eagles' nests were in the same
places, the only change being more droppings near
the edge of the cliff. That made walking slippery and
treacherous, the rocks smelling like a mossy log.

"No rain to clean things," Juarez remarked.

The three reached the ledge without difficulty,
though it was late afternoon and a chill was settling
aggressively on the exposed outcrop. They circled the
cone of rock. There were no eagles on the other side,
where the ledges were small and stubby. Only hawks
circled below the clouds, looking for prey or sitting
in the branches of trees just below. There were also
no caves or fissures at their level, nothing suggesting
an entrance. They returned to Eagle Lookout. Stockbridge heard the birds nesting above, a cacophony of
sounds as the young ones were learning to hunt on
their own now that they had come of age and size.

"It seems to me the only direction Ben Keeler could have gone is up," Molly said.

"I agree," Stockbridge replied. "Juan, I see what must be your tracks from the other day."

"*Sí*, those are ours, partly covered."

"There are no subsequent tracks in the droppings to indicate that the trapper came down."

"No."

"Then we have to go up," Molly said.

"You have climbed, *señorita*?" Juarez asked.

"No, and I haven't shot the derringer in my pocket either. Life is full of new challenges and we don't appear to have other options. Not if we intend to find this man."

"What about him?" Juarez asked. He was pointing at Stockbridge.

"Juan," Stockbridge said, "the man you were with up here was a thief. I killed him. His friends may be after us."

"*Señor, you* kill and *others* kill. Maybe Juan should leave."

"Juan, it's not like that," Molly said. "Dr. Stockbridge was protecting a woman and her children. The other men are scoundrels. If he stays here, no one will get past him. We can't afford to lose our horses."

"Molly, that's not the only risk to consider," Stockbridge said.

"What else? Are you afraid I might slip? I could have gone off the road and over the cliff anywhere back there." She moved closer. "Doctor . . . John . . . I have spent over a year in a bathroom. Before that, as a maid. I'm not ashamed, but I am more than that. I *want* to do this."

Juan bundled himself against the chill, fur fluttering against his chin. "The lady, like the country—she is free."

Stockbridge was not accustomed to being argued with. People rarely argue with any man holding a medical bag. Only his wife ever stood up to him, in her quiet way.

And didn't I usually come around to her way of thinking?

"Dr. Stockbridge?" Molly prodded.

He looked up along the cliff. "Those ledges . . . the droppings. There's nothing to hold."

"I've cleaned worse off some of my clients."

"That dress? It's bulky—"

"If I fall, it's a cushion."

"And the birds themselves? These are predators we're talking about, protective predators with merciless talons."

"Again, some of the men I've bathed . . . ," she began. She held up her hands. "These gloves are leather, and I've got good soles on these shoes. Keeps me from slipping on soapy water."

He looked up, then back at Molly.

"This thing makes a lot of dangerous noise," he said, raising the double-barreled. "You mentioned a derringer?"

Molly went back to the surrey, reached into her bag, and retrieved the handgun Nikolaev had given her.

"Fire it. See what scatters."

Molly nodded and aiming away from them, she discharged a bullet up the face of the cliff. There was a general flapping of wings above the clouds.

"They think there is rockslide," Juarez chuckled. "Dumb birds."

"I figure you've got about ten minutes till they settle and return," Stockbridge said. "Keep it handy in case you need to discharge again."

"I will," she said, slipping it in the pocket of her dress. "And thanks . . . John."

"What do we do if we find a way in?" Juan asked. "There are legends about—*things*."

"Legends get inflated," Stockbridge said with a glance at Molly.

She looked back at the surrey. "Maybe I should get the lantern in case there *is* an opening."

"You know what? Maybe dumb Juan, too. I'm going also."

Juarez walked to the surrey to get the lantern. It was small and metal and hung from a pole on the driver's side. There were matches in a metal compartment in the bottom. Juan undid his belt and threaded it through the eye hook on top of the lantern. Stockbridge was relieved that the Mexican had offered to go. He did not know what they would find up there. But even if it were a ledge with Ben Keeler's frozen remains, he was glad Molly would not be alone.

The Mexican strode over to the rock wall, leaned his rifle against the cliff, and stood beside Molly.

"To be with you, I am happy to climb a cliff!" he said.

"That, *Señor* Juarez, is the most flattering compliment I have ever received." To test the rocks, Molly stood on her toes and pulled, then set herself back down and turned to Stockbridge. "I believe we can do this!"

"Godspeed," he said sincerely, though mostly he had said that to keep from saying anything else.

Molly took the lead and Juan stood below her in case she slipped; he waited until she was five or six feet up before he joined her.

The crags, though slippery, were fat and jutted far enough from the cliff to give them strong handholds and footholds. In the silence under the cottony clouds, Stockbridge could hear their every grunt and curse, and there were many of each from both climbers.

For all of Molly's enviable bravado, it was not an easy climb. He also could not help but wonder what his enemies and the newsprint writers would think if they saw him now.

The fearsome John Stockbridge rockbound and helpless like Prometheus . . .

"The cliff is not very stable!" Molly called down as she rested for a moment.

"What do you mean?" Stockbridge asked.

"I feel a little give every time my weight is on one ledge, either hand or foot. Like they are levers for the ones above."

"Molly—"

"Don't worry, John. I'll drop right into your arms," she said, putting an end to his misplaced efforts at chivalry.

It did not take more than a few minutes for Molly and then Juan to disappear into the low cloud layer. Stockbridge did not call up for fear of distracting them. They would let him know when and if they found something.

It was just Stockbridge and the two horses, both of whom were at ease. There was an occasional flutter of wings, but the eagles did not seem interested in returning just yet.

His eyes served no purpose gazing upward, so he turned toward the road. He did not believe the Confederates would consider searching for him up here. They would look in Buzzard Gulch, or perhaps figure that he had stayed on the trail and headed west—the direction he was headed in the first place. Those men, McWilliams and Pound, must have told the others as much.

There were also the Keelers. If the Rebels sought them out, they would not tell where he had gone. And if he hurt them—

No, Stockbridge thought. If anything, Cuthbert would use them as bait to get to him. It was a troubling notion, but he had picked this course based on what he knew, and a man who was not a demigod—or a legend—could do no more.

There was an occasional trickle of rocks but nothing large, nothing alarming, the natural result of the two climbing. Finally, it stopped. The only sound or movement was the wind.

And then he heard Molly's muffled voice call from somewhere up above.

"John, we're at the top, and we've found something!" she said.

"What is it?"

"An opening, about five feet across," she replied. "We're going to see where it leads!"

Stockbridge did not bother to tell them to come back and wait for morning light. He could tell from the sudden, moving effulgence of the lantern through the clouds that they were already moving north, away from him.

And then the light vanished.

IT WAS A cone like Molly had seen in magazines depicting volcanoes, only smaller. The warm air rising from inside was stale, and the odor was rank. Molly saw no evidence of a fire. Inside, beginning where Molly and Juarez were hunkered, a slope angled down, like a coal chute. The glow of the lantern did not reach to the bottom.

"How did something like that get formed?" Juarez asked.

"There are ridges. Do you see them? Made by rain. Maybe snow freezing, then melting and running down."

"You see much," Juarez said admiringly. If he was

not yet in love, it was the closest he had been in years.
"God, when he make this place, He was not in a hurry."

"But we are." She crouched. "I'll go first. You
hand the light down."

"You have to go down on your—"

"Seat. Yes, I know." She swung her left leg over the
rock lip, tested the slope with her heel. "Seems solid."

Braced on her palms and feet, Molly eased her way
down until she reached the end of the lantern's glow.
She gave her eyes a minute to adjust to the darkness.
There was nothing to see *except* darkness. She lay on
her back and extended an arm over her head.

"Juan, lean in and pass down—"

She fell silent as she heard a noise, like scraping.
She heard a moan.

"Señorita?" Juarez said.

"Shhh! Hello!" she called down. "Is someone there?"

There was no answer.

"Ben Keeler? Are you there?"

A voice, weak and soft, replied, "Merciful . . .
God . . . in His bright, blue heaven . . . *yes!*"

Molly turned to the opening. "Juan! Tell Dr.
Stockbridge we found Mr. Keeler. He's alive!"

"El milagro!" he cried. "A miracle!"

As Juarez relayed the message down the side of the
cliff, Molly turned back. "Mr. Keeler, are you hurt?"

"Yes . . . *trapped*. Please don't go!"

"I won't!" Molly turned again. "Juan, you're going
to have to come down with the lantern! I can't see him."

"I will bring it!"

Using one hand to hold the lantern and the other to
guide him, he walked down on his back as Molly had,
using his feet to break the slide. His approach threw
more light on the chamber below. It was a grotto of
stalactites and stalagmites that reflected millennia of
dripping water. Amidst them lay the crumpled figure

of a man with a few small bones and some tools scattered about. There was a pelt spread beside the man, with rocks bundled in each corner. He must have thrown it, used it to trap mice or other small animals, dragged them over, then eaten them raw. The caked blood around his mouth bore that out. The cadaverous look of his cheeks and drawn forehead suggested that the animals had not been much of a meal.

The lantern came down farther. It revealed a tunnel on the far end, dark and foreboding and full of rocks. The bottom half of the man's legs were beneath them.

"We're going to get you out!" Molly said as she continued down, Juarez following with the light.

"Thank God. Thank God," Keeler repeated over and over. "I—I tried . . . but the rocks were too big. . . . I couldn't reach . . ."

"Keep talking. How did this happen?"

"I was coming out—steep walk. I was pulling on crags to help myself. They all fell." He added forlornly, "And all for nothing. Days of dead ends."

Molly walked toward the man as Juarez slid helplessly the last few feet, hitting bottom and scrambling quickly to his feet. The circle of light bobbed and slid as he ambled over, rubbing his backside.

The woman stopped beside Keeler. "I'm sorry I didn't think to bring water."

"I'm all right." He patted the wall just a foot away. "It gets wet . . . from clouds and groundwater."

Molly saw his tongue, bloodied and gritty. He had licked the wall to survive. He was lying in his own waste.

"Are you in pain?" she asked.

"My feet are under a bunch of rocks," he pointed out.

"I've done some mending in my day. If they were broken, you wouldn't feel anything."

"I feel them."

"Good," she said. "There is a doctor waiting."

"How—?"

"He met your wife and children searching for you, came looking himself."

"Alice! She's—"

"Home now. She's fine."

"Thank God! My horse," he implored. "Is he . . . still out there?"

Juarez had arrived then. "He was taken away days ago. No one knew you were here, *señor.*"

"You're the hermit," Keeler said.

"Juan Juarez, mountain man."

"I've heard of you. Thank you."

The Mexican walked around Keeler and examined the wall closely. The rocks were piled about five feet high, and the smallest was the size of a cannonball. They would be difficult to move by hand. They would have to move and dislodge themselves by falling.

Using spit and a handkerchief, Molly wiped the blood and grime from Keeler's face.

"What's it look like, Juan?" she asked.

"I'm seeing."

The Mexican gently pushed the rocks on top. Each time they shifted, Keeler winced.

"Lo siento," Juarez said.

"No . . . need to apologize." Keeler forced a smile. "I'm grateful to y'all."

"What were you looking for down here?" Molly asked to distract Keeler.

"A legend. I'm getting on. . . . I wanted . . . security for my family. A nice home. An education for the children."

"What did you think was here?"

"There's a story I've heard many times . . . of a passageway through the Rockies clear to Ute Mountain

on the other side. No one ever found it. I figured that
the man who did could show the location to the railroad or maybe one of the old overland stage lines.
Such a man . . . would be wealthy."

Juarez set the lantern down, then retrieved the
pick that was in Keeler's gear.

"That damn pick— Pardon me, miss," Keeler said.

"I've used the word myself."

"The pick was outta reach. I would've chopped if
I could've."

Juarez swung the tool sideways a few times, like a
scythe. "I have not used a real tool in so long!"

"You'll do fine," Molly said.

"*Sí, señorita*, sorry. I can do this, but you will have
to be ready to pull him away *rápido*. I swing at the
rocks, they will slide. Maybe this way."

Molly nodded and stepped back from the trapper.
She knelt by the top of his head after bunching her
dress under her knees.

"I knew this would come in handy," she said as she
settled in and looked Ben Keeler up and down. He
was twisted slightly on his side, like a ribbon. She
turned him very gently so she could take both of his
hands in hers. The gloves gave her a secure grip.
"You heard what Juan said, Mr. Keeler. I don't know
if you have any broken bones under there, but I do
know that when I pull, whatever is injured will scrape
and hurt."

"I would suffer hell to see my family again."

That touched Molly unexpectedly. She was cold
and arm weary from the climb, and hungry, but she
was determined that they would not leave here without this man.

Juan could see that they were ready, and after de-
termining where he should stand, he took a swing at
the wall, at a juncture of two rocks near the bottom.

Molly's eyes were on the rocks on top. If any began to move, she would start to pull.

Nothing happened, and Juarez swung again.

There was a rumbling, and while Juarez grabbed the lantern and jumped back, Molly braced herself. As the rocks began to groan and finally to knock one against another, she tugged hard. Keeler came free, she fell back, and the cascade cracked rock upon rock as they made a new pile low across the tunnel opening.

The rumbling, however, did not stop locally. Though all three were free of the cave-in, the chute itself was jarred by the concussion. Almost at once, the surface of the slope cracked and came apart, along with sections of the cavern roof. The collapse lasted just a few moments, but it filled the grotto with dust that left them coughing and unable to see.

"Is everyone all right?" Molly cried.

Both men answered affirmative, but the good news was short-lived. As the dust began to fall, Molly could see that they had lost their only way out.

CHAPTER TWENTY-ONE

IT WAS STRANGE and unfair, thought Promise Cuthbert. Why were the moments of one's life that clung to the soul never in balance?

The happy moments—like cousins' weddings and births, the first, clumsy shave that made a boy feel like a man—those brought him small, lingering smiles and a warm glow. But the hateful moments—the death of those close to you, the destruction of a home and mementos and one's past—those burned hot and contorted his features into something supernatural, into constantly shifting shades of blackness fed and flushed with ruddy, pumping blood.

Cuthbert and his two companions drummed across the plain, leaving Buzzard Gulch and its petty men behind but not forgotten. They were smoke in the brain, fuzzy visions replaced by the flames of hate. Even the smug Nikolaev was fading. He would be dealt with in time. Replacing those men was an increasingly sharp image of Dr. Vengeance, black-and-white lines from a newspaper becoming bloodred in his imagination. It did not matter that this man had become the reflection of every pain and wrong Cuthbert had ever suffered. All he knew was that this *thing*, this monster must not only be vanquished; he must be so thoroughly beaten that not even a particle survived. Shot, cut, burned, thrown partly to the wind, partly to a river, spread so far that he was lost to all but the yellowing print of rank journalism.

Now and then, as they rode, Cuthbert would howl from deep in his throat. He could not control it. He frightened one of the men who was with him, not for what he might do but for what he might shame or threaten the others into doing. Alan DeLancy wanted vengeance against John Stockbridge. But what might this man and his ox-dull companion, Tunney, do to anyone who was associated with the man?

Was this the road to true armistice that the captain had always threatened? A bloody, wide-ranging battle that would end with the Rebels victorious?

The thought worried the sergeant—a concern that weighed as heavily as the pain he felt from the losses inflicted on the Red Hunters.

The three were riding toward the hundred acres of land that had been set aside for homesteaders. It was not especially arable land, so the state had allowed for it to be sold, cheaply, to folks who basically just needed a place to live. This was where the dairy farmer had a small place, the tanner, the cooper—

The family of the fur trapper.

The horses complained at the pace by occasionally whipping their heads from side to side, but Cuthbert did not care. At some point the animals would lie down and refuse to go farther. The Apache, he had heard, would light a fire under them to get the animals back on their feet. Cuthbert would not do that.

He did not have the time or the patience. He would run until the animals dropped. Then he would run until he had to walk and then until he was forced to crawl. He would not stop.

But the horses did not give out. The fur trapper's home was the nearest of the settlements. That had been a practical matter: It was also nearest to the trail that wound into the mountains, where Ben Keeler practiced his trade. The three men knew it was the home of the Keeler family because of the pelts used for window shades. That was too expensive an extravagance for anyone but a trapper.

The men did not bother to conceal their approach. The men secured their animals to an empty tanning frame out front, then separated. Each man held a Colt in his hand. There were two females and one boy inside. Even if they each had a gun, there were no openings in the pelt shades for gun barrels. They would have to pull the furs aside, exposing themselves to seasoned fighters.

DeLancy went around to the western side, Tunney to the east. Cuthbert headed toward the front door. He strode like an ancient Titan, with purpose and a sense of invincibility.

There was no patio, just the oak panels of a narrow front door with a railroad tie lying before it. There were dried horse patties on the edges, where the undersides of boots were scraped.

The door opened just as Cuthbert was about to pound on it. A sallow-faced woman stood on the other side, in the unnatural darkness. She had flour on her hands and a sad turn of mouth. She was not holding a gun. Noticing the one in Cuthbert's hand, she stepped back.

"What is it?" she asked in a small voice.

"Where are the others, your children?" Cuthbert demanded. He was still burning from an internal furnace.

A fur shade was raised. Behind her, ghostly in the light coming through the uncovered window, a young lady and a younger boy stepped into view. The girl was holding a tray with dough on it, and the boy held a basket of eggshells bound for the compost heap.

"Set that all down," Cuthbert barked at the children. "Now on the floor."

Lenny and Rachel hesitated.

"Do it, children," their mother said.

They did as they were instructed—more or less. Rachel had stiffened and put the tray of unbaked bread on the wooden table behind her, where she and her mother had been making bread and cutting a few poor carrots. For a moment her back was to the men. To Cuthbert, she seemed to be deciding whether to resist.

She did not. When she turned back, brushing her hands on her apron, the only change was that her chin was slightly upraised. Cuthbert let it pass. He marked it up to the defiance of youth. That was not a bad quality out here.

"Get on your coats and wraps and come out here, all of you," he said next.

The woman hesitated and the children made no sign of moving.

"What do you want from us?" Mrs. Keeler demanded. She was now showing the same chin her daughter had presented a moment before.

"All right," Cuthbert said, suddenly feeling—and showing—some respect for the two women. "What we're going to do is take a ride up into the mountains. To our compound."

"Why?" Rachel asked.

"Because, Miss Keeler, it is preferable to being shot for *not* coming!"

Mrs. Keeler glared at him. "Why are you doing this?"

His mouth twisted. "Don't push your luck. I told you all you need to know. Now, come willingly or be dragged—I don't care which."

Without turning, Mrs. Keeler said, "Rachel, go get our things."

The girl hesitated. *Now* she was annoying.

"Rachel, go!" her mother repeated.

The girl pivoted and did as she was instructed.

"Just clothes," Cuthbert told the family. "If I see a gun, whoever's holding it dies with the same in their hands."

Mrs. Keeler's eyes fell to his gun. "Bravely spoken."

He smacked her with a hard backhand. She staggered back. Rachel and Lenny both ran forward, but Mrs. Keeler stopped them.

"Yankee sass," Cuthbert said. "No culture, no respect. Just crude, animal prickles."

The woman's cheek burned, and her lips pursed tightly. She thought better of replying in kind. "Let a man be known by his actions. You're one of those men, the ones who were with Grady."

Cuthbert's eyes flared. "Don't you *dare* speak his name! You don't have that *right*."

"In my own home? On my own land? I will not only say his cursed name, but I will speak what he was: a bandit, no better. From hiding, he ambushed and tried to rob two women and a boy."

His face a mask of hate, Cuthbert cocked the firearm and pointed it at the bridge of her nose. Lenny jumped forward and stepped between them. He bundled her in his arms, his back to the gunman.

"Captain, don't!" DeLancy yelled. He had come around from the side when he heard the shouting. "Not that and certainly not here. We have a mission."

"A mission," Cuthbert repeated, almost reverently. *Just like in the War, the Red Hunters shoulder to shoulder.* DeLancy was right. The captain could not let this sack of bones in a housedress stop the mission.

Cuthbert released the hammer, stepped back, then used the gun to motion the two Keelers out. They waited while Rachel joined them, her eyes on Cuthbert like a she-wolf's on a ram. Rachel helped her mother with her fur coat, which hung on a peg beside the door. Rachel tossed Lenny his own wool garment, then grabbed the rabbit-fur cloak her father had made for her.

"Private Tunney!"

"Yes, Captain?"

"Go to the stable and get whatever horses they've got!"

"Yes, sir!"

Rachel put her arms around her mother and hugged her. Lenny stood before them, shifting from foot to foot, his fists at his side. He looked like he wanted to say something, do something. What stopped him was not cowardice. He was thinking about his mother's grief if he got himself shot and died. Rachel seemed to sense that and, reaching out with one hand, lightly rested it on his shoulder and pulled him in.

Watching them, Cuthbert said, "I had family, too. A wife back home and brothers in blood out here."

"I'm sorry," Alice Keeler said sincerely.

"The tears of a Yankee," he scoffed. "Where you from? New York? New England?"

"Pennsylvania."

"Gettysburg," he muttered. He stepped closer again,

his gun hand shaking, eyes livid. "We should have had you there. We pushed all the way up, but you had the guns and you had the numbers. It wasn't for lack of courage or resolve. You had the *damn guns!*"

DeLancy came over. "Save it for who deserves it, sir."

"*None* of them is innocent," Cuthbert sneered. "Somewhere in their clan, they got our blood on their bayonets. I want to wipe it on their hair, on their pale faces, on—"

"Captain," DeLancy quietly coaxed him, "the mission."

Once again, the Confederate leader eased back.

Save for the slapping of Tunney's boots, the cawing of a few crows, and the gentle whoosh of the cold wind, there was no sound. Not until the big man returned leading two saddled horses and wearing a pleased grin.

"Lookee!"

His two companions looked over.

"Grady's horse!" Tunney said proudly.

DeLancy saw Cuthbert's eyes turn to feral slits. The captain raised his right hand and pointed his Colt at the Palomino.

"Captain!" DeLancy yelled.

Tunney stopped. At this distance he was not quite sure where the six-shooter was aimed.

"Sir!" the private said with a sudden look of panic.

Cuthbert held his shooting stance. It was not thought but instinct that told him to reunite the horse with its owner the quickest way he knew how. But some part of his brain took control and told him the way to remember Grady was by chasing Stockbridge down on the back of the Palomino.

Once again, the hammer was released, and the Colt went down. Both Tunney and DeLancy exhaled.

"The lady's with you, on point all the way to the

cabin," the captain told DeLancy. "Put the boy on my mount and the girl on the nag. I'll bring up the rear on Grady's horse." He looked at the huddled Keelers. "Any of you try to break away, any of you talk to each other, any of you try to slow us down and you get to die in your home, on your land. Nod if you got that."

The heads of the three Keelers moved slowly up and down—the children only after their mother had done so.

Within minutes, the horses and riders were on the trail headed toward the mountains.

CHAPTER TWENTY-TWO

JOHN STOCKBRIDGE FELT the rumbling of the rock-slide in the soles of his feet and along the iron bar-rel of the shotgun instants before he heard it. He thought, at first, it was coming from somewhere out-side this cone of a promontory, perhaps from the poking and pulling they had done on the other side.

He was already moving toward the trail to steady the animals; the rumbling ceased before he reached them. After taking a moment to settle them, he turned back toward the cloud-shrouded cliff. That was when he saw dust darkening the clouds.

"Molly!" he called up.

The word was smothered by the ugly brown haze above.

"Molly! Juan!"

He listened. The silence was thick as death. He was about to shout again when he thought he heard a cry. There were sounds that could have been talking.

Low, monotone, possibly afraid that something else might fall.

Stockbridge stepped back. There had been a sloping path inside—he had heard that much. Molly and Juan had used it to enter. It was possible that their combined weight had been too much for the ridge. Or maybe something they had done to try to free Ben Keeler had caused a rockfall.

He looked up along the cliff. If he went up and there was another collapse, they would lose the animals for sure—and he might be injured. That would help no one. If there were instability in the structure, he might only make it worse. He did not even have a rope to throw them.

Too many field surgeries, too many sudden military skirmishes, had left the military doctor confident in his ability to improvise. This was a hard-learned lesson to the contrary, a rebuke to the legend of Dr. Vengeance. So was his having let the others go up there unprepared.

Being angry at myself for that is not going to help get them out.

More pebbles fell. Grass from one of the nests came fluttering down, along with several twigs.

"The cone is unstable," he thought aloud as he looked up "You climb up, you could fall. You climb up, *it* could fall."

And yet the wall falling might be exactly what he wanted—as long as it fell down or out. There was likely enough fallen stone inside to block it from tumbling in.

Stockbridge recovered his hat, stepped a few feet from the wall, and raised his shotgun. A loud sound, along the wall, would rattle the exterior surface. The outside stones might give way and fall toward him.

That did not give Stockbridge a lot of room to duck and dodge, but he had to take that risk.

The horses and surrey were well enough back that they might not be struck. But there was a good chance the horses would panic, so he hurried over. He tied the reins to each other, with very little slack, and then he took the blanket from inside the carriage. He bound the left foreleg of one horse to the right foreleg of another. They protested, but a three-legged horse wasn't going anywhere.

Stockbridge rushed back to the cliff and raised his shotgun so it pointed north along the wall, the barrel aimed away from the horses and from himself. He did not believe in prayer, but he offered a silent one now. It was not, after all, for himself the words were intended. They were for two souls who had taken his cause as their own and for the family who needed their man.

Stockbridge was about to try to tear down a part of God's abode on earth. He did not dare to pray for a favorable reply.

He shouldered the shotgun and fired twice. The powerful blasts punched through the clouds and echoed above. The rolling boom faded right into the sudden, rising, louder thunder of rock. That roar became a quaking that shook Eagle Lookout above and below. Stockbridge jumped back and to the north as far as he dared. Chunks of the cliff fell away, tumbling outward, landing around Stockbridge with a force that caused the ledge itself to crack. He hurried over to the horses, the two of them rearing and trying to bite each other. Stockbridge put the shotgun down, grabbed the conjoined reins, and pulled down, his weight on them. In addition to forcing the horses into a semblance of calm, he was away from the center of what was now an avalanche. His back was pelted with ricocheting stones, mostly pebbles that did nothing more than tear small rents in the sleeve of his coat.

After what seemed an eternal span, the cascade stopped well before Stockbridge was aware of it. The airborne particles were thick, and his hearing was cottony. The unexpected calm of the horses, like the sudden end of a squall, was the first indication he had that the cataclysm was over.

With the ground beneath him steady, Stockbridge raised himself. He slowly let up on the horses' reins, and when they made it clear they weren't going anywhere, he undid the blanket and tied it around his waist. If anyone was injured, it would make a good tourniquet.

Stockbridge felt confident leaving the animals. If anyone came looking for them, they would not leave without exploring the rockfall.

Grabbing the waterskin strung from his saddle and tying it to his belt, Stockbridge picked up the shotgun and waited impatiently for the haze to clear. The air remained stubbornly white and heavy, and he could hear nothing.

Impatiently waving his hat from side to side, he finally started through the granular mist. The nearer he came to the cliff, the more he could see. The first things he saw—gratefully—were rocks. They were piled high on the outside in an angled mass, like some ancient ziggurat. The cone had collapsed outward, as he had hoped, though he could not tell if any rocks had fallen inside. Though stones were still falling, most of those came from somewhere above the clouds, to the east. There was nothing left on this side to collapse.

Reaching the base of the structure, he put his hat back on. Coughing from the powder, he held his breath and leaned forward. He held tight to his shotgun and used his free hand to grip the rocks as he walked up the side.

"Molly!" he called out. "Juan?"

There was no answer, and he began to fear that as many rocks had fallen in as out; it was impossible to tell. It would not be the first time people had been injured or killed because John Stockbridge did not have time to bother with the law—either the laws of man or, in this case, the laws of nature.

Small stones dropped from under his feet, almost spilling him over several times. He had gone about ten feet up before the air began to clear of dust. He was nearly at the cloud layer when he heard moans from inside the cone. He moved faster, his toes and heels digging in, until he was at the top of the pile and could see inside.

The tester of airborne grit was underlit by the lantern. Through it, Stockbridge discerned three figures lying on the ground. The rockslide had not formed a pile inside, but the collapse of the ridge had left him with something resembling titanic steps. His descent was inelegant. He sat on the top block, hung his legs over, jumped, and repeated. He did this four times until he was on the ground.

All three figures were ghostly white, covered with rock dust. One figure, the farthest, had spots of red on his head. As he neared, again waving his hat, Stockbridge could see that it was Juan. Molly was the nearest. She was the one who had been moaning. Between them, lying quite still, was the man they had been attempting to rescue.

Stockbridge got on his knees beside Molly. She was on her right side, that arm beneath her and the other with its fingers wrapped in the outstretched hand of Ben Keeler. Stockbridge poured water into his palm and then onto her eyes. The cool water caused her lids to flutter. She blinked, then rolled her open eyes toward the face looking down at her. Her pasty lips parted.

"I heard . . . a shot . . . ," she said. Her voice was caked and raw, but the smile that came with it was like the sun.

"Everything's all right. Can you sit?"

"I . . . I think so. All parts of me ache . . . so nothing is broken."

It was curious reasoning, but Stockbridge knew she was right. Except for ribs and skulls, most broken bones left an area numb. He set the shotgun down, put his strong hands under her left arm, and helped her slowly into a sitting position.

"Would you believe," she said slowly, "this is how I started the day? Yi Huang helping me sit? Funny thing is . . . I feel better now."

It was probably the shock of what had happened that was making her talk. With a reassuring hand on her shoulder, Stockbridge left her sitting there, and he went over to Juan. The man was on his face, unconscious, apparently having struck his forehead on the ground. Stockbridge carefully turned him over and poured water on his face and in the wound. It was a bad cut, but Stockbridge did not see bone. He used his serrated knife to cut off a swath of blanket and, dampening it, laid it on Juan's forehead to try to cool the swelling. He felt the man's arms and legs; nothing appeared to have been broken there.

Then Dr. John Stockbridge turned his professional eye to Ben Keeler. He did not want to bring a body back to the family.

The trapper was on his back. This close, Stockbridge could see, then hear him breathing. The doctor's sigh almost became tears. He poured a few drops from the waterskin into the man's mouth. Ben's tongue responded, and he swallowed the water down. Stockbridge set the skin aside and quickly examined the man's body.

The trapper was emaciated and dehydrated; that much was immediately apparent. His clothes were rags, and both ankles were cut and swollen. He did not know if the man could walk, though there were no protrusions suggesting a break.

"His feet . . . were trapped," Molly said. "But he could feel them."

Stockbridge nodded. They would have to carry him, probably using the blanket as a stretcher.

"Hey! What happened?"

Stockbridge looked to his right and saw that Juan had risen on an elbow. The damp towel was in his hand, and he was facing the back of the cave. Then he noticed his rifle, smashed beneath the rocks just beside him.

"The wall fell in," Stockbridge said. "It barely missed you."

Juan turned. "Doctor?"

"Keep that cloth pressed to your forehead," Stockbridge said. "You've got a nasty cut."

"*Sí, señor!*" Juan replied. He did as instructed and smiled at Molly. "You are good?"

"Good enough, Juan."

Juan's eyes fell to his side. "Better than my poor rifle. I'm sorry," he said to the gun. "You were a good companion. You provided for me, in your youth."

Stockbridge continued to check Ben Keeler carefully for cuts, bleeding. He did not look at the man but read his body with his fingertips. He had perfected this skill during the War, as it caused less pain to wounded soldiers if movement was minimal. It also left his eyes free to watch what nurses were doing for others.

As Stockbridge worked, Juan sat, then rose.

"Aiii . . . ," the Mexican wheezed.

"Watch yourself," Stockbridge cautioned.

"At least you left a blanket for me to fall on," Juan said, pointing at the ground.

Molly stood next, leaning on a fallen rock to help get her feet under her. She reminded Stockbridge of a tightrope walker he had seen with his wife and son at a circus in Denver, her arms slowly rising while her body wobbled uncertainly. In the midst of the rubble and disorder, it was an unexpected thing of beauty.

Stockbridge finished his examination. A second dribbling of water into Keeler's mouth was finally enough to elicit a sound.

"Thank you." The man's baggy eyes, undilated from the dark, opened a moment later. "And God bless you."

"Maybe one day," Stockbridge said. "Ben Keeler, you've got a lovely wife and two beautiful children who are waiting to see you."

Tears spilled from the man's blue eyes. "I—I never thought I would hold them again."

Giving the man his privacy, Stockbridge rose and recovered the blanket, which he spread beside him. Together, the three gently eased Keeler onto the floral-patterned quilt, Keeler making sounds—not pain but with apparent delight at feeling something soft for the first time in months.

They agreed that Molly would go first, guiding and helping to steady Juan, with Stockbridge in the rear.

"I heard a bang and a bang," Juan said as he discarded the compress, then spit on his palms to get a good grip on the blanket. "I see now—you shoot the mountain down, *señor*?"

"In a manner of speaking."

"Like Joshua," Juan said.

Stockbridge dismissed the analogy with a frown. "On three?"

The others agreed, and as one, they raised Ben Keeler knee-high. Molly went back to collect the lantern.

As they walked, Stockbridge kept careful watch on Juan. Blood dribbled down the bridge of the Mexican's nose. The man was so *game*, which caused Stockbridge to stew about what Juan had called him. He did not like the press creating Dr. Vengeance when they should have been reporting actual news, and he liked even less when a good, unassuming man like this elevated him—or anyone—to an exalted level, let alone that of a biblical patriarch. It was both grandiose and embarrassing.

It was necessary to lay Keeler down from time to time as the men followed Molly up the big steps of the broken slope. They had an easier time going down the stacked boulders outside into the fast-fading sunlight.

Ben Keeler raised a bony arm to protect his eyes from the setting sun.

"Oh, glorious day!" he cried, and again began to weep.

With slow and patient effort, they finally got the man to the surrey. Molly took care to wrap the blanket around him before they tucked him into the backseat.

"We can at least make it to Juan's cave before sunset," Stockbridge said. "I think we should stay until morning, give everyone a chance to heal."

Juan beamed in the dying sun. "After so many years, you will be my first guests."

Stockbridge paused and examined the man's cut. "I'm going to have to cauterize the wound, Juan."

"What is that?"

"I heat a stick in fire and use that to stop the bleeding."

"I really *must* travel with needle and thread," Molly said, climbing into her seat.

Juan snorted. "You will hurt me to make me better. Are you *really* a doctor?"

Stockbridge smiled. "I swear by Apollo physician I am."

Juan made a confused face as he climbed into the surrey beside Molly. There was not nearly as much room on Eagle Lookout as there had been before, and it took some jockeying before they were able to turn the carriage around. That done, Molly waited while Stockbridge mounted his own steed and led the way down the mountain.

CHAPTER TWENTY-THREE

During the four-hour ride, Cuthbert found himself ranging between seething fury and quiet determination. Every time he seemed to settle, his mind would think of the blow the Red Hunters and New Richmond had received, and he would be in a storm all over again.

The man will die. He will die slowly. He will die soon. He will die by my hand.

There was no thought beyond that, not even how the Red Hunters would go on with just four members. But those concerns were foremost in DeLancy's mind, especially what they would do after they killed their quarry. Word would get out that the Red Hunters had stopped one of the most suddenly famed gunslingers in the West. Other gunslingers would come looking for them to prove their own mettle. Without Grady Foxborough on point, without Woodrow Pound for silent kills, without Liam McWilliams for sheer brass, the unit was greatly compromised. It

wasn't a matter of recruiting more men. You had to
have been a Red Hunter to understand the mission,
the fealty, the old South built fresh in the new West.

The dark shadows of late afternoon had already
fallen on the cabin when the men and their prisoners
arrived. The proud sign announcing New Richmond
was in shadow, the burned-in letters dark, almost
mournful, and disapproving.

The Keelers had not spoken during the trip, not because they had been instructed to by Cuthbert but
because they were praying, pensive, or angry. Even
Lenny realized that the last might get them killed.
They said nothing when the men stopped to water the
horses and relieve themselves, Rachel making a point
of ignoring the looks of Zebediah Tunney when he
flashed a crooked, partly toothless smile at her. She
did not know, or care, whether it was an oafish effort
to show kindness or a prelude to something awful.

She had ignored DeLancy, too, when he had noticed Tunney noticing her and used his head to motion him elsewhere. If that was an effort to earn her
respect or admiration, she rejected it.

Rachel's real concern was not what could happen
to her but what was happening to her mother. As the
trip wore on, the woman seemed to crumple inside.
She had held up for so long during the long summer
and fall, always in anticipation of her husband returning, that there was nothing left. When she had finally
put them all on their expedition, it was not so much a
journey of hope but of desperation. Rachel feared
that if they did not succeed, Alice Keeler would not
survive this ordeal.

And then there was the strong, proud Dr. Stockbridge. Alice Keeler's expression seemed to become
more and more lost as she wondered where he was.
She had transferred her flagging energies to him, held

his strong arm to support herself, put her dying faith in his uncanny, almost supernatural stature. Since he had ridden out that morning, Alice Keeler had seemed alive for the first time in weeks.

Then this.

That lunatic Promise Cuthbert had rudely kicked dirt on Alice's spiritual campfire. Even if the man with the shotgun was near, there were three men with guns holding the three Keelers captive. Rachel herself did not believe that Dr. Stockbridge would risk cutting their captors down if it would endanger any of them, and her own hope of rescue had faltered with that. She began to feel that their only chance of surviving lay with her or Lenny.

Rachel did not have a gun. But she did have something she had tucked into her apron back at the kitchen table and transferred to her coat before they had departed. The long, slender, newly stropped knife that she had been using to cut carrots. She did not know what she could do with it, or when, or how. What she did know was out here on the plains, there were still too much sun and too few hiding places to afford her any chance of getting away. Perhaps that would come later, at their destination. From what she had seen of the mountains, the woods, Rachel felt there might be an opportunity to escape. So the young woman waited. She had the stout heart of her mother, but she was also the same determined dreamer as her father.

The Cuthbert party reached its destination by late afternoon.

The captain had half hoped, half expected, but mostly begged the Lord God Almighty that they would encounter Stockbridge along the way. It would have been like that one rare, wonderful occurrence when the men, returning from Buzzard Gulch or Gunnison, had run into a stag watching out for the herd and cut it down. That was one reason they always rode out with rope. With the rope tied to the antlers, two horses could drag the carcass back, urged on by heroic coaxing from the riders.

Hope, like that rope, was something Cuthbert just carried.

Rachel's spirits drooped when she laid eyes on what Cuthbert had referred to as "the cabin." It was a fortress, awesome in its natural majesty. She understood almost immediately why these men had chosen the location. She had heard her father tell about the Confederacy and its plantations, and seen pictures in books. The South had been a land of plenty, just as this was a land of great timber and rivers and mountains. Men who had irretrievably lost one would naturally seek the other. Seek it and hold it with the kind of unyielding ferocity of Captain Cuthbert.

Alice Keeler was unstirred and probably unaware of the place, but Lenny looked in open awe from the cabin—whose likes he had never beheld in his short life—to Rachel to the mountains to Rachel as though seeking her approval, his big eyes asking, *Is it all right to be overwhelmed by all this?*

She gave him a little nod, though she was unsure whether he could see it as they passed beyond the sign. There were unlit lanterns outside the main cabin, making it seem even more majestic, as though it were hewn from the very rock that rose behind it.

Still as agitated and restless as when the caravan had left the homestead, Promise Cuthbert dismounted and ordered everyone off their horses. Rachel slid from hers so swiftly that the Confederates feared she might make a break for the mountains. Instead, she walked briskly to her mother, who remained slumped in the saddle. Rachel helped her off by supporting her under the arms.

"I'm all right," the woman soughed in a soft, beaten voice.

Lenny ran over next. Ahead, a dark figure struck a match and ignited a lantern. He wore a bloody apron, and Rachel suddenly saw her own future in servitude here. These men had been slaveholders. She feared that the fate of the Keeler family was to never leave this place. No one on the homestead would know where to find them, even if they troubled to look; every family had their own worries. And from what she had heard, Sheriff Tom Neal did not do anything unless it had to do with the nine structures that stood on the one wide, empty street that was Buzzard Gulch.

"Move!" Cuthbert urged, his voice like a whip as he came forward.

The Keelers started walking, Rachel helping her mother, pretending to look at her but actually taking in the immediate property.

Her brother was on their mother's left, Rachel on the right.

"Lenny, will you give Ma your shoulder?"

"Sure, sis," he said with characteristic pluck.

Rachel stepped from under her own burden. She turned to Cuthbert.

"I would like to use the privy, please," she said.

Her unexpectedly conciliatory tone seemed to sit well with the former captain.

"Private Tunney?" Cuthbert said.

"Yessir!"

"Escort the lady to the necessary. Sergeant DeLancy, Franz, and I will settle the other two inside. Tunney can see to the horses when he's brought Miss Keeler back."

An orange glow from the lantern had suffused the grounds around the cabin, and Rachel could see the giant's pleased smile.

"Yessir." Tunney broke from the ranks and reached for the girl's arm.

Cuthbert stopped him. "No. You do not touch. Do you hear me?"

Tunney hesitated. If he was considering disputing the order, Cuthbert's thumb went to the hammer of his Colt, discouraging that.

"I hear you, sir," the man replied.

Cuthbert's eyes lingered on the girl for a moment. "Only don't let her out of your sight. She's got mettle, this one."

Tunney nodded at the captain and threw a beefy arm ahead. "That way, girl."

Shivering from the cold and thrusting her hands into her pockets, Rachel needed to feel the knife handle as she trudged across the hard earth in the direction Tunney had pointed, the big man padding after her.

The girl's heart began to drum hard as she considered, fresh, what she was contemplating: running. Getting away would be a problem on its own, and then there were potential reprisals. She had to believe that Cuthbert would want to hold on to his remaining hostages rather than harm them from spite.

Rachel and Tunney reached the structure, which was larger and sturdier than their own windy shack at home. She opened the door, expecting to be submerged in the odor—but found it not as acrid as expected, no doubt because of underground runoff from the mountains. She went to shut the door, only to have the man's big paw block it.

"Captain said to watch you."

"He didn't mean that, I think."

"I think he did."

Rachel's heart thumped faster. She lowered her shoulders, which shoved her hands deeper into her pockets. But she did not lower her face. Her eyes were locked on those of the Confederate.

"Please close the door."

"You do what you come to do, or I'm taking you back. I won't say it again."

There was no condition in this hard, cruel land under which Rachel had imagined she would take the advice of any of these men. Yet the man was right. She would do exactly what she came to do.

Tunney loomed very close, his arms out around the sides of the structure to keep her from running. Blood was rushing so fast and hard that Rachel was afraid of passing out. Holding the blade cutting side up, she simultaneously stepped forward and ripped through the pocket with a determined thrust. The carrot knife plunged deep into the man's wool coat and into his belly. He seemed more surprised than hurt as he looked down.

"What is this?" he muttered.

It was a moment, a distraction Rachel needed. She pulled her arm back and drew the blade from her pocket. Using the man's chest as a guide, she pushed the blade into the bottom of his jaw. He had just started to reach for her throat or shoulders—she did not know which—when the tip pierced the soft tissue and entered his mouth and stuck hard in the palate. The man tried to cry out, but the sound was trapped behind his closed mouth. Rachel withdrew the knife, turned it lower, and pushed it into the man's throat. She heard herself snarling and could not imagine those sounds were coming from her.

Blood gushed over her hand and down the front of her coat, which was pressed close to his. It coated the man's trousers on its way down, splashed over her old shoes, dripped onto the dry earth, and ran down the hole in the ground—all the way to hell, she hoped.

Rachel released the knife and left the blade where it was. She stepped to one side. Tunney breathed hard, the wound burbling. He wobbled for a moment, his thick fingers rising, trembling, trying to find the hilt. They froze below his neck, his eyes rolled back showing white, and he dropped to his knees before flopping forward. His head landed facedown on the hole.

The girl's hands were open claws at her side, bloody as a hawk's talons. She was breathing hard through her nose, afraid to release her lips lest she scream. Except for the trickling of blood into the water below, she heard only the shuffling of the horses outside. She realized that someone would come out in a moment, wonder why they were there, and look for Tunney.

There was no time to think or plan. For a logical girl like Rachel, that was a bigger hurdle than putting a carrot knife in the throat of a man who had abused her family and wanted to watch her urinate.

Reaching down to recover the knife, she stepped over the body and leaned from the outhouse. The horses—her horse—were where they had been left. Slipping the knife in the pocket that wasn't torn, she ran as hard as she had ever done toward her father's horse. Almost without stopping, she pushed her foot into the stirrup, swung into the saddle, and reined around hard.

The horse whinnied. There was a shout from the house. It was DeLancy.

"Tunney?"

The sky was nearly dark, the ground even darker. It would be difficult to see, but it would be impossible to stay. Kicking the horse, Rachel sped toward the sign that boasted the name of this place to the uncaring mountains. She thundered below it, waiting to hear a gunshot that might take her or the horse down. But she had enough of a head start, and the report never came. There were only shouts and oaths, especially when someone saw Tunney lying on the ground.

Please, God, do not let them hurt my family, Rachel thought as she raced up the trail. That was where she hoped to find John Stockbridge, where her father's map indicated he might have been headed.

Tearing along the trail to the higher elevations, Rachel thought she heard the clop of hooves behind her. She was not surprised. She had been considering what to do. Get as high as she could, first of all, where thick trees and blackening skies would help conceal her.

She galloped until the wind blew spittle from the horse into her face. Stopping hard, she swung to the ground and dismounted. The ground sloped down toward her left, the west, and up toward her right. Reaching her bloodstained hands toward the trees that lined the hill, she pulled herself along. Without support, she would have slipped back along the slanting terrain. Grab and release, grab and release. Moving from tree to tree, she was able to draw herself along the hill like a monkey she had seen climb its cage in a traveling carnival. Her knees scraped bark, her dress tore each time she stepped on it, and low thistles raked her flesh. She grunted, she inhaled hard, and she cried in the brief moments that fear took hold. But she never stopped. Even though it was now fast-fallen night around her, the trees were near enough that she could proceed by feel.

She heard two riders somewhere below. Cuthbert and DeLancy, no doubt. She blew out her cheeks and pulled even harder, more mountain cat than monkey now.

They will not get me.

Rachel did not know how far she had gone when the land suddenly became level. The trees were no longer slanted but upright, and she started running between them, unaided, her hands out, making sure she did not crash into any of them. She did not want to render herself unconscious and wake back at New Richmond. She would rather fall from a cliff and die.

The flat plateau was soon relatively grassy and the trees grew sparse, and she found herself running in a clearing. She was fading, wheezing through her dry mouth, stumbling ahead until her legs finally crumpled beneath her.

"No!"

The girl raised herself to her hands and knees and began crawling. She continued to scrabble along the hard earth until she got some of her breath back. That was when she heard something that made her heart soar. A sound she did not hear often, below. A sound that spoke of help and salvation.

The rush of a nearby river.

CHAPTER TWENTY-FOUR

THE WEARY RESCUERS reached Juan's cave shortly after nightfall.

They made a very slow, careful trek down the mountain. The collapse of the cone had weakened cliff walls up and down the trail, and the path was littered with stones of varying sizes. The lantern provided limited illumination, and to negotiate the last half mile, Stockbridge was forced to fashion a torch. He would have preferred not to. There were people hunting them, and the two lights, moving behind the trees, created flickering that could not be missed.

But there was no choice. The only good thing was that the Red Hunters would need a light, too. The advantage was Stockbridge's. He could rain scatter-shot down on them more effectively than they could pick him off in the dark.

Upon reaching the Mexican's home, they carried Ben inside. While Molly made him warm and comfortable on Juan's fur bed, the Mexican brought the horses into the cave, where they would be safe from mountain lions. Juan left them saddled for now and went back out with the lantern to find a place for the surrey on the north side of the cave. Inside, Stockbridge tended to Ben's bruised, torn feet while Molly held the torch. He used what was left of the water to wash the cuts and then tore strips from the blanket to bind them. He used the rest of the fabric to fashion a pillow.

"I don't know how I can ever repay this kindness," Keeler said. "God will bless you both."

"Just rest," Stockbridge said softly, his voice echoing through the cave. "Don't think of anything but getting strong."

"And getting home," Keeler added.

"That, too." Stockbridge smiled down at him.

The doctor and Molly left then, taking the torch with them. Juan came from around the north side with an armful of branches. He placed them in the two firepits and lit them with the torch. The mouth of the cave glowed orange behind them.

"This is brighter than any nighttime's ever been," Juan said, looking from his fires to the torch. "Merry, like a fiesta!"

"How's your head?" Stockbridge asked, setting his shotgun nearby, against a rock, and looking closely at the cut.

"It is *nothing*," Juan said emphatically.

"It's not nothing, Juan. It's still bleeding. You've got blood on your sleeve where you've been wiping it."

Juan's mouth twisted in surrender. "You going to burn me?"

"The injury has got to be closed, *amigo*."

The Mexican sighed. He looked at Molly for support, found only sympathy. He backed up against the side of the cave mouth, bracing himself. "Okay. Do it."

Stockbridge selected one of the sticks. He rolled the tip around in the flames, against a rock, getting rid of any splinters and hardening the point. Blowing on it, he stood and approached the shorter man. Gently, he pushed Juan's long hair from his brow.

"This is going to smart a little," Stockbridge warned. "Count to three."

Juan shut his eyes, drew a breath, held it, and said, *"Uno—"*

That was as far as he got before Stockbridge laid the charcoal black brand against the wound. It sizzled for the moment he held it there, Juan at the same time hissing through his teeth, blood vaporizing and filling their nostrils. Juan continued his sibilant exhalation even after Stockbridge had withdrawn the ember.

"Ow!"

"Perfect," the doctor said, examining the cauterized cut.

"*Madre de Dios*, that was worse than *getting* the cut," Juan said, fanning his forehead with a hand.

"That's because you were knocked out, Juan."

"Maybe you should do that," Molly said.

"Hit my patients? I confess to being tempted, from time to time."

Molly had been watching the operation with interest. Stockbridge's calm professionalism was not surprising. That was how the articles had described his killing. She preferred this. It stirred different things inside of her.

Juan refrained from scratching what had not really bothered him before but now itched. He reached for his rifle to support himself, remembered that it wasn't there, and put his hands on his hips.

"I have to get food. Fish, I think, because I do not have to shoot them or see them."

"You're going fishing . . . in the dark?" Molly asked.

"Sometimes I get hungry late. I will take the torch—anyone looking for you will only see me."

The Mexican retrieved a small net made of twined roots set in an oval frame made from willow. The handle was the leg of a mountain lion. It was withered, the skin mostly gone, but the claws were intact.

"I shot him in my cave," Juan said proudly.

"Impressive," Molly said, shuddering a little.

Juan took the torch and walked off in the direction of the Oónâhe'e River.

"He's a good man," Molly said as Juan and the torch disappeared around the southern side of the cave.

Stockbridge nodded in agreement. With the birch twigs hissing and popping behind him and Ben Keeler snoring in the cave, Stockbridge had done all he could do now—except to turn his attention to the woman at his side.

"Are you comfortable?" he asked.

Smilingly, she nodded. "You wouldn't happen to have a smoke, would you?"

"I never took it up," he answered.

"A pipe would suit you," she said. "In my line of work, I need it. Relaxes me."

"You haven't met many good men, have you?"

"I have not. But I haven't had it as bad as some women. Yi—she's one of the nicest people you could ask to meet. Because she is Chinese, and a domestic, and polite—no matter what is said to her—no one knows she's alive. I think that may be worse than having to fight for some measure of dignity. What about you? Dr. John Stockbridge used to spend every day healing. Now, it seems, people come around either to kill you or be killed."

"That's about the scope of things. And I can't seem to talk them down."

"You've tried, I'm sure."

"Just yesterday, matter of fact. To one of the Red Hunters. A black man. He seemed reasonable and left."

"Woodrow Pound. What do you mean he 'seemed' reasonable?"

"He came after me again this morning, and I had to shoot him. Men don't know how to tamp down their own fires. They only know how to burn."

"Maybe you should retire this, then." She cocked her head toward the shotgun.

"I was on my way to do that when all this happened, with the Keelers. I want to move away, move on. But it's probably an illusion. There would come a day when someone would recognize me or see a picture of me in an old magazine and learn who I really was." He smiled. "You know, I even thought about going to a city like New York or Boston and just giving in to the whole thing, writing Dr. Vengeance adventures that never really took place and selling them to the magazines. I fancy that I could work up to writing a memoir, maybe take up pipe smoking. Be invited to parties and dinner—"

"Have men applaud you, and women fight to be on your arm?"

"It would be different from the way I've lived, the way I'm living now." He shook his head. "I don't know. If you can't have your old life back, maybe a complete change is the best thing."

"Sometimes, even if you *can* have it back, change may be the best thing."

"Change," Stockbridge mused. He glanced behind him at the cave. "We've got one man who surrendered the company of men for this . . . and another who wanted to bring a new world *back* to his family. I guess there's no rule, is there?"

"No."

Molly could not remember the last time she had enjoyed a relaxed conversation with a man—any man, let alone one who was smart and had a sense of humility. She wanted nothing more than to lay her head on his shoulder or lap, sit by the fire, and feel safe and wanted, for just a while. Raspy Nikolaev looked out for her, but she made him a lot of money. This man was different. He did things because he was good.

And what about me? Molly asked herself. She had come out to help this man; was it because he had been courteous to her on a dirt road in Gunnison or because she yearned for more? The idea of "Molly Stockbridge" seemed stillborn. *Yet—*

There was a saying Molly had read in a magazine, *"Time and tide wait for no man."* She had never had the opportunity to apply it to her own life—until this moment. Her heart pounding more than it had on Eagle Lookout, she was about to brave a related topic, ask if Stockbridge ever thought he might remarry, when Juan's voice broke from a distance away.

"*Señor* Stockbridge! I have *found* someone!"

Stockbridge was immediately on his feet. Scooping a burning stick from the fire, he walked past the cave to see what the yelling was about. He peered into the darkness at two shadowy forms. Within moments he had discerned the silhouette of the fishnet Juan had been carrying.

"Juan? Who is with you?"

"I don't know who she is, Doctor."

"She?"

The figure was clinging to Juan's right arm, barely able to walk. Stockbridge could not imagine what a woman would be doing up here alone.

"Doctor . . . ?" a woman's voice said at the same

moment that her knees gave out and she stumbled forward into the light.

"Dear God," Stockbridge said as he recognized the dim contours of the girl's face. "Rachel!"

The physician hurried across the few yards that separated them, dropped the stick, and scooped the girl under her other arm.

"She is a friend?" Juan asked.

"Ben's daughter," Stockbridge said.

The young woman went limp, and the men walked her back. Molly was waiting for them at the bend. She stepped aside so they could pass.

"Did I hear you say she's Ben's daughter?" Molly asked.

Stockbridge nodded as they laid the dirty, exhausted girl beside the campfire. He was shocked by her appearance. Her face, hands, legs were ripped and torn, like a fox that had tried to escape hounds through thick bramble.

Molly went into the cave and came back with the waterskin. There was a great deal of dried blood on the girl's hands and dress—more than would have come from rushing through woodland. Molly washed them while Stockbridge checked to make sure that she had not been molested by something other than what was clearly a mad flight. The attentions revived the girl. Her eyes shot open, and she shook her head as her hands moved reflexively in front of her, pushing and sweeping as though she were still running.

"Had to . . . get . . . away!"

"Rachel, you're all right. You're with friends," Stockbridge said softly.

She reminded Stockbridge of men he had treated in the War. They would come to after a concussion on the battlefield and, without thought, just an instinct to survive, would thrust a bayonet or call to retreat or shout to a comrade about an unseen danger.

The girl blinked her eyes. The doctor leaning close was the first thing she saw. Her expression of pinched panic turned to overwhelming joy and tears of relief. She heaved herself forward and hugged his neck.

"Thank you, Lord. Thank you."

"What are you doing up here?" Stockbridge asked.

Her trembling fingers clutched his long hair as she wept into his cheek.

"I killed a man, Doctor. I . . . I *had* to. . . . I stabbed him. . . . God save me. I stabbed him over and over and over. Blood was everywhere!"

"Was someone chasing you?" Molly asked.

"Not . . . chasing. Trapped. *Cornered*."

Stockbridge completed his examination. He smoothed her garments and nodded at Molly that Rachel was all right. Then he regarded the girl with as kindly an expression as he could find.

"Rachel, where are your mother and brother?"

She eased back to the hard earth. Juan had removed his gloves, placed them in the net, and hurriedly crafted a makeshift pillow to slip beneath her head.

"Three men came to the house. They forced us to go with them to a place in the mountains. It is not far from here, I think."

"A large cabin? New Richmond?" Molly asked.

"Yes, that was the name. I took a horse and I rode, and then I ran and ran."

"Did they follow?" Stockbridge asked.

Rachel nodded. The doctor regarded Juan, who nodded knowingly and went back to watch the road from behind the edge of the cave.

"Was one of the men Promise Cuthbert?" Molly asked, her voice hard.

Rachel nodded. "Cuthbert . . . DeLancy . . . Tunney. Those were the names."

"Who did you kill?" Molly inquired.

"Tunney. I went outside to . . . to . . . He followed me, was watching. I had the knife from our kitchen." She looked at Stockbridge. "They wanted to use us to kill you."

"Your mother and brother are still there?" Stockbridge asked.

"Yes. I don't think they will be hurt. Not yet. But"—she began to sob again—"I don't know. I was afraid for them, for all of us, and I had to do something!"

"What you did was not just right. It was brave," Stockbridge said. "Very brave."

Her eyes stared up at him, imploring. "We have to do something."

"We will," he said. "Rachel—I have something to tell you."

"Pa?"

"We found him. He's here—weak but alive."

The girl's face was suddenly alive. She was overcome again, only this time with joy.

"Take me to him!" she cried, struggling to rise. "Father? *Father!*"

Stockbridge and Molly helped her up, caught up in the moment and wanting to soften her pain by reuniting Rachel and Ben Keeler. As the two women shuffled into the cave, Stockbridge looked out into the darkness beyond.

That turnoff from the main trail. That was where the two Keelers were. He had to go there.

Stockbridge turned toward the cave as Rachel reached her father. In the faint glow, he saw her fall beside him.

"Father!"

The shape of Ben Keeler formed itself from the

furs. He sobbed, his hands reaching up and grabbing Rachel's. The two came together in an embrace that both warmed and saddened Stockbridge. He remembered the last time he had held his wife and children. They were already gone, but they were his loves, his life, and no less. Since that moment, he had known in his soul that every villain he met would wear that creature's cold expression. Every wrong he encountered had to be met by right.

Promise Cuthbert was about to learn that.

Stockbridge did not linger but strode to his horse tucked deep in the cave. As he walked it out, Molly came running after him.

"Wait for us," she said.

"Ben and Rachel—they cannot be left alone here."

"Then wait for me. Juan can stay."

"No."

She pulled at the shoulders of his coat. He looked down at her dark features, only the bright eyes clearly visible.

"I've come this far, John. Don't make me chase you!"

Stockbridge was tired and angry, and he was horrified by the descent of man into something less than a beast. He was even ashamed of what he had become—Dr. Vengeance. He was about to debate her when the question became moot.

There was a voice calling from down the trail.

A voice that sent fear racing along John Stockbridge's backbone.

CHAPTER TWENTY-FIVE

O N THE OUTSIDE, the man who loomed ahead on
Peak Road was indistinguishable from the rock
cliff beside him. On the inside, however, Cuthbert's
scream still rang in his skull.

"She killed Zebediah!"

If there was a state of mind beyond madness,
Promise Cuthbert had found it. No longer man but
devil, he was flushed red, with invisible horns of hate
rising from him like the heavy, weathered body of the
most vicious stag, an animal of mythical venom. Until now, pulling the yoke of the fallen South had been
his sole burden. Now he hated at an even greater
magnitude.

"You *bitch*!" he had screamed over the gutted body.
"You *demon*!"

DeLancy had been the one who had described the
corpse. He had already mounted and ridden after the
fleeing girl. Still crying out, his lungs and fire seem-

ingly bottomless, Cuthbert jumped on his own frightened steed. He turned sharply toward Baker.

"Keep those two here! If they try to leave, kill the
boy!"

With that, the officer—who saw himself as an
avenging angel, not a devil—galloped after DeLancy.

Alice and Lenny Keeler remained huddled together behind the cook, unsure what had happened
at first—but quickly realizing that Rachel had somehow killed the man who was guarding her and was
attempting to escape.

"She cannot outrun them," Mrs. Keeler said fear-
fully.

"She's not on foot," Lenny said, having peered
past Baker and counted the horses.

"God protect her," the woman said.

"God already protected you," Baker replied. He
turned to the woman. "I would've bet a gold bar
against you living another minute. I never seen the
captain like this, not even in War."

"Then, sir, please—you have to let us go," Mrs.
Keeler said. "At least let the boy go."

"No, Ma!"

"I won't cross the captain," Baker had said.

The degeneracy of these men, of this situation, was
beyond anything Mrs. Keeler had ever known outside
the pages of her Bible. In the absence of any other
succor, she turned Lenny away from the door and
went to the hearth, where they fell to their knees and
prayed.

The pursuit of Rachel Keeler did not last long.
Darkness and an unforgiving terrain forced Cuthbert
and DeLancy to turn back before the Keelers had
sent very many humble words to their Maker.

The horses clomped back hard, Cuthbert dismounted harder, and he entered the cabin like a storm. Without preamble, he went to where the Keelers were praying and grabbed Lenny by the neck. He yanked him up and threw him toward DeLancy. It happened so fast that Mrs. Keeler was still on her knees before she fully realized what had happened.

"Take him, Sergeant," Cuthbert roared. "Go out and—"

"*No!*" Mrs. Keeler screamed. She threw herself at Cuthbert, wrapping her spindly arms around his legs as if stopping him from moving and stopping time from moving were somehow possible.

He kicked her off and drove the toe of his boot into her belly.

"Ma!" Lenny shrieked.

DeLancy had the boy by the shoulders and held him firm. Cuthbert swung toward Lenny like a wolf on a cornered hare.

"Take that little shit out and have him call for his sister," Cuthbert hissed. "Put a knife to his throat if you have to, but get him to yell loud. *Loud*, you hear?"

"Yes, sir."

"I want him to cry so loud that, by God, heaven itself will shut its cursed ears."

"Captain, yessir. But we got other unsettled business out there—"

"Stockbridge? You afraid of him hearing, Sergeant?"

"You know that ain't it. I see him, I shoot him dead. But to do that, I need my arms free. It might be better if we tied the boy to a tree, y'know. If he stops screaming, we cut her." He had nodded toward the woman.

Cuthbert had stood ominously still, like a Ketchum Grenade about to blow in every direction.

"We do not wait for Stockbridge. We attack. Do you remember how that was?"

"I do remember, sir—"

"We seek the Yankee murderer out, and we do not allow him to set foot on the soil of New Richmond. Do you understand?"

"Yes, sir."

"Get on your horse, *with* the boy, find the girl, and bring them back. Tie her to your horse and drag her here if you have to. If Stockbridge shows up, kill the boy if you need your arms free. Then kill him."

"No . . . ," Mrs. Keeler wept. "God, no . . ."

Both Alice and Lenny Keeler were sobbing. The woman was on the floor in a huddled mass, behind Cuthbert. She was reaching helplessly toward her son. The boy's legs refused to support his weight, and DeLancy hooked an arm around the youngster's throat. The boy gagged as the Southerner held him up by his head.

The fire momentarily spent, Cuthbert settled into a state not unlike steam.

"Is there anything else?" he whispered to his man.

"No, sir," DeLancy replied. "You will have them all."

The sergeant walked out, hauling the boy with him like he was a hog-tied calf being lead to his branding. Baker stepped aside to let them pass. There was a brief relaxing of Cuthbert's mouth when they had gone.

"We will see to Private Tunney later," Cuthbert said to Baker. "For now, put the rest of him in the outhouse and close the door. I won't have him eaten by wolves."

"What about our patch?" Baker asked.

"I won't have the red palm on a crap house. *Not* there. We'll do it later."

When DeLancy mounted his horse and dragged the boy up in front of him, Baker went about his own grim business.

"What a bastardly business this is," the cook muttered as he went outside.

ONCE BEFORE, SERGEANT Alan DeLancy had been forced to face a world that had been turned on its side and emptied of everything of value. After the War, nothing seemed to matter. Nothing until Captain Promise Cuthbert had summoned and reassembled the Red Hunters. The reunion was like a returning faith. It gave every man purpose and restored his dignity. To them, as during the War, the law of the land had no influence. The honor of the South was all that mattered. That renewed heartbeat had sustained them, given meaning to their lives.

Many of the men who were a part of that sacred mission had perished today. But, he reminded himself, as long as he and Captain Cuthbert and Cook Baker survived, so did the Confederate States of America. This boy, his mother, his sister—they were all unfortunate casualties of War, a struggle for which the South did not ask and a fate that had befallen so many mothers and children of Dixie.

The boy had squirmed when they started out, and it was only the cutting edge of DeLancy's knife nestled tight beneath the youngster's Adam's apple that quieted him. DeLancy was aware of the trickle of blood on his own hand but kept his hold steady as they rode into the darkness. The blood concerned him a little; it might make his hand slippery if he went for the old Griswold & Gunnison pistol at his side or the rifle in its saddle holster.

"Shout your sister's name, boy," DeLancy said into his ear.

"My throat—"

"You won't bleed out . . . yet. Now, *call*!"

"Ra . . . chel!" Lenny cried, the pain and fear causing the name to catch.

"Louder."

"Rachel!" Lenny screamed.

"There ya go," DeLancy said approvingly. "Again!"

"Rachel! Please answer! *Rachel!*"

They rode up the trail, moving slowly because of the darkness. A rain gully or mole mound could drop them, so DeLancy let the horse pick his own way. Two decades seemed to vanish as DeLancy—then himself a boy—was back on dark roads in Union-held territory, looking, smelling, listening for men or campfires or spit-roasting meat. The years fell away and defeat did not now, as then, seem like it was possible. The mind just did not accept the idea of a world without the South.

Or the Red Hunters.

As they rode, DeLancy also arranged a signal with the boy. When he relaxed the pressure of the blade, Lenny could go silent and save his voice, put a sleeve on the wound. When force was reapplied, the boy had to shout.

Before long, they had entered the higher elevations. The wind was low but steady, blowing down from the peaks, and amidst the scent of pine and the rot of dead things, DeLancy picked up the faint scent of a fire. There was no glow that he could see, but it was definitely coming from ahead and higher. He knew of but had never met the Mexican hermit Juan Juarez, who lived up there—the man Grady said had shown him Eagle Lookout. If the fire belonged to the

Mexican, he would show his ugly face when he heard the boy. The man reportedly did not like visitors.

DeLancy applied pressure to the boy's fair skin.

"Rachel! *Rachel!*"

The smell came and went as the trail wound through rock and woods, each time returning stronger. Finally, DeLancy was on the last section of trail before the old man's cave. The smell here was powerful and of more than just fire. There were horses here.

The sergeant stopped. Without releasing the reins, he reached his right hand to his holster, drew his gun, quietly cocked the hammer, and aimed. With his other hand, he pressed the blade to the boy's throat.

"Rachel!"

A figure came from around the bend.

CHAPTER TWENTY-SIX

T HE CRY WAS haunting, horrible. It briefly rooted
Stockbridge and Molly where they stood. Their
debate about Molly staying or going ended abruptly.

"I know the voice," Stockbridge said quietly. "It's
Lenny Keeler."

He picked up his shotgun and started toward the
trail. As he reached Juan's position, the Mexican
grabbed his sleeve. He spoke, his voice an insistent
whisper.

"*Señor*, wait! You cannot go."

"I must."

"No, I mean—*you* cannot go. Whoever is here,
they will expect *me*. Maybe they see the fire, not even
sure Rachel is here."

Juan made several good points.

"Is there a way to come up behind him?" Stockbridge asked.

Juan shook his head.

Molly came up quietly and laid a comforting hand

on Stockbridge's shoulder. Or maybe it was meant to be persuasive, to make sure he stayed. Juan was right, but Stockbridge did not like the idea of the man putting himself in danger . . . again.

The wilderness echoed again with a plaintive cry.

"Rachel! *Please* . . ."

Stockbridge heard his own son's voice in his head, felt his gut burn with a desire to avenge every boy who had ever been wronged by any man.

You're supposed to be able to look up to men. *They're who you want to grow up to* be.

Juan began to move.

"That has to be one of the Red Hunters out there," Stockbridge whispered. "He may shoot you out of hand."

Without looking back, Juan said, "Then you get to burn me again."

"Just hold on a second." Stockbridge turned to Molly. "Better get Rachel out here. We may need her."

Molly hesitated, but only a moment. She hurried back to the cave.

The hermit moved out then; Stockbridge had no choice but to let him go. Any struggle here, now, would be heard by whoever was around the corner.

Juan was tired and sore, and he hobbled rather than strode forward.

"Hola?" Juan said into the dark.

Now he saw not just the shape of a big rider and a mount but four legs hanging down the sides. Two riders. The boy and a Red Hunter.

"Juan Juarez?" a man's voice asked.

"Sí. Who is it that asks?"

"Never mind. Anyone else with you up here?"

"Who would be with me?"

The rider held up the gun so Juan could see the

familiar outline, even in the dark. "Mister, the way it works is I ask and you answer. I'm looking for a girl."

"The one whose name you say? Rachel?"

"That's right."

"Rachel Keeler?"

DeLancy straightened visibly. "Yes. Is she with you?"

"She is," Juan said. "And *caramba*! What a terrible sight she is!"

"Don't you worry about that. You got a rope?"

"Rope?"

"A lasso . . . a riata?"

"*Sí.*"

"I want you to go back, put it round her neck, and bring her to me."

"*Don't!*" Lenny whimpered, then cried out as the knife dug deeper.

"Is that her brother with you, the one she was babbling on about?"

DeLancy exhaled. "Stop yammering. I said bring the damn girl, dirt!"

Juan lingered at the insult. Then, shrugging, he turned back toward the cave.

"Hey, wait," DeLancy yelled.

Juan faced him.

"How'd she come to be here?" DeLancy asked.

"I found her at the river," Juan replied. "I brought her."

"She walked?"

"*Sí.*"

"Then you stay. She can walk here," the former sergeant said.

"But the rope."

"Tell her where it is. I don't know if I trust you."

"I don't have a gun. I don't have a fight with you."

"Keep it that way."

"Okay. But she's hurt. She's slow."

"I got time. I also got her brother. Now goddamn it, tell her where the damn rope is and to tie it around her neck!"

Juan sighed and faced the cave. *"Señorita* Miss Keeler, I think you heard everything, *sí?"*

"Yes, Mr. Juarez," a voice answered faintly.

"The rope is holding my spare blankets in a bundle—"

"I see it."

There was nothing after that but silence and expectation on the narrow stretch of trail as the two men remained motionless. The boy was breathing hard but was otherwise silent. DeLancy lowered the gun to rest his arm.

After a minute there was the faintest sound of shoes scraping on the dirt. Like a wraith risen from her tomb, a haunted figure came around the bend— still in shredded garments, her hands still bloody, her eyes wide but dead, her mouth slack. There was a rope around her neck, the end hanging down her chest almost to her knees.

"Oh, sis," Lenny said involuntarily.

The Southerner did not bother applying the knife. He was distracted by a circle of light behind the girl and by his jumpy horse. There was someone following Rachel Keeler, and the gun came up again. He was half expecting John Stockbridge, ready for a showdown like the newspaper from Gunnison described. But it wasn't Dr. Vengeance. It was someone Alan DeLancy did not expect and dared not shoot.

"Molly?" the Southerner said.

"Hello, Sergeant," the woman replied. She was carrying the torch so DeLancy would see her face. She was smiling as though pleased to see him.

"Molly, what in blazes are *you* doing up here?"

The woman and Rachel stopped along the side of the cave.

"I waited for the captain at the hotel, but I found out he was in jail," Molly said. "No one told me that he had been released, so I came up after him."

"Up . . . here?" DeLancy said.

"Mr. Nikolaev loaned me his surrey. I heard a commotion on the trail, saw a girl run off, and followed her."

"I didn't see you," DeLancy said.

"Nor I you."

The gun came down. "Well, now, your friend is out of jail, and you can do him a real service. Bring that girl to me."

"Of course, Sergeant," Molly said, as though she were instantly part of whatever plot the Red Hunters were working.

"Hey, South of the Border," DeLancy said, "stand with them so I can watch you. Keep your hands out front."

"Ah, he's okay," Molly said. "Just a little unsociable."

"I do not do nothing," Juan assured him, holding up both hands to show that he was cooperating fully.

"Sergeant, can you ease up on the boy?" Molly asked.

"That's not your concern."

"He's bleeding on your horse. It doesn't seem happy."

"Just give me the end of the rope, please, Molly. Then you can go back and get your surrey and follow me down. I know it'll do the captain good—a *lot* of good—to see you."

Molly gave the girl a gentle push, and they walked forward, Rachel moving stiffly before her. The girl looked up at her brother as she neared, and he turned his eyes toward her.

"Lenny, I'm so sorry," the girl said, her lower lip trembling.

"I love you," he replied, tears cutting through the dirt on his cheeks.

Reaching the horse, Molly told Rachel to stop. The woman came around, took up the end of the rope, and handed it to DeLancy. He did not see the derringer she had palmed though he simultaneously felt and heard the bullet that pierced his temple. The .22 caliber projectile was not enough to kill him, though his arms went slack. The knife and gun fell, and DeLancy listed to the right, following them to the ground.

Startled by the shot, the horse reared. Molly dropped the derringer and grabbed the bridle while Rachel reached for her brother before he could fall. She embraced him and pulled him toward her, turning her back to shield him from the horse. The animal came back down just a foot from the two. Juan ran over and seized the other side of the bridle before the horse could go up again.

Flat on his belly, DeLancy slurringly called Molly a name the others had never heard. Though stricken, he struggled to get to his hands and knees. The wound in the side of his head was bleeding moderately, the shot having cracked his skull without penetrating to his brain. He felt around for his gun.

His hand landed, instead, on the boot of John Stockbridge.

"Stay still, DeLancy," he ordered. "Molly, leave the torch, take the Keelers to the cave. Juan, the horse."

The woman laid the flaming brand on the dirt. Rachel gently but firmly placed her own sleeve to her brother's throat wound as they headed for the cave, followed by Molly, Juan, and the horse.

When they were gone, DeLancy turned his face

up. "Letting . . . a woman do your . . . bloody work . . . ?"

"You'd be dead if I hadn't," Stockbridge said. "Come with me. I'll try to patch you."

The sergeant sneered. "Go to the devil!"

In the dark, unseen by Stockbridge, the man's probing hand had found his firearm. He brought it up and aimed, the barrel glinting briefly in the torchlight. Almost at that instant, a shot exploded, and the sergeant died on the ground, cut nearly in half by the shotgun blast fired two feet above his back.

The report echoed, causing a few rocks to lose their hold on the mountainside. They clattered beside the man's dead body. The sound lingered as it rolled down the trail—loud enough, Stockbridge suspected, to be heard at the compound of Captain Promise Cuthbert.

He hoped so.

Molly came running around the corner to make sure Stockbridge was all right. She arrived to find him moving the man to the side of the road, against the cliff, and covering him with loose rocks. That would have to do for now. Before leaving, he retrieved the gun and stuck it in his belt.

"The kids all right?" he asked.

Molly nodded.

Stockbridge and Molly returned to the cave to find Lenny in the back, lying beside his father, both crying urgently and clutching each other. Rachel was kneeling beside them, sobbing but giving them their time together. She had removed the rope and retied the furs. She was quite a girl, Stockbridge thought.

The doctor and the woman went back outside, where Juan was finding a spot for DeLancy's horse.

"You can leave it, Juan," Stockbridge said. "I'm taking him with me."

"To below?"

"That's right." Stockbridge saw Molly give him a look that was already familiar. "This time, I'm going alone."

"Were you not paying attention just now?" Molly said. "The sergeant didn't shoot because it was *me*. I got close because he knew *me*."

"And when he found the gun, he could just as easily have shot *you*."

"The captain won't do that."

"He just lost another man. How many does that leave him with?"

"The cook," Molly answered.

"The cook. His world has been burned down again, and you think he won't shoot anyone who comes along that road?"

"That's right, Dr. Stockbridge. I don't think he will shoot me or you out of hand. For one thing, he'll assume, in the dark, on that horse, it's the sergeant coming back. For another, he will want to make you suffer. Or me. Or anyone who may have had a part in this, including the Keelers. If you're going to face him, you'll need someone who knows the cabin, who can find Mrs. Keeler if he's got her tucked away, and who has a prayer of getting her out."

Stockbridge stood still the whole time she was speaking. What she was suggesting was not his way. But that was not the sentiment that came from his mouth.

"All these men who died here. It's because twenty years later they're still hostile toward an old foe. Is that what is going on with you, Molly? Is Cuthbert every cuss who crawled on his belly but made sounds like a man?"

"Maybe. And if it is, I don't care. You yourself said

that men can't tamp down their own fires. Why should it be any different for me?"

"That man I just shot is why!" he said, gesturing back at the road. "I gave him an offer to save himself, and he voted it down. Same thing with the captain. I don't seek his death. That's for the sheriff, a judge, a jury to decide. All I seek is the safe return of Alice Keeler and a reunion for the family."

"Fine words, John, but unless the articles are all wrong, you got to kill the man who wronged you."

"Killed, not murdered," he said. "Adam Piedmont had his chance. So did DeLancy. So did Pound. So did McWilliams. I wanted justice. *They* chose death."

"Men like Cuthbert have no respect for the law, for the church, for anything decent," Molly said. "He deserves to die."

Stockbridge exhaled, noticed Juan standing beside Molly with the horse. His back was to the campfire, his face in shadow.

"You did not ask, *Señor* Stockbridge, but I tell you anyway. Back at Eagle Lookout, the *señorita* saved a man's life. She is strong. And also I am coming, too. You say what you want about this captain and his men. They may have been, each of them, *el ladrón*, a thief, but you see how they were also a pack, like the wolves. When they work alone . . . they die. We go as a pack, we are stronger."

Stockbridge did not know what to think, let alone how to answer. Then there was a new problem.

"If you are going to where they have my mother, I am going, too."

The voice came from Stockbridge's right, from just inside the cave. It was Rachel.

"No, dear," Molly said. "You should stay with your father, your brother."

"I agree—they are going, too," Rachel said.

"Rachel, just because Juan and I are doing this—"

"We are coming," Rachel said with finality. "I ran away on my own." She looked at her hands. "I took a life on my own. I will do it again if I have to."

Stockbridge was tired, and he was also growing impatient. He wanted to jump on the dead man's horse, charge down the mountain, shoot Promise Cuthbert on his back dead, kill the cook if necessary, liberate Mrs. Keeler, and ride on—all without breaking his stride. He wanted to be free of this pain and confusion, his and everyone else's. Reason was failing him, and he feared that if he lost that, he might also lose what was left of his humanity.

"Rachel, I agree with Molly," Stockbridge said as rationally as he could. "If we did all of this only to lose you three now—"

"We feel the same, sir," she told him. "We are in your debt, all of you, more than I can ever express. But you do not have to look out for the Keeler family. Pa is back. We are concerned about our mother. If—if *we* did all of this for nothing, if this does not turn out, we want her to know at the very least that we were reunited, if only briefly. That all the Keelers were together at the end."

Molly and Juan both looked from the girl to Stockbridge. The doctor knew it was not only pointless to argue but counterproductive, a waste of what energies they had left. The last two Red Hunters would also be tired—

There are *just two now,* he reminded himself. *And those two do not know what we know.*

An idea began to form, one that gave him hope.

"Molly, you'll be driving the surrey?" he asked.

His sudden acquiescence seemed to surprise her. "Yes."

"Juan, you'll be covering the rear, in case the cook or Cuthbert is already on the road, hidden somewhere?"

"If that is what you think, *sí*."

"And I can shoot," Rachel said.

Stockbridge exhaled slowly. "All right. We must leave at once. If Cuthbert starts to worry about his man not returning, he may take it out on Mrs. Keeler." He looked from face to face. "I will ride in front with the sergeant's horse. You will do nothing unless we are fired upon. Is that understood?"

There was no argument after that. He told Molly that he wanted her to describe the compound. When she was done, the doctor took Juan aside and quickly gave him a set of very clear and careful instructions— along with something he would need.

CHAPTER TWENTY-SEVEN

S TANDING UNDER THE New Richmond sign he had
S carved with his own hands, smoking and bundled
against the night, Promise Cuthbert felt a familiar
calm suddenly come over him, the kind of peace he
used to know before a battle.

He had heard the distant shots. A little pop and then
a big one. Neither was the six-shooter Alan DeLancy
carried. Cuthbert already knew that the last remaining
field veteran among his troopers was dead.

Yet Cuthbert was strangely unmoved. Death had
finally caught up with them all, after almost a score
of years. He dropped the cigarette, turned, and
walked back inside.

Cuthbert was not entirely surprised. They were
spent, all of them; that was part of it. Not just from
this day but from nearly twenty years of unendurable
pain. It was a bittersweet relief to realize he no longer
had to carry the burden of the lost South. There were
no soldiers left to fight for it, to rebuild parts of it, to

stand shoulder to shoulder with him, keeping the memories of shared history and camaraderie alive.

It was done. *He* was done. Now there was only one mission left, and that was to kill the man who had done this to them. He did not even have the desire to cut him apart, as he had been considering before— stringing him up and dressing him like Baker would gut a deer.

Stockbridge dead. That was all he wanted. If it meant killing the woman, he would do that. She was very, very expendable. If it meant exchanging his own life, he was prepared to make that deal, too. To live here with just the cook seemed unutterably hollow. What would he do, write odes to the lost world? To the end of civilization as he knew it? There was no way now New Richmond could be that eternal light.

The walk back to the compound was not long, but it was long enough for him to look into the abyss in his gut and see what was still alive in there.

Nothing.

No, that is not true, he told himself.

John Stockbridge. The name was still unbearably discordant in his ear. The picture in the magazines was burned in his heart, in his mind.

Die. Die. Die!

The brief calm was passing, the storm rising again. Bloodlust was returning. The man kicked open the unlatched front door, and he stared at the woman who sat on a rocking chair, her wrists tied to the wooden arms. He considered cutting her throat here and now. His big, dangerous eyes sought Baker. The cook was standing by a counter in the kitchen area. He had been looking out the window toward the sta- ble and the mountain beyond. Perhaps he, too, was looking at the home he had given up to come to these shores.

Baker turned sharply when the door flew in. Cuthbert glared at him and growled just one word: "Knife!"

T HE UNLIKELY CARAVAN moved slowly down the mountain trail. On point, Stockbridge had to watch the road, listen for sounds from the surrounding terrain. From the War, from living out here, he knew the difference between man and animal noises, the weight of a footfall versus the weight of a paw large or small; the breathing of a bear as opposed to the breathing of a man; the white eyes of an owl and the lesser eyes of a man. He paid especial attention to smells. A horse or an unwashed man was quite distinct from a wolf or a coyote or a bear. Not only did those have their own distinctive odors, but there was always a coating of blood and flesh, fish and fowl on animal coats and muzzles, even on their tongues. Coyotes had a wicked, skillful pack habit of getting close enough so you could smell their breath.

He had smelled the blood on Rachel's hands when she arrived. He had recognized the caked, dried smell on his own fingers from the War.

Juan's job was to make sure the surrey stayed on the often narrow trail. But Molly was good at that, even with three passengers.

The Keelers were quiet in their seats. The children had propped Ben in the back, one of Juan's furs on one side and Lenny on the other. The man held Alan DeLancy's six-shooter in his right hand. His job, as explained by Stockbridge, would be to cover the sides of the surrey. The doctor did not want the man shooting his daughter, who sat beside Molly. The rifle that Alan DeLancy had carried in his saddle holster she gripped tightly in her lap.

Stockbridge suddenly raised his arm. "Hold!"

They had not yet turned the sharp curve that opened onto the final descent to the cabin. There was a glow coming from behind the tree line just below.

"Something burning outside the cabin," Molly said.

"Any idea what?"

"I can't tell. It's near the front of the place—there's only a portal there, the name of the place, no gate."

"What's that name?"

"New Richmond," she said.

The explanation caused some concern. If Cuthbert was burning their ties to the old Southern capital, he was already resigned to death. Then a worse thought occurred to Stockbridge. There was no more wrenching welcome he could give Stockbridge than the burning corpse of Mrs. Keeler.

Stockbridge moved the little caravan forward. It was a horrifying prospect. If true, it was something of which these children would never be clean. Marriage, children of their own, grandchildren—the reek would be in their nostrils, would burn in their eyes every day of their lives.

Stockbridge hoped that even in a deranged state Promise Cuthbert had not decayed so irredeemably low.

As they reached the last stretch of road, about a half mile long, Stockbridge was somewhat relieved that Molly's sense of things seemed to be right. From what he could tell through the trees, the fire was high among the trees, flaming from the ground to about fifteen feet up.

It was dark, but growing brighter as they descended due to the blaze. He half turned toward the others.

"I'm watching ahead. You look *and* listen to the sides of the trail."

A palpable tension fell on the group in a way that the smoke did not. That pall twisted skyward—the anxiety and trigger-tightening readiness was low, chest high and buzzing.

And then, just below the burning signpost, Stockbridge saw something that caused hate to rise anew. There was a figure lying across the trail. It was spread-eagle, on its back, head toward the burning sign. Each of the four limbs was lashed to a tree, creating an asymmetrical sight—less like a human than like a marionette that had been carelessly flung aside.

It was Mrs. Keeler. She was writhing weakly and trying to cry out, but there was a cloth stuffed deep in her mouth and tied around the back of her head.

Stockbridge stopped and leveled his shotgun ahead while he looked furtively from side to side. Molly halted when Stockbridge did. She and then Rachel saw the woman a moment later.

"Mother!" the girl cried, simultaneously leaning forward as if to get out of the surrey.

Molly shoved her back with a strong hand. "No!"

Behind the girl Ben and Lenny stirred. Molly turned and warned them back. "Don't get her killed! Let John handle this!"

"Listen to Molly!" said a voice from among the dark trees to their right.

Promise Cuthbert came forward a little, into the glow of the burning entranceway. He was pointing a rifle at Mrs. Keeler's head. "Baker?"

"Here."

The new voice came from the opposite side of the trail. The cook stepped from the shadow of a large boulder. He was holding a six-shooter on the woman.

"Captain Cuthbert," Stockbridge shouted, "what do you want?"

"First, monster, that you not use my rank. You make it poisonous."

"All right."

"Second, you put your shotgun under your chin. I want you to end your wretched, unnatural life. Then and only then will I instruct Mr. Baker to cut the woman free. Everyone else will be allowed to go then."

"Molly, too?"

"Molly especially," Cuthbert said bitterly.

"Can I trust him, Molly?" Stockbridge said loudly enough for Cuthbert to hear.

"He—he never lied to me," the woman replied. "But, John—"

"There, *John*! Straight from the mouth of Jezebel," Cuthbert said. Then, heaving like a dragon ready to blow fire, he shouted, "*I trusted you, Molly! I cared for you!*"

"I only bathed you," she responded coldly.

Cuthbert stiffened, then laughed maniacally. "That's good. Very good. But I know you. You're trying to make me mad so I turn the gun on you. Stockbridge kills me, and the little lady beside you—she takes a chance at getting Baker. But that all depends on me being *stupid*! Do you think I'm stupid?"

"You are many terrible things, but not that," Molly agreed.

The man continued laughing. "Still pushing, still goading. Well, whore, it won't do you any good. Be grateful that I still have enough affection for you not to shoot you out of hand." He tilted his head, chuckled. "I notice the surrey is riding heavy. Who do you have in back—I can't see. The other Keelers?"

"Yes!" Lenny cried out. "Me *and* my pa!"

Hearing that, Mrs. Keeler struggled helplessly at her bonds.

Cuthbert shook his head. "The boy. He went up with Alan DeLancy. Maybe we need another execution before Dr. Vengeance dies. Tell me—did *you* kill my sergeant, Molly? That shot—was he killed with a concealed derringer?"

"No, I killed him," Stockbridge replied. "With my shotgun. I offered him amnesty—he declined."

"DeLancy was a hero to the last, a true son of the South." With a final hiss of dragon fire, Cuthbert glared at Stockbridge. "I'm waiting. If I have to wait much longer, I will put a bullet in this woman's leg. Then another. And you won't be able to treat her, Doctor. Because if you move off your horse, except to fall dead, I will kill her."

Not wishing to provoke the Southerner, Stockbridge lowered the shotgun and swung it up clockwise so the barrel was under his jaw.

"John, no!" Molly screamed.

"Molly, see that Rachel looks away," he entreated with great solemnity. "Also her brother."

"John—?" she implored.

He put the barrel against his jaw. "Do what I asked. And nobody do anything stupid. I'm accepting this man at his word."

Hesitating, but only until she heard the hammer of Cuthbert's gun go back, Molly instructed the two Keeler children to do as Stockbridge had asked.

Rachel wept and Lenny quietly implored his father to use the gun, but Molly repeated the doctor's full order in a way that left no room for further discussion. The children turned away and shut their eyes, both of them crying.

Molly looked ahead, expecting to see Stockbridge do *something* other than what he had agreed to. The idea that he would bow to this fiend, even to save her and the Keelers, was unthinkable.

There was a sudden, sick, low gurgling sound to the left of the trail. At first, she thought that a big cat had grabbed Baker—but they would have heard rustling, a cry, *something*. Cuthbert must have thought the same thing because he looked over, though the gun remained pointed at Mrs. Keeler.

It was a reflexive move on Cuthbert's part, the instincts of an old soldier, and it cost him. By the dying light of the burning sign, Stockbridge lowered the shotgun, targeted Cuthbert, and fired. The blast whizzed over Mrs. Keeler on its way to the chest of his target. The Confederate captain cried out and crumpled even as, across the trail, Baker fell forward, clawing at his sliced throat. Juan stepped out into the faint glow, Stockbridge's serrated bread knife in his hand, the cook's blood warm and dripping from the blade.

Juan looked over at Stockbridge, not with triumph but grim resolve. The plan had worked the way the doctor said it would.

"If we are stopped," he had instructed, handing Juan the blade, *"stay far enough back so you can hunt your way around and tend our flank."*

It was a lot to ask of the man, to kill, but the Mexican understood it might be necessary. He, too, had grown instantly fond of the Keelers. Stockbridge had trusted that he would do what was necessary, and not stain his conscience, to protect them.

Even as both Southerners fell, Stockbridge dismounted quickly and ran ahead to put himself between the badly injured Cuthbert and Mrs. Keeler.

"Cut her loose, Molly!" the doctor cried without taking his eyes off the fallen officer.

All of the Keelers followed her from the surrey, Lenny lingering to help his father out. While they gathered around Mrs. Keeler, freeing her and helping her up, Stockbridge stood over the panting, bleeding Promise Cuthbert. The man's middle was open, and there was no chance of saving him. But the victor did not gloat. No one had won here.

"One man," Cuthbert gasped. "One . . . damn . . . Yankee."

"And a Mexican," Stockbridge said. "And a woman. It's no longer a world built for you, Captain."

"No," he agreed. "I thought . . . I thought I could . . ."

The man's lips froze, his eyes locked on the flickering remnants of a flame burning just out of his sight, and his chest fell still.

"It's a fool's errand to hold tight to the memory of a ghost," Stockbridge said to the dead man. "I should know."

He looked over at the Keelers, who were gathered on the rough trail, propping one another up, hugging and crying and saying over and over how much they loved one another. Ben even made room for his Palomino, who nuzzled his master.

Molly was standing beside them, with Juan. She excused herself and came toward Stockbridge while Juan went back to see about the horse he had left behind.

"You made plans of your own," she said. It was not an accusation but an appreciation.

"You and Juan were right about what you said—a pack, a team."

"But the doctor used it surgically," she said with admiration.

Just then, to their right, the sign collapsed in a heap.

"New Richmond is no more," Molly said.

"Not as it was, no."

"What do you mean? Could—could you settle here?" she asked hopefully.

"I was thinking that if they can bear up with the memory, it would be a place for the Keelers to relocate. Ben can go back to his trade, maybe teach his boy. He would only have to be gone a few days, maybe a week at most. Better for all of them."

Molly laughed lightly.

"What is it?"

"Nothing," she said. "Always thinking about others."

"That's what doctors do."

Molly reached out and took his left hand, held it gently in hers. "Not everyone is a patient, Dr. Stockbridge."

He squeezed back lightly, then excused himself and went over to the cook. The man was dead, but he had known that already. Stockbridge just did not want to stay with Molly then, there, like that. Seeing the joy of the Keelers, and hearing their heartfelt thanks, feeling their love as he walked past, Stockbridge felt old stirrings, longings, pain.

He needed time alone. Not just to grieve but to think.

CHAPTER TWENTY-EIGHT

As soon as the Keelers were settled in the surrey, Juan turned back up the hill—on foot.

"You Keelers have more need of horses than I do," Juan said. "I will be fine. I do not need another big mouth to feed, and to tell you the truth, I do not like the smell."

"At least take this," Rachel said, and gave him the rifle to replace the one he had lost. He thanked her and looked longingly at Molly.

"What I said about horses does not apply to you. You will come to visit?"

"As often as I can, though may I make a suggestion?"

"*Sí?*"

"Come down for a bath now and then," she said. "On the house."

"I don't know what that means, 'on the house.' But if you offer it, I think I like it."

"You'll like it," Stockbridge said. "It means free."

"Then that is good, because I have no *pesos*. Not a one."

Molly took the horse, and after some discussion about whether to remain here the night, the group decided against it. Stockbridge told the Keelers his thoughts about the disposition of the house.

"I will consider that in earnest," Ben said, "and I—we—appreciate the gesture."

"Wouldn't *you* want it?" Mrs. Keeler asked Stockbridge, looking from him to Molly.

"There's not much doctoring I could do from way out here," Stockbridge answered.

"Maybe you'll move into town, then?" Lenny asked. "We don't have a doctor."

"Your ma's a pretty good nurse," Ben said.

"Well, there you have it," Stockbridge said. "I'd probably go broke with all the fine women who live hereabouts."

They rode back to the homestead, additional horses in tow, arriving with the first light of dawn breaking behind them. Molly left them with the horse and retrieved the surrey, which Nikolaev would expect to have returned.

On the way, they passed the mounds that Stockbridge knew and Molly suspected held the remains of Red Hunters McWilliams and Pound.

"Look, Pa," Lenny said as they passed, "lightning-struck cactuses." Then he continued with a boy's restless curiosity. "You see a lot of lightning up in the mountains."

"Up there it's too high," Ben replied. "It's below you."

"Gosh. Just like that fella we read about in that book, Ma—what was his name?"

"Zeus? The Greek god?"

"No . . ."

"Thor," Rachel said, "the Norse god of thunder."

"Yeah!"

Stockbridge felt a plug rise in his throat as he thought of all the talks like that he had missed . . . and would never have. He thought of a different god, the one who had let him down. The blockage broke as bile rose. That was the way of it. Missing his family followed by hate.

What a way to live a life, he thought.

The six of them reached the homestead without needing to stop at the watering hole. In a group, and then individually, the Keelers thanked both Molly and Stockbridge. They saved their special appreciation, though, for another parting moment with John Stockbridge.

"I can never put into words what I feel," Ben Keeler said, his strength returning quickly, thanks to his family.

"Sharing this reunion has been thanks enough, in a way *I* can never express," Stockbridge assured him.

"I love you," Rachel said next, hugging Stockbridge. His embrace was warm and reflected her own.

"I love you more," Lenny said, hugging him tighter. Stockbridge's embrace was followed by an affirming pat on the young man's shoulders. "Don't forget to start a new book when you're able. I expect to buy one from you in the store someday."

"It will be about you," Lenny promised.

"And Molly and Juan, too. I was just the man who made the most noise."

It was Mrs. Keeler's turn then. She faced Stockbridge, put her hands on his arms, and looked up into his eyes. "That kind of 'noise' is what moves mountains and people, for the better. Don't ever stop, John Stockbridge. Please don't stop."

"I'm not sure I can," he admitted.

Ben and the children left to find a place for the new horses. Mrs. Keeler went back inside—her step lively and a song in her throat—while the doctor and Molly rode off, side by side, into the rising sun. They stopped at a stream to tend to the horses—and their own thirst, which by now was pronounced.

It was fitting, thought Stockbridge, that the nourishing water was a branch of the Oónâhe'e River.

The remainder of the ride back to Buzzard Gulch was short and untroubled. They stopped at the sheriff's office to recount what had happened. Tom Neal was still on his first cup of coffee when the two walked in. He had his impaired foot on the desk, his full attention on the narrative.

"First, Dr. Stockbridge, it's a pleasure to meet you," Neal said. "Second, I believe what you and Molly have told me. I can't say I'm sad or surprised. The way those boys left here yesterday morning, they was asking to die. I'll go out later, get some folks to come with me—see about burying whoever's left to bury." He then looked Stockbridge down, up, and midway. "Yes, it's certainly quite something to meet you, sir. You ever think about deputy work?"

"No, Sheriff, that's one thing I do not think about."

"Shame. With Raspy looking to grow his business and others muttering the same, we could use someone who don't have to do more than parade along the street to keep undesirables from coming here."

"I think you'd find I attract them, Sheriff."

"Like mud to a stagecoach. I hear you. See who can beat Dr. Vengeance. But on the plus side, think of the folks who would come out of their way to spend money here."

"It's all very tempting," Stockbridge said, "but for another man."

The two left to begin the last stretch of their ride, from the sheriff's office to the Pap Hotel. It was also, for both of them, the most difficult, especially because of Sheriff Neal's parting words.

Seeing them to the front door and limping over to the hitching rail, he watched Molly climb into the surrey, then turned to Stockbridge and said, "You know what Buzzard Gulch could use more than a deputy?"

"A gambling parlor to compete with Gunnison?" Molly said to head him off from where he was going.

"No, ma'am. A doctor. We got to go to the aforementioned town for that. Not too bad a ride if someone's having a baby—which they haven't here in about a year now, I think. But grievously long if they're belly-shot or hurt some way the barber can't handle. When he isn't also bartending, I mean."

"I think you can probably do better than someone who just killed six men," Stockbridge said as he mounted.

"I don't know. You tell a kid to behave while you check his ears, I think he'd listen. You know something else? I think Molly would make a real good nurse. She already seen most of the town without its shirt."

The woman had lost the buggy whip somewhere along the way, or she would have used it. They had left the blanket at the cave, or she would have thrown it. Instead, she turned away and started down the street.

Stockbridge felt a more-than-subtle change in Molly on that final stretch of dirt. He had been wondering if her strong outside would break, just a little, maybe when the dangers and violence of the previous day were finally over. This sudden quiet did not seem to be that. She was sitting straight in the seat of the surrey, attentive to the road. Hers was not the posture or face of a woman who had been tapped dry.

This was something else.

Stockbridge kept his silence. He did not know what to say.

*A*ND A RUSSIAN.
When Stockbridge had been going down the list of those who made up local America for Promise Cuthbert, he had neglected to mention Raspy Nikolaev, a figure whom the doctor had not yet met. John Stockbridge discovered that the man was like a dust storm: big, inexorable, and unforgettable. Nikolaev was a welcome force of nature, since parting with the others had been difficult for the doctor.

The Russian emerged from his hotel, smoking a morning cigar and scowling hard at the condition of his carriage. His expression softened when he noticed the condition of Molly Henshaw, then changed altogether when he laid eyes on and recognized John Stockbridge and his Parker Brothers from the *Line & Telegram.*

Nikolaev was gentleman—and businessman—enough not to linger on the surrey or the physician. Instead, the cloud of his displeasure passing, he helped Molly from the surrey and kissed both of her dirty cheeks.

"You are okay?" he asked.

Molly nodded tightly. Now she dared not speak or even part her lips. Nikolaev's eyes softened. He looked over at Stockbridge, who remained in the saddle.

"I am Rasputin Nikolaev, proprietor," he said, bowing. "You are Dr. John Stockbridge?"

"I am."

"Will you come in for breakfast, sir?"

"Thank you, but I think I'll resume my travels."

Molly hadn't looked at him since they left the sheriff's office. But now she made a point of turning away.

"What of Promise Cuthbert?" the Russian asked. "When I saw him last—"

"The captain has taken his last bath," Molly said.

"I see. I can imagine what kind." The Russian did not look at Stockbridge. He did not have to.

"It wasn't like that," Molly said softly. "Not at all."

"I see," Nikolaev said again. "I'm sorry. Whatever it was must have been awful."

Molly nodded and started toward the hotel.

"Thank you, Molly," Stockbridge said to her back.

Molly stopped. "You are welcome."

Stockbridge felt a tug on his heart—even Nikolaev put a protective arm around her without quite knowing why. Stockbridge tipped his hat to the man and resisted the urge to race away at a gallop.

Instead, he pulled the reins around and retraced his steps back down the street. As Stockbridge rode he felt *something* settle upon his chest suddenly and with an uncustomary weight. It was something other than the emptiness he had felt for so long.

He proceeded slowly, half expecting to hear Molly call his name.

Do I want that? he yelled inside his head.

Just before he reached the sheriff's office, Stockbridge stopped. He stood there looking out at the plain that would take him past the homestead, onto the mountain trail, through the Rockies—

Maybe I'll find Ben Keeler's legendary pass, then go through it and beyond to the blue Pacific, he thought.

Do I want that? he asked himself.

He remained there like a statue in a town square.

Then, against every bit of iron plating that had been hammered over him over the past few years, and fighting his own muscles, Stockbridge turned his head around.

Rasputin Nikolaev was standing in the street holding the sobbing Molly Henshaw to his big chest.

"Shit," Stockbridge said.

He could still ride on. Neither of them saw him.

"Shit."

With a yank on the reins, Stockbridge turned the horse that was not even his back toward the woman who was. He did not quicken his pace but rode slowly. He did not want her first sight of him to be that of a knight charging in the lists.

Nikolaev was the first to see him. He looked up and smiled. He held the secret a little longer before turning Molly around by her heaving shoulders. The woman's face changed like Denver weather, going from tears to laughter in a single beat of her heart.

Molly remained where she was standing until Stockbridge stopped beside her and extended his right arm, the one that always held the shotgun, which he had shifted to his left.

"I believe I need a woman for this," he said.

Laughing, she reached up, and he pulled her onto the horse, hugged her close to him in front. Stockbridge looked down at the beaming Russian.

"Thank you, Mr. Nikolaev."

"For what?"

"For not putting up a fight."

"Against Dr. Vengeance?"

Stockbridge grinned. "He's retired, sir. It's Dr. Stockbridge now."

"We could use a good doctor!" the Russian said.

"So I've heard," Stockbridge replied as he turned the horse around.

"Wait! Molly, your things! Will you be back for them?"

"I—I don't know!" she called back.

"But—you need *clothes*!"

"I know where I can get her some furs," Stockbridge yelled over his shoulder as he rode from town toward the homestead and the future.

Ready to find
your next great read?

Let us help.

Visit prh.com/nextread

Penguin
Random
House